He was in the room!

She had neither heard nor seen him, but *he* was what had awakened her—his being, his force. She knew it the way a wild animal knows when a hunter is in the forest.

She strained to see through the shadows but detected nothing.

Without warning, an arm shot out from behind her and snagged her waist, reeling her back, while the other looped terrifyingly about her neck.

Petrified, Mary abruptly found herself crushed to a man's body, a body that was the texture of iron—a lean, pulsing, driving form, arms that were clad in leather and smelled of woodsmoke and legs that might well have been carved from granite.

"Hello there," a voice murmured huskily into the mad swirl of her hair.

Dear Reader,

Once again, six Silhouette **Special Edition** authors present six dramatic new titles aimed at offering you moving, memorable romantic reading. Lindsay McKenna adds another piece to the puzzling, heart-tugging portrait of the noble Trayherns; Joan Hohl revives a classic couple; Linda Shaw weaves a thread of intrigue into a continental affair; Anne Lacey leads us into the "forest primeval"; and Nikki Benjamin probes one man's tortured conscience. Last, but certainly not least, award-winning Karen Keast blends agony and ecstasy into *A Tender Silence*.

What do their books have in common? Each presents men and women you can care about, root for, befriend for life. As Karen Keast puts it:

"What instantly comes to mind when someone mentions *Gone with the Wind*? Rhett and Scarlett. Characterization is the heart of any story; it's what makes you *care* what's happening. In *A Tender Silence*, I strived to portray two people struggling to survive in an imperfect world, a world that doesn't present convenient black-and-white choices. For a writer, the ultimate challenge is to create complex, unique, subtly structured individuals who are, at one and the same time, universally representative."

At Silhouette **Special Edition**, we believe that *people* are at the heart of every satisfying romantic novel, and we hope they find their way into *your* heart. Why not write and let us know?

Best wishes,

Leslie Kazanjian, Senior Editor
Silhouette Books
300 East 42nd Street
New York, N.Y. 10017

LINDA SHAW
Love This Stranger

Silhouette Special Edition

Published by Silhouette Books New York

America's Publisher of Contemporary Romance

SILHOUETTE BOOKS
300 East 42nd St., New York, N.Y. 10017

ISBN: 0-373-09540-6

First Silhouette Books printing July 1989

All the characters in this book are fictitious. Any
resemblance to actual persons, living or dead, is
purely coincidental.

Printed in the U.S.A.

LINDA SHAW,

the mother of three, lives with her husband in Keene, Texas. When Linda, a prolific author of both contemporary and historical fiction, isn't writing romantic novels, she's practicing or teaching the piano, violin or viola.

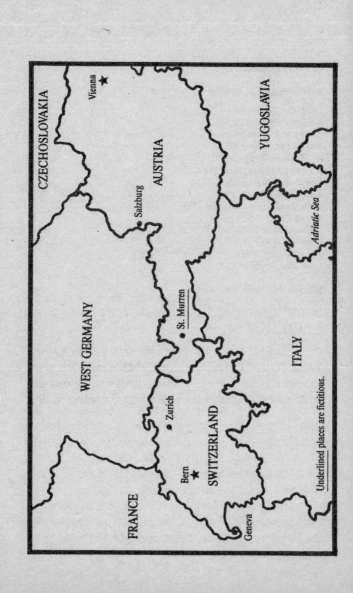

Underlined places are fictitious.

Chapter One

The helicopter circled wide over *Zurich-Kloten* and hovered above the tarmac like a mutant dragonfly that lost its way.

Overhead, the late afternoon sun had burned away the mist. The snowplows were scraping the runways clean of the first good powder of the season, and the smell of winter was bright and crisp in the late-October air. The big commercial jets were backed up for takeoff, and their great underbellies glistened crimson and violet and aquamarine as they nosed upward and, with a thunderous roar, lifted and soared into the waiting clouds.

Karl Bauer ran a regular helicopter charter from St. Murren across the Austrian border to Zurich.

"...clear for landing," crackled in his headset as an ambulance, lights flashing, raced toward him and came to a screeching halt. Its doors opened like wings as if it, too, were preparing to ascend.

Karl set the chopper down gently. Crouching low, bearing a portable stretcher while the rotorwash threatened to shred the legs of their pants and snatch their hair from their heads, paramedics ran toward him.

Motioning them on, Karl glanced at his watch. A flight from the ski resort at St. Murren didn't amount to much time-wise, and he usually made at least one trip a day. The chateau had always attracted its share of the social set, especially in its better days: the bored superrich, the jet-setters, the political hotshots, European royalty, the inevitable film stars from America. Someone was usually needing quick transportation and had the cash to pay.

Today he was right on schedule, and Mary Smith was the charter, though Mary Smith was neither rich nor a jet-setter. She wasn't even a film star. She was the nutritionist for the chateau, and if gossip was to be believed—he had supreme faith in the resort's grapevine—she had set St. Murren's new American administrator back on his heels today by turning up pregnant. She'd set everyone on their heels!

Now the ambulance would rush her to emergency in a Swiss hospital, and Karl suspected Jed Kilpatrick, St. Murren's American house physician who had chartered the chopper, of having more than passing medical interest in the case. In the three years since the lanky, fortyish doctor had come to St. Murren, Karl had known him to be moody, withdrawn, depressed or all three at once. But never had he seen him bone-deep afraid. Not until today.

If he was nothing else, Karl was discreet. "Good luck," he called cheerfully as the paramedics lifted Mary onto the stretcher and returned to the ambulance at a brisk trot.

From the stretcher Mary couldn't spare the strength to reply but sought the strong, sure grip of Jed Kilpatrick at her side. Once in the ambulance, pressing her lips into a pale, determined line, she waited until the conveyance was wailing and careening through the streets of downtown Zurich.

"Do me a favor," she said to Jed despite the panic that had her by the throat, "don't ask how I'm doing."

With his unruly black hair and cracked leather bomber jacket making him look more like a pilot than a doctor, and the lines at his eyes fanning in a permanent squint, his cheekbones windburned and tan, Jed scowled. "You're not going to go to pieces on me now, are you, Mary? I'd hate to have to hurt you in front of all these people."

To Mary, their favorite mock insult was a lifeline in a torrent of insanity. She arranged a brave smile. "Yeah, yeah, yeah. I know."

His smile was a flicker of white in his taut face. "You're pretty fresh for a Maryland kid."

"That's because I had such a great, all-star chauvinist teacher," she retorted. Then: "Jed, can they stop the baby from coming?"

During the past ten years Jed had held many a fate in his surgeon's hands, but Mary guessed that none of them, not even the one that had ended up wrecking his life, mattered as much as the one he could now do nothing to help.

His own mortality bent his shoulders. "Of course they can," he said helplessly.

The vehicle swayed from side to side. Up front, the two-way radio spit raspy static, and the siren blared its schizophrenic howl. The paramedic's face was a mask as he monitored her pulse.

"What's the count?" Mary heard Jed inquire in halting Swiss-German.

The man did not respond except to say, "I speak English, sir."

Swearing softly, Jed unzipped his jacket and reached for the man's stethoscope. Too surprised to protest, the attendant watched as Jed placed it about his neck.

Mary closed her eyes as Jed moved the instrument skillfully over her aching middle beneath her blood-stained coat. Her perceptions drifted in and out of focus, and she attempted to sort them. How had she gotten here? she wondered erratically.

Then she recalled the confrontation with Juliet on the stairs and her own fall when the girl swung around in crazed denial—down, down, down. Something had torn loose inside. She was hemorrhaging. Even now, Jed's quiet voice kept filtering in and out of her consciousness like the moon through roiling clouds.

"Hand me that pack," she heard him order over the siren's scream. "Hurry, man! Call ahead to obstetrics. Find out who's on duty in OR. See that they have plenty of AB-positive plasma on hand as I ordered."

Groping for the reassurance of his fingers, Mary shook her head. "I want *your* blood," she declared. "I trust it."

Bending, he kissed the contours of her face and smoothed back her hair, smiling unhappily down at her. "Then it really would be my baby. Then you'd have to marry me."

Mary's hand fell weakly to the stretcher. "Is this another of your infamous proposals of marriage, Dr. Kilpatrick?"

"Hell, no. Why would I want to be saddled with a cheeky little wench who can't even dance?"

"But I can do the splits." She giggled halfheartedly. "Even pregnant, I can do the splits."

His hands shook as he blotted a tear trembling on her lashes. "There you go, discriminating again. I've explained a thousand times, Mary, I can't get pregnant. If I could, I could do the splits."

Mary thought if she could only hold onto the sound of Jed's rich voice, the Harvard intellectual's accent tucked into a rebel's sultry drawl, she would make it. But his voice kept blending with others—familiar sounds that were much more distant, an ocean away, a continent: John's cruel sarcasm, Eve's glamorous treachery, her mother's naive love, her own stubborn search for independence.

Ghosts, all of them with their chains, phantoms rattling through the chambers of her pain-clotted brain. Why hadn't she been more clever? How had she ever believed she could pull off such a stupid, impulsive deception?

It had been the perfect way out. Lying there, temptingly innocent in its stiff, India-white envelope beneath the telephone bill and the electric and water bills, along with a copy of *Foods for Life* magazine, was a letter from John's divorce lawyer.

From the living room of the century-old Smith estate overlooking Chesapeake Bay where she had lived since her marriage, Mary had heard the lid open on the brass mailbox outside. The flap of which, she thought belatedly, was still embossed "Mr. and Mrs. J. Smith, III."

With a whispery *thunk*, everything slid inside. Nervous, she smiled across the room at her in-laws, soon to be ex-in-laws. They smiled stiffly back at her.

"Eve, John," she said, slipping into the facade of poise that everyone in Annapolis expected her, as a Calvert, to always possess. "Could I get you more coffee?"

The John J. Smiths, II continued to balance third-generation Spode china cups upon their knees. "Of course, darling," Eve said, her tone calculating. She crossed her glamorous legs and lifted the china cup to her lips with fingers that dripped diamonds. "This is much too important a matter to rush."

She might have done better to marry John's parents, Mary thought from behind glasses that rode at an intellectual half-mast upon her nose. At least Eve and John liked her. Rather, they liked her genealogy. Genealogy always had been her best asset—those enviable roots stemming from the Calvert families who traced their own names back to Maryland's Cecil Calvert, Lord Baltimore, God rest his soul.

The Smith's roots were much less spectacular. They had found their place in the world by mere sweat and hard work—three of them standing in an undistinguished row, all Johns with numbers after their names like the world wars. John, I, her husband's grandfather, had been a builder of roads, but he'd had the bad judgment to run away with his brother's wife. John, II, a staunch dues-paying union man, fortunately had no brother to betray and was single-handedly responsible for the Smith-Blakey technical millions.

Lacking a name, the Smiths thought John, III should marry one. Having a name but no money, Mary's family had thought she should marry John. The truth was, she and John shouldn't have married anyone, least of all each other.

Mary spotted Poppy putting the vacuum cleaner away in the hall. Keeping her back to the Smiths, Mary signaled her maid with wild gestures and outlandish sign language.

"I'll get the mail, Poppy," she calmly intoned while making grotesque faces. "Mr. and Mrs. Smith could use some fresh coffee, I believe." This, serenely, demurely: "Eve, John, would you please excuse me for a minute?"

Poppy was the unquestioned boss of the Smith household. Mary had long ago given up trying to change this law of nature. With an aloof sniff, the woman always let it be known that personally, she wouldn't have let the white-trash millionaire Smiths into the house at all if they hadn't owned it.

As anxious to escape the maid as John's parents, Mary hurried to the front door.

Her leather thongs slapped urgently upon the soles of her feet, the sound echoing in the quiet house. Sweeping open the heavy oak panel, she ran out onto the sun-splashed stoop with the relief of a prisoner having narrowly escaped the guillotine. She waved to the stout figure in regulation U.S. Postal shorts who was trudging down her sidewalk toward his idling mail Jeep.

"Jim!" Shading her eyes, she cheerfully motioned him back.

Jim Carabatsos lifted his cap to mop a band of sweat from his forehead onto his sleeve, his grin making his lopsided face resemble that of a friendly mountain goat.

"You're early today," she called out, laughing. "It's barely ten o'clock."

"Had to get an early start on the heat," he said. "Geez, it feels more like July than the middle of September, don't it?"

"The U.S. Government's been too good to you, Jim, giving you that cute little Jeep to ride around in. Time was when delivering the mail was a test of character."

Laughing, Jim gripped his bulging stomach as if to keep it from sliding to his knees.

"You're a mean woman, Mary," he said as his over-sized shadow lumbered alongside him. "D'you know, you're the only one on my route who fusses about my weight?"

Years ago Jim could have insisted that she put the mailbox down at the end of the drive on Fairfax Avenue; he delivered the entire residential section to the naval base. But then they would miss this pleasant daily ceremony that had evolved between them. She wondered if he didn't enjoy the long ascent beneath the shady oaks up to the mansion that had been built by the first John J. Smith at the turn of the century.

She waged a battle with the wind for wisps of her hair that she'd wound into a topknot and held down the swirl of chambray that billowed about her legs.

"I'll have you know, Jim Carabatsos, that I'm fragile these days."

"Fragile like an army tank."

"Don't let the Navy hear you say that."

Having reached into the mailbox, she drew out the bundle of envelopes and circulars and flipped idly through them as she talked, seeing nothing of interest until she spied the magazine.

"Lookie, lookie, lookie," she cooed, and riffled eagerly through the pages to locate the index.

Drawing a fingernail down the list, she located her own name and turned to page twenty-nine. She held it at arm's length for him to admire.

"Well?" she demanded enthusiastically, giving the magazine a shake. "What d'you think? Is that great, or is that great?"

"I think *you're* great—you're one smart lady, Dr. Mary Smith."

He dutifully admired the article and read the caption beneath her tiny photograph: "Mary Smith, Ph.D., a regular contributor to *FFL*, is well-known for her contributions to the field of nutrition. Her postgraduate research was conducted at the Harvard School of Public Health, and her studies of the immune system have received critical acclaim. She is presently on the staff of Fields Laboratories."

What the caption did not say was that she was also the wife of one of Annapolis's most upwardly mobile yuppies, Mary thought. No vital statistics here: five-feet-nine, brown hair, brown eyes, slim to a fault, more concerned with her organic garden than fashion.

"You're my most devoted fan, Jim." She laughed with a total lack of modesty, then grimaced. "What am I saying? You're my *only* fan."

He laughed. "I know a good thing when I see it."

"Come on." She gave a sniff. "I earn enough to keep a prairie dog alive, if he doesn't stir around too much. What's smart about that?"

The words tripped off the end of his tongue: "But you're going to come out all right in the divorce, aren't you?"

Seconds passed clumsily by. Jim had stepped across a social boundary that wasn't his to trespass, and he knew it. He glanced awkwardly at the sprinklers hissing on the estate grounds, then back at her.

"You were supposed to be discreet and pretend you didn't know that, Jim." Sighing, Mary plucked a strand of hair and pulled it to the end of her nose. "But of course you had to know. Nothing's secret to a mailman or a banker, is it?"

"You mean, this isn't going to be one of those civilized divorces?"

"Civilized? He and Penelope Barnes deserve each other."

"Bitter, bitter."

Merriment disguised her ire. "Nothing bitter in that, Jim." She laughed. "I simply pray every night that their lives will be a living hell."

His amusement joined hers in the warm fall morning, and as he hitched at his belt, a voice called from the interior of the house in cultured, mother-of-pearl tones, "Dar-rling, what's keeping you? You know we have to be at the first tee by eleven."

Except for a roll of brown eyes, Mary made herself the mistress of a multimillion-dollar estate, the descendant of Cecil Calvert, estranged wife of John J. Smith, III who was heir to the Smith-Blakey fortune. The girl in her had disappeared. She was thirty again.

"John's parents," she whispered as she climbed the steps. "We've been having a serious discussion about you know what."

Closing the magazine, she slipped it wearily beneath her arm and placed the letters into its fold. With a lift of brows over the rim of her glasses, she signaled him goodbye and moved into the two-story hall where the staircase swept grandly upward and a priceless grandfather clock mocked the firing squad of Smith portraits frowning from the opposite wall.

"I'll be right there, Eve," she called, glancing back with her smile still stiff on her face. "Thanks, Jim. See you tomorrow."

"Yeah. Have a good day, Mary Smith."

Stepping quickly out of her life, for he moved only in the periphery of the people on his route, Jim wanted badly to add that he would think about her lovely smile the rest of the day. But Mary had already left his world for her own. He pushed his stack of mail aside and climbed beneath the steering wheel, wondering if good old John J. knew that his soon-to-be-ex-wife had been getting bills from an obstetrician.

To look at her, one would never guess. Not with Mary's five feet nine inches and incredible bones. And those ridiculous clothes she and Annie Hall wore— pleated trousers so baggy she had to hold them up with suspenders, or a man's football jersey over an ankle-length plaid skirt. She wouldn't look pregnant until she went to the hospital to have the baby.

He released the hand brake and backed up to turn around. Mary might even move out of the big house after her divorce was final. Too much house and too much land for a single woman. At this moment a gardener had stopped his riding mower in the shade while his assistant adjusted the sprinklers so that they laid out plush, wet arcs. Another was making a late pruning of the hundreds of shrubs that framed the house and bordered the steel fence circumventing it all.

But she would be a fool to leave the Smith estate. She should do like any other woman in the world would and soak old John J. for every copper penny he had in the settlement, house and all. But no one could accuse Mary of being like any other woman, that was for sure.

When the front door of the haughty old house clicked shut with finality, Mary thought it sounded appropriately like a hammer being pulled back on a gun.

She would as soon face a loaded gun as John's parents. Hesitating outside the door where they were wait-

ing, she stalled for time and absently tapped the edges of
the mail upon the tabletop while she stared back at the
generations of disapproving Smiths on the walls.

She made a face. They certainly wouldn't be sorry to
see her go. *Failure*, the pinched edges of their mouths
called her. *You are not one of us.*

"And you couldn't pay me to be," she retorted inau-
dibly to the original John J. with his chin whiskers, stiff
cravat and flinty, get-the-hell-outta-my-way eyes. "You
may have been a prince, Grandpa John, but your grand-
son's a human reject."

"Blessed are the meek, Mary girl," her tweed-suited
father had routinely counseled her from his safe, schol-
arly world of T. S. Eliot and Mozart. "Practice the
Golden Rule and love thy neighbor. Go the second mile,
and owe no man anything. No one ever violated princi-
ple and lived to be happy about it."

Too bad he hadn't explained that the people honor-
able enough to appreciate the meek were few and far between. And she *had* gone the second mile, over and over,
and where had it gotten her but farther down a dead-end
road?

She peered into a beveled mirror over the table. A
woman grimaced at her, one she didn't find ugly but not
particularly attractive, either—not in the way her sisters
were pretty. She didn't look at all like her mother. So why
did she have to act like her?

"Look out for number one, girls," Treenie had always preached, as she breezed superficially through life.
"No one else will, and you can't eat genealogy or drink
blue blood." Treenie and Mary and the two other girls,
Joanna and Dotty, had been going through their father's personal effects after his death. "A woman cries a
lot of tears in a marriage," she counseled. "She can suf-

fer more easily when a servant brings the Kleenex, believe me.''

Fingering one of the envelopes, Mary realized she had missed seeing it before. A foreign stamp? Frowning, she pushed her glasses higher onto her nose. *Austria?* Puzzled, she turned it over and read ''St. Murren'' embossed upon the back flap. Who could she possibly be receiving a letter from in St. Murren, Austria?

Yet, the address was neatly typed: Ms. Mary Smith, Fairfax Avenue. No street number, no zip code.

With a poke of her fingernail, she ripped the envelope open.

Dear Mary Smith,

How pleased we were to learn of the possibility of your return to St. Murren as the resort's nutritional consultant.

Our staff is all new, as you may have heard by now, and our present nutritionist unfortunately was part of the recent air tragedy in Paris. We are quite desperate to have someone for this immediate season. You come highly recommended and could, as the saying goes, write your own ticket.

Should you decide to join us, please notify us immediately, and we will arrange for your airfare, room and board. The Olympic trainees are holding their usual session with us, and it promises to be an eventful season.

We do hope you will send your affirmation. If not, could you let us know so we may search elsewhere?

Cordially,
Haman Stone, St. Murren

Baffled, Mary worried a strand of hair. St. Murren, though momentarily having financial difficulties, was one of *the* resorts in Europe; anyone who read the latest slick magazines knew that. How could they have the misconception that she had once been on their staff?

A computer mistake, more than likely. What should she do? Return the letter? Tell Jim that he had delivered it to the wrong Mary Smith? Should she attempt to forward it to the right Mary Smith?

She sighed. How many Mary Smiths could there be in Annapolis? Hundreds. Thousands!

Yet, it was just possible that she actually had been recommended by someone on the basis of her qualifications, and that Haman Stone had simply misunderstood and worded the letter incorrectly. Perhaps he was making a legitimate offer.

The baby kicked her for being so naive. "Never fear, my darling," she teased, "I'll take you with me. After coping with your grandparents for eight years, Austria cold-turkey would be a piece of cake."

"Oh, there you are, dear."

Startled, Mary glanced guiltily upward as Eve Smith glided along the corridor. In cream-colored shorts and matching silk blouse, a cashmere sweater looped smartly about her shoulders, she hardly resembled the bitchy woman who could put an entire restaurant on its ears because a vegetable was cold.

"John and I were wondering if you'd run off with the postman, darling," she purred.

With a bland smile Mary hastily slipped the letter from Austria into the pocket of her chambray dress.

"Impossible," she quipped. "He only rang once."

Eve was too busy admiring her reflection in the mirror to catch the point. Adjusting one of her diamond earrings, she turned sideways, drew in her breath and scrutinized her flat stomach. She said, still admiring her stomach, "We're running quite late, dear."

Eve was the only person Mary knew who played golf in silk. "I know, Eve. First tee at eleven."

"And that gorgeous little golf pro gets so upset if I'm a minute late." Meeting Mary's eyes in the mirror, Eve bubbled with laughter. "He vows upon his mother's grave that I'm more sexy than any twenty-year-old he knows. Isn't that adorable? Just between us, dear, I think the child is half in love with me and can't help himself. Every woman on this side of town is simply dying to get her claws into him. If I miss one session, they'll move in like hungry wolves."

"A real hardship, Eve," murmured Mary as she hesitated outside the living room door and sniffed a suspicious whiff of smoke that met her at the door. Damn it!

Caught hands down as the women walked in, John II hastily rose to stub his cigarette in the Boston fern and stood rocking back and forth upon his toes in cherubic innocence.

"Ladies!" he boomed exuberantly.

Though Mary had lived in the house eight years, she had never attempted to remodel any of the rooms, and she secretly despised this particular one with its heavy paneling and darkly varnished trim.

With a clink of silver and china, Eve poured herself more coffee and gazed about as if lost. "Where do you keep the artificial sweetener, dear?"

Walking over, Mary lifted the top of the sugar bowl that had been millimeters from the woman's fingertips.

"Oh!" Eve laughed. "Thank you, dear." Ripping the packet open and looking about, then offering the torn paper to Mary who wearily accepted it, she stirred and said, "Did I hear you and the postman discussing another of your little articles, Mary?"

"Hold it right there."

As John moved jovially toward them, Mary watched the rusty hair on his tanned thighs turn to gleaming copper. The Smith men were extraordinarily handsome; one must give credit for that. And though John had overindulged himself in the fruit of the grape, he was still astonishingly fit.

He fashioned a camera's field of vision with both hands. "Two of the most beautiful women I know." He laughed a smoker's raucous laugh.

"I'm nearly seven months pregnant, John," Mary wryly reminded, and positioned herself before the windows. Why had they come? And why didn't they leave?

"I don't think you're going to have a baby at all," Eve said with a ruthless inspection, head to toe. "You're not even showing. It's unnatural."

"She must see our doctor," John said.

"The baby is perfectly normal," Mary declared. "I don't want another doctor, John."

It was her own fault, of course, that John's parents knew about her horrible behavior when she learned she was pregnant. She had locked herself in her room and cried for days, and when her husband's parents stood outside and demanded to know what was wrong, she made the mistake of telling them. Over and over John had warned that under no circumstances was she to ever have a baby. He wasn't going through all that morning sickness business and the swollen waist and puffy ankles and splotchy skin, he said. He wasn't going to tolerate interrupted sleep and weeks on end with no sex rations. No sir, not John J. Smith III. So what had she done after eight years during one of those sacrificial offerings of her body?

"And it *is* John's baby," she added tightly, meeting their unspoken accusation head-on. "I don't care what he told you."

"That's actually what we came to talk to you about, darling," Eve said, and moved to stand beside her husband as if they were a firing squad of two.

At her words, John cleared his throat and awkwardly pulled at his nose. "What we want to know, Mary," he said gruffly, "is how you feel about having the baby now?"

A tiny spasm of alarm began tightening dangerously at the base of Mary's spine. Running her tongue across her lips, she carefully removed her glasses and slipped them into her pocket. The envelope from Austria crinkled like a forgotten ally.

"What d'you mean, how do I feel about having the baby?" she asked warily.

"Oh, I'm the first to admit it, dear," Eve said with a blithe wave. "Johnny has behaved absolutely abominably in all this. I'm dreadfully ashamed of him, and so is John, but he is our son, Mary, and we can't very well give him to Goodwill, can we?"

That was the first sensible thing she had heard in weeks, Mary wanted to say, stifling laughter.

"Hell, just say it, Mother." John spread his legs as if he were bracing himself for a storm, and drew in a long, speech-making breath. "You never wanted this baby, Mary. You can certainly understand our concern. Look at you. You're living here in John's house, forcing him to get the divorce—"

"Which is another thing," Eve said as if it were a matter of national security. "It would have been so much better if you would've gotten the divorce yourself, dear. Don't you agree?''

"Now, Eve," warned John, "we agreed not to go into that aspect of it."

Anger smoldered deep in the pit of Mary's emotions. Was she such a namby-pamby that people thought she would tolerate such interference in her personal affairs? If she had an ounce of backbone, she would scream at them to get the hell out.

She strode to the silver tray and slammed the top back onto the sugar bowl. "I refuse to get the divorce. I never wanted a divorce. I don't believe in divorce."

They were staring at her back as if she were showing symptoms of some terrible disease. "But you can't raise a baby by yourself," John said bluntly. "Face it, girl."

Mary stacked the used cups and spoons upon the tray. She flicked away granules of artificial sweetener from the waxed tabletop. Where was that overpaid Poppy when she was needed?

"I'm perfectly capable of having and raising a baby, Mr. Smith," she said tonelessly, and pushed the cups to the left, then to the right.

"Of course you are," Eve said. Gliding forward, she took Mary's shoulders.

Unable to bear the woman touching her, Mary stepped back and looked in disbelief from one to the other.

Eve went on to say, "What John's trying to explain, dear, is that you have your whole life ahead of you. I think you know how much John Senior and I want what's in your best interests. And the best interests of the baby. Times have changed since you were single, Mary. Perhaps if you had come from a family with money, we wouldn't be so worried, but we both know that Treenie, charming and delightful woman that she is, won't be able to help you financially. If you would allow us, dear, we would consider it a sacred privilege to take the baby when it comes and raise it with all the advantages that John's child deserves."

Mary stumbled in shock as the room seemed to come alive around her.

"We've had a little paper drawn up," Eve said, "and we can assure you that the child would have the best education, the best of—"

To prove her point, she produced a heavy sheaf of legal documents bound with blue from her handbag.

Mary's greatest shock was how, in the space of a few seconds, life had changed and she was helpless to control it.

Torn between the fierce maternal instincts that burned in her breast and the compulsion to fly at John's parents and scream for them to get out of her house, she knew she couldn't even do that. The house belonged to them, not to her. She was as helpless as before.

But not quite. She told herself to smile. Hysterics wouldn't help now, nor temper, nor nastiness.

"I really appreciate what you're saying," her low, calm voice said, "but actually, I don't think that will be necessary, Eve."

A look of surprise passed between the couple. Outside the living room door, Mary glimpsed Poppy eavesdropping shamelessly.

"What do you mean?" Eve was inquiring incredulously.

"I mean that I just couldn't consider it, Eve," she said. "And to push me—"

"Push you!" Eve's rage mottled her glamorous complexion and flared her nostrils, pinching her features until the darling golf pro wouldn't have recognized her. "You think *this* is pushing? Look here—"

John attempted to temper his wife's rage. "Sugar—"

"Keep out of this, John! Look here, you pathetic little church mouse, we've tried to be nice about this, but you make it impossible. We have resources at our command and the money to pursue a matter indefinitely. Are you getting my drift?"

Mary was aware of her breath being caught, of her scalp being numb, of the tips of her fingers tingling. Eve was exactly right; if she and John wanted her baby, they were capable of building a case against her that even Treenie couldn't refute. And they were vindictive people, rich and mean. The worst part was, they would rationalize their act until it truly would seem a sacred duty of monumental proportions.

She jammed her hands into the deep pockets of her dress, and her hand closed upon the crinkling ivory envelope. She didn't move. She hardly dared breathe as she kept the smile frozen upon her face. It was madness!

Or was it? Could she make it work? Could she accept the job in Austria and pull it off for one, short season? There would be problems, yes, terrible risks, but none as dangerous as remaining where John's parents could get their hands upon her baby.

Slowly lifting her head, she waited until she could speak without showing fear.

"Eve, John—" she forced her eyes to remain level with theirs "—I know you mean well. I know you've given this a great deal of thought. I'm deeply... touched." A vile taste formed in her mouth. She swallowed it down. "As it happens, I have plans that will take me out of the country for a while. I've been waiting for the right moment to tell you."

The announcement was tantamount to taking the rings upon Eve's fingers and flushing them down the drain. John was so stunned, he immediately lit a cigarette with shaking hands and took a whistling drag on it.

Eve's face twisted. "You *what*!"

"Eve, Eve," John consoled, coughing. "Get a hold of yourself. I'm sure Mary's not that stupid. Look, Mary—"

Their scorn and hatred and contempt and bitterness was a poisonous gas in the room. It was everywhere, in the smell of the foul cigarette, in the stain of Eve's coffee cup.

"Actually, I'll be leaving quite soon," she told them with a calmness she could hardly believe of herself.

Eve began to deflate like the Wicked Witch of the West melting into her shoes. Her diamonds flashed fire as she waved her hands before her face. "Can't you ever think of anyone besides yourself? This is the only grandchild we will ever have, Mary. You can't rob us of that. We won't let you."

What were they talking about? The only grandchild?

Cruelly, she reminded, "Penelope is having a baby, Eve. Why aren't you having this conversation with her instead of me? I'm sure John would be delighted if you would take her baby to raise."

Angry tears ruined the perfect mascara. "But Penelope's baby isn't John's baby!"

Mary had known about Penelope when she married John. Everyone did: the childhood sweethearts, the hottest team around, the talk of the university. She could remember the precise moment she'd learned that John was seeing his old flame again. Their marriage was four years old at the time, and she remembered when her own feelings for John, whatever they had been, had finally succumbed.

But this? He would not love her own baby, but he would love Penelope's illegitimate baby? Whatever died in her now had no name. Innocence? Hope?

"I've already begun my arrangements," she told them quietly, and closed her hand resolutely upon the letter in her pocket. "I'm quite pressed for time just now, Eve. If you'll excuse me . . ."

Eve reached for the support of her husband, who was ashen with rage. Mary had no illusions about the chances she would be taking. But she had some savings put away. She would take the job and work as she had never worked in her life. At least an ocean would be between them and her.

And the baby? She had no doubts whatsoever that St. Murren would immediately rescind its offer if it had the slightest inkling she was pregnant. And it was a pretty tacky thing to do, wasn't it? Accepting the job?

Luckily, she was carrying the child extremely well, and the work would last for only a couple of months or so. If the staff *did* learn she was pregnant before the season was finished, she would simply have to win their loyalty so it wouldn't matter. Even if she didn't win it, could she possibly be worse off than she was this very moment?

Eve had recovered enough to hiss through her teeth: "You selfish little bitch. You can't leave it like this. What're you going to do about our grandchild?"

While tears welled inside her, while she needed more desperately than ever before in her life to be warm and safe and held and told that everything would be all right, Mary smiled. She smiled and smiled. She was still smiling when she walked out of the room through the door where generations of Smiths stared at her with cold, hard censure.

"Have it, of course," she said.

She hesitated a moment, then, turning, left them and began to climb the stairs.

Chapter Two

Like the movie credits of *Star Wars*, elongated, stretching and rolling out to infinity, walls swirled past in the periphery of Mary's vision.

Somewhere outside, an impatient dusk was crowding down upon Zurich, but here, lying on a rattling hospital cart, headed for surgery, there was no night or day. In a garb of hospital green, strangers moved alongside her. Their voices blended with sounds she did not know—the clatter of wheels, strange doors opening, murmured commands ricocheting back and forth like BBs from a pop gun. Only Jed was real as he floated in a gauzy pool of light beside her head.

"You look terrible," she said with a weak smile.

"You're talking? I've seen better looking faces spray-painted in subway terminals."

Mary laughed, but closed her eyes as the pain stretched a band of flames around her waist. "I hate John," she vowed. "I hate the world. I hate you, I hate this baby. I hate *everything*!"

"That's my girl." His tease sounded as if barbed wire were wrapped around his throat. "Taking it all in stride."

He gripped her fingers hard as his legs kept pace, and Mary clung to him because for the next moments he was her only connection to life. At the foot of the cart, doors crashed open and more walls swept past. She was in a room tiled in blue, an evil-looking light leering overhead as alien faces peered curiously down at her as if she were some earthling specimen brought in for observation.

"Who are these masked strangers?" she quipped, seeking his face and whispering, "Don't leave me."

He lifted her knuckles to his lips and kissed them, his promise finding her as the crow's feet framing his eyes tightened with determination. "Wild chipmunks couldn't drag me out of this room, lady."

A nurse slipped a surgical gown onto Jed as he waited for them to transfer Mary from the cart to the table. Everything he saw and smelled dredged up his past like silt that had drifted to the bottom of the Dead Sea. The woman stretched before him represented life and the future, a thing he would have said, two months ago, did not exist. More than anything he had ever feared, he feared losing her.

Over Mary's head, the anesthesiologist was smiling at her upside down.

Jed wanted to grab him by the collar and yell, *You have my life in your hands, doctor, and you damn sure better not make any mistakes! Not like I did!*

"Are you sure you know how to do this?" Mary was feebly joking with him. "I can take the truth."

"I'm not going to put you very deep, Mary," he told her. "Just a really great high."

"I'll be a junkie."

He laughed. "A brief visit to la-la land."

"Hello, Mary." A doctor unknown to Jed flexed his fingers into snapping surgical gloves and leaned over the table. "I'm Dr. Werner, Mary. You're going to be just fine. Are you allergic to anything?"

"Codeine and pain," she murmured. Twisting, she groped across the empty space. "Jed?"

He leaned very close, his face half hidden behind his mask.

Meeting Jed's eyes at close range—those rust-gold eyes framed by spiky black lashes that could surprise her with their infinite shades and moods, that could strip her to bare bones or cocoon her in a swath of safety—Mary thought of a thousand things she should've said long before: *Thank you for being who you are. Thank you for understanding my old-fashioned ways. Thank you for not finding me ugly, for putting up a fight to keep me, for refusing to let go.*

"Don't try to talk," he said.

Her fluttering fingers quarreled with his. "There's something I have to tell you."

"It can wait."

"No. John's parents. If they find the baby... if anything happens to me, Jed, promise me they won't get her. You take her. You raise her. She's our baby. You—"

A nurse pricked her with an injection. "Ouch." Mary squinched her face.

"Her?" teased the nurse. "You're sure of a girl, are you?"

"No doubt about it."

Jed knew, even as he groped for a professional objectivity that eluded him, that he had been here before. He had known the same terror of losing and, until he met this smiling, contradictory woman, he *had* lost. He had run from that loss blindly, crashing through one wasteland after another until he had nowhere left to go. Because of her he had turned, finally, and faced his fear, had embraced it as an old and gouty friend.

"I promise I'll take care of the baby," he said hoarsely. "*Our* baby."

"Our baby. Relax now, darling. Let your injection take effect."

"I only wanted to make things better." She began to ramble as her worries swirled blissfully away into a lavender Valium mist. "I thought I was doing the right thing. I didn't mean to cause trouble. I love you, Jed. I think you're wonderful. Everything is so wonderful."

To Jed's amusement, the nurses exchanged twinkling looks over the tops of their masks. Chuckling, he said, "I love you, too, even if you are drunk as a skunk."

"How drunk can a skunk get?"

"Can you count backwards for me, Mary?" The anesthesiologist prepared to find her vein. "From one hundred?"

"Ninety-nine." Mary licked her lips and smiled. "If you let me die, Doctor," her voice slurred happily as it floated out to meet Luke Skywalker and Darth Vadar in a galaxy far, far away, "I'm going to drag you down to the floor and break both your arms and legs and then I'm going to hurt you. Ninety-eight, sixty..."

St. Murren had sent a car to Zurich to meet her flight. After first stepping off the long flight from the States into a strange new world, Mary had expected some kind of initial gesture from the resort—a train ticket waiting for her, or a fare on a local puddle-jumper, even one of the staff picking her up while they conducted hotel business.

As she disembarked and staggered up the ramp beneath the weight of her shoulder purse and a carryon, she was beginning to despair of taking one more step when she spied, beyond the flurry of people, a piece of cardboard held high above the crowd.

"St. Murren" was scrawled upon it, and beneath it a curly blond head was swallowed by a jaunty yellow cap. A blessedly friendly face was surveying the passengers as they passed.

Thank goodness! "I'm Mary," she exclaimed as she ran up to him. "Please say that's for me."

He was a healthy decade younger than she, but his gray eyes roamed expertly over her height, ending in approval of her slim red maxi-coat and the neat wool trousers and lace-up flats beneath.

"I'm Stepan." Laughing, he slipped the card beneath his arm and reached for her tote, adding in the perfect English she was to learn that almost everyone in Europe spoke, "Welcome to Zurich, Mary Smith."

"My life is in your hands." She was more than glad to turn over her luggage when it came.

"You made a wise decision, *fräulein*."

The little flirt! Mary thought, liking him.

He steered her adroitly through the ordeals of the airport and out the terminal gates. When she was finally snuggled into the back seat of a limousine that reeked of leather and a recent Gauloise, she began to unwind and relished the luxury of being cared for. She had done it. She was actually here. A powerful engine was spiriting her to somewhere different from anything she had ever known or done before.

Gooseflesh appeared on her arms, and she hugged herself and the baby.

Watching from his mirror, Stepan inquired, "Are you comfortable, *fräulein*?"

Starting, she laughed, then stretched away her weariness. "Could a person be uncomfortable in heaven?"

"I thought heaven was America."

"You haven't been there recently, have you?"

"I don't have to. America came to us."

"Oh?"

"Haman Stone." He rolled the name on his tongue as if it left a bitter taste in his mouth.

Not understanding, Mary let it pass and gazed out at paradise—the folds and crevices of snowy slopes, rooftops rising out of misty hollows and fruit orchards shivering until spring. Soft dusky clouds drifted high in the sky, and the setting sun spattered them with scarlet and orange and rust.

Ahead soared the majesty of the Alps, with snow as white as a bride's veil wrapping its crests. Stepan steered the car into breathtaking climbs, and she held her breath that she would wake up in a few moments to find it had all been a mistake. Maybe all this wonderful stuff would turn into a pumpkin at the stroke of midnight and leave her with nothing but the bitter fruit of her deception.

She crossed her legs, then uncrossed them, straightened the creases of her slacks and arranged the hem of her coat.

"You know Haman Stone, *fräulein*?" he presently inquired, tossing the question over his shoulder and watching her from his mirror.

The corners of Mary's mouth turned downward in a shrug. "We've corresponded. Why?"

"No reason, no reason."

Then why had he asked? "Do you know him?"

He pursed his lips. "Everyone around here knows Haman Stone. People..."

"People what?"

But he only smiled in a maddening way, and Mary wanted to say that if he didn't intend to finish, he shouldn't have begun. "Don't people like him? Don't you like him?"

"St. Murren is an ancient village, *fräulein*. The château is very old. An American has never owned it before."

Ah! The good old American bull market with its arbitrageurs buying up companies as if they were only so many apples and oranges on a grocery shelf. St. Murren resented Haman Stone. Surely she hadn't stumbled into some "ugly American" situation, some no-win, Yankee-go-home thing.

"Actually—" she smiled her most trustworthy smile "—I've sort of put my neck in a noose taking this job. If you know a good way to get on the boss's good side, Stepan, I promise I'll make it up to you in the tip."

He gave the bill of his cap a tug that made it clear he had said all he had to say.

There had been times after her brash announcement to John's parents that she wished she'd held her tongue and waited them out. One of her main problems—if it hadn't been such a cliché, it would have been silly—was that she didn't have a thing to wear!

"If women can pretend to be men, why can't I pretend to be unpregnant?" she asked the mirror every day, as she critically inspected her middle.

Maternity shops were out, so she'd haunted the secondhand stores and garage sales. At Rudy's Second Time Around on Third Avenue she discovered a marvelous, cream-colored Gloria Vanderbilt jacquard chemise that the clerk swore on her mother's grave had been donated by the sister of a soap opera star on *All My Children*. The waterfall of soft pleats from neck to hem made her look blessedly flat-tummied.

She also unearthed a sweet, rusty brown Patty O'Neil with a dropped waist and scalloped sleeves and hem. The most exciting find, however, were the two Bill Blass separates she located at an "honest to goodness final, final clearance"—a dazzling red bateau-neckline cardigan that hung to her knees and a black trumpet skirt. For a person who had never been a clotheshorse, she could squeak by at even the dressiest occasion. And with her Banana Republic slouchies and Guess? knockabouts for work? And a long lab coat to schlepp around in? Perfect. Her sins were forgiven.

The river and the road and the railway were weaving a crisscrossing tapestry. Stepan had begun to climb again.

After one harrowing turn the ground fell dramatically away, and there, nestled breathtakingly in the valley, was St. Murren, all eight hundred years' worth of it.

"Oh!" she said as she glimpsed quaint cobblestone streets, a tiny church and presbytery magnificently weathered, a small bistro with a gay yellow and green awning, houses' doors opening right onto the streets.

High above the village, in a buttress of the mountainside, its windows catching the last fire of the sun, was the château itself. With just enough castle in the design to please the romantic but enough of the classic, eighteenth-century hotel to satisfy the most practical, it seemed to literally hang upon the side of the mountain. Each corner of honey colored stone was set off by a turret whose shaft was shrouded with ivy and whose top was capped with a snow-tufted, dunce cap affair that flew the hotel's banner.

"Welcome to the war zone," Stepan announced as he swooped the huge car down into the valley and up again with a surge of power.

"It can't be that bad," she retorted.

"You want to bet?"

The château's gardens, Mary saw as they skimmed up the harrowing climbs, were elaborately formal and interspersed with small islands of woodland left in its natural state—holly gleaming among tangles of shivering hawthorn and birch. Dozens of Ferraris and Rolls-Royces and Jaguars and Lamborghinis gleamed from the parking lot. Valets wearing smart, short-waisted red jackets were fetching cars for dark-haired men and beautiful women, some of them dressed for the slopes, some in street clothes for a shopping trip in the village.

Her own limousine didn't stop beneath the flagstone of the front canopy but swung around to the side entrance. Servants' quarters? Quite a step down for a Ph.D., eh?

Still, a doorman was on duty, and he opened the door and helped her out while Stepan climbed out to fetch her luggage. Cinderella was definitely in her scullery stage!

"Take care, *fräulein*," the doorman warned as he helped her alight.

After placing a larger tip than necessary into Stepan's hand, Mary detained him with a troubled touch of his cuff.

"What you said before?" she prompted softly, not wishing to be overheard and wishing she knew more, much more. "About the war zone?"

But half Stepan's mind was on the bills he was pocketing. He hardly looked at her and his tone was much less civil than before. "What, *fräulein*?"

She bit her lip and clenched her hand against her coat. "Nothing."

Before Stepan could shrug, the doorman brusquely urged her up the steps. "This way, please."

"May I help you with the luggage?" asked a bellboy anxious for a tip.

With a helpless glance over her shoulder at Stepan, who had already forgotten her and was swaggering toward a group of drivers who knew much more delicious gossip than a mousy nutritionist arriving from the States, Mary sighed.

Well, heck! If she was walking into a combat situation between Haman Stone and the people of St. Murren, she would simply refuse to be a part of it. She would stay out of the cross fire, create her own identity as a conscientious objector.

Folding her coat strategically over her arm and hugging it to her waist, she held herself very, very tall and sucked in her stomach.

"I'm here to see Mr. Stone," she brusquely announced to the guard posted at the entrance, and wondered if she had "hired help" written across her forehead.

"Of course." With a precise, old-world click of his heels, the man motioned her forward. "Good luck."

There it was again—the insinuation that she was in for trouble.

Once inside the luxurious lobby, Mary was only grateful that she had at least one status symbol in her Vuitton bag. Too much was going on for her to receive more than a superficial impression of the château's immense size. Its old clientele had traditionally been the millionaires who came for the anonymity of the private grounds and interior opulence. For a dignitary to occupy twenty rooms was nothing.

But times had changed. As she moved forward, gasps suddenly zephyred across the spaciousness, causing her to stop. A number of photographers were hastily clearing a lens line, and tungsten filaments were exploding in quick succession.

Spinning full circle, she saw, descending the wide, dramatic stairs like an empress, Mavis Duvall in all her Oscar-winning glory.

People stood taller as the famous Duvall head, held at its most flattering angle, came into view. Her glamorous hand was gripping the leashes of a trio of straining terriers, her eyes were hidden behind enormous dark glasses and her famous, flaming red hair was wrapped in a white turban reminiscent of Gloria Swanson. Surrounding her, front and back, was a phalanx of bodyguards who had gone to the same gym as Arnold Schwarzenegger.

The crowd swept forward as one, fans with autograph books extended sending a red alert rippling through the staff from the receptionist's booth to the elevator operator.

Mary watched a tall, demure blond step out of a cubicle labeled "concierge." With a face hardly out of her twenties but with the poise of a matriarch, she glided forward and spoke to first one, then another of the dark-suited security men sprinkled through the lobby.

"Miss Duvall," a voice shouted, "is it true that before you left America you filed for divorce on charges of assault and battery?"

Mavis Duvall appeared oblivious to the question. One bodyguard placed himself between the superstar and the people. In a thick Austrian accent, he said, "Miss Duvall iss not giffing interviews today."

"Had you signed a premarital agreement?" a reporter insisted.

"Was there another woman?"

"Is your husband really worth a billion dollars?"

The bodyguard spread his massive legs and braced his fists against his sides. "No more questions," he declared.

For a crystallized moment the crowd was completely silent as it pondered the giant. No one was inclined to argue and, with a murmur, they drew back. The château's security sighed with relief.

As the superstar reached the landing, the snap of her fingers caused an instantaneous flurry among the valets to fetch her car.

Mary winced. She would be responsible for satisfying the quirks and vagaries of all these people? "Boy, have you gone and done it this time, Mary Smith."

"Mary?"

Starting, Mary blinked up at a tall man who looked about forty, his face pleasant and heavily peppered with freckles. His hair, thinning at the temples, was furiously red and so curly it appeared to have exploded from his scalp. Dangling from a pocket of his ski pants was a cap, and hooked into the neck of a heavy sweatshirt was a pair of dark glasses.

"Yes?" she said, trying swiftly to place his face with a memory that refused to come into focus.

His smile faltered as she turned.

"I'm sorry," he said, laughing sheepishly. "I didn't mean to be rude. I mistook you for someone else. My mistake."

"You're forgiven," she quickly retorted, and shot him a bright smile. "But I really am a Mary. Along with another million women, I think." She gripped the hand he had extended. "Mary Smith, the new nutritionist. I just arrived, and I'm so lost I think my adrenaline has evaporated. Is it like this all the time?"

His smile was as warm as a new coat. "The nutritionist, eh? Well, welcome to Olympia. The guests? You kind of get used to them. You remember the heavy tippers and hope you'll never see the prima donnas again as long as you live. I'm Scutter Brown, one of the ski instructors. Actually, I teach the American kids who're in training for the Olympics. Where's your luggage, Mary? I'll help you with it, and if you have nothing better to do afterward, we can fall in love."

Mary couldn't help liking the man. Who wouldn't, the rogue! "I think Big Foot ate it. My luggage, not my love life. Though maybe that's the answer to what happened to that, too."

"Strange you should say that." He boldly made an assessment of what she would look like beneath her sweater and pants and winked. "Something got a hold of mine, too."

"I think—" Mary pretended to disapprove as she pulled her glasses low upon her nose and peered over their rims "—that I've gotten off on the wrong foot with you, Mr. Brown."

"Then let me change feet." He leaned closer. "I'm thirty-four going on forty-three, have never been married but would like to be, possess no bad habits except an insatiable sweet tooth, and you'd love my mother. You don't have to give me your answer today. In the meantime, what can I do for you?"

Their easy laughter made Mary forget to ask why he had mistaken her. "You could steer me toward Haman Stone's office."

"Oh."

Before she could wonder if she'd imagined the heart-beat of hesitance, he was off with a spring of energy, his long skier's legs covering the lobby floor.

Mary hurried to keep up. "Tell me, Scutter, why do I keep getting those looks every time I mention Haman Stone's name. Is the man with the Mafia or something?"

Scutter indicated that they should turn down a narrow corridor. The carpet was lusciously deep, and the sounds of the lobby seemed far away from here. They stopped before an important looking door of stained oak with a brass plaque bearing Haman Stone's name.

In an irreverent voice, Scutter said, "You've never met His Holiness?"

Laughing, Mary whispered from the side of her mouth, "Don't tell me I'm supposed to kiss his ring."

"A mere genuflection will do." His eyes flirted outrageously as he talked. "You do understand, of course, that Premier, Incorporated, presently very high on Wall Street's big board, has been circling Europe like a vulture for months. It's picked the bones clean on a half dozen privately owned establishments like this one."

She had guessed something along those lines. "The takeover's all the rage."

"Rage, yes. Body counts are taken every day. It makes you feel guilty to be an American. Does that answer your question?"

Mary made sure her shrug could be taken either way.

"If you do have a job, you've taken a whopping cut in salary, American or otherwise." He jabbed a thumb into the front of his sweater. "*Moi* is a prime example. Now there's a nasty rumor going around that Stone sees St. Murren as a giant step toward tycoondom. He and the three stooges, his lawyers, go from resort to resort, filtering out potential enemies and installing their own people."

"That's why everyone has such a bad taste in their mouths."

"They crave Haman's blood, my dear."

"Well," she said, wishing that Austria wasn't so far from Annapolis, "there aren't many heroes in the money game, Scutter."

"He'll adore you."

"Who? Haman Stone? I doubt it."

"Then *I* adore you."

When she pulled a chiding face, Scutter laughed and held up both hands. "Okay, okay. Look, I'd stay and see you through the ordeal by fire, but I have a student waiting for me. See you at dinner tonight?"

Waving at him with one finger, Mary huddled behind the security of her bag. "If I'm still alive. Perhaps."

He hesitated a moment before walking backward to the bend of the corridor, as if rearranging things around in his mind. "Good luck, Mary Smith," he said, before he gave her a small signal of sympathy and disappeared.

She had been better off with only the Smith generations to disapprove, but it was a little late for that choice wisdom now, wasn't it? She had made her bed, and if she didn't want to lie in it, the least she could do was leave it as neat as she had found it.

As if by magic, the door to Haman Stone's office opened. A rather prim man of fifty with features as smooth and flawless as a boy's looked at her as if he knew every act, every thought, every word of her entire life.

"Oh!" she gasped involuntarily, and retreated a step.

"You're Mary Smith," Stone declared in a voice several sizes larger than he was. "Come in."

After Scutter's cynical talk about vultures, Mary had expected claws and a beak. His elegant pin-striped suit was hand-tailored, reminiscent of the ones Eve bought for John from Savile Row. She could imagine him fretting over a microscopic dot of soil, should it commit the unpardonable sin of clinging to his person.

Boyish face notwithstanding, his blue eyes were those of a human computer and just as emotionless and impersonal. His smile was merely a formality; it never reached his eyes. When it came to business—and everything would be business with him—he would be totally ruthless.

Mary felt as if she had suddenly been snatched from a casual game of Chinese checkers and pitted against a chess master.

"Thank you," she said, and extended a frozen hand. "I'm very happy to meet you, Mr. Stone."

In lieu of a smile, a tiny grimace appeared momentarily upon the trapdoor of his mouth. He touched his fingers briefly to hers and waved her into an office that was in the process of being rid of its Old World charm and remade into one that would suit his more sybaritic, utilitarian tastes. Fifty feet deep, dark paneled walls rose out of a sea of white carpet. At one end stood an onyx desk on a stainless steel base. Upon its gleaming surface rested a telephone and nothing else.

Three immaculately suited men stood near one wall. They did not speak as she entered. They did not smile.

"Did Stepan have any difficulty finding you at the airport?" he inquired without inviting her to sit.

The lack of the invitation was redundant. There were no chairs except his behind the desk.

"Everything went quite nicely," she said, and smiled with grim determination to see it through. "I'm afraid I fell a bit in love with the scenery on the—"

"I'm glad *one* thing went well." He spun on his heel like a metallic soldier wound too tightly.

With a nervous little gait, he moved behind his desk and thrummed his fingers upon the surface in an irritated drumroll. "I've had to be rather ruthless in bringing the château up to standard, I'm afraid. Which has resulted in a small mutiny on my hands."

He exchanged a look with the three stooges. Nothing short of death by hanging could have induced Mary to ask what he was talking about.

"The chefs are threatening to quit," he declared as he removed some papers from a drawer and idly flipped through them. "And the gardeners are demanding more money. The maids shirk their work, and I'm sure they're stealing me blind, but they're so clever, I can only suspect. And the doctor..."

Without warning, he pinned her with the lie-detector eyes. "My purpose of this little chat," he said, "is to clarify certain house policy matters up front, Dr. Smith. Considering our unique circumstances here, anyone on my staff is under personal obligation to me to report anyone indulging in damaging gossip or any kind of behavior that would undermine the purposes of the administration. Fraternizing with villagers is expressly forbidden. At least until the unrest subsides. As far as Americans employed here, the only one who would pose a problem is the house physician who has an arrangement different from the staff."

Mary smiled blandly. "Of course."

"This administration inherited the man, actually. It's my personal opinion that he's behind much of the ill will in the village, but that is yet to be proven, of course. If you receive any knowledge of this, Doctor, I expect you to inform me."

"I understand perfectly," she lied, for she couldn't care less about some doctor who was obviously going out of his way to cause trouble. He probably should be given a medal for bravery.

"There are no exceptions to this policy."

"Certainly."

He smiled genuinely for the first time. "Please don't be overwhelmed. These are only minor irritations that will soon disappear, I assure you. I'm certain you'll have no such problems during your stay here."

Except with you, sir. "I'm sure I won't."

"Annelise, we've been waiting for you. Have Dr. Smith's bags been attended to?"

Starting, for she had heard nothing, had had no sense of anyone entering or being in the room, Mary jerked around. Slightly inside the door, regal in the way that a simple skirt and sweater and real pearls are regal, the concierge she had noted earlier was adding her up in the ledger of her eyes.

With hardly any stretch of the imagination at all, Mary could imagine the younger woman at the top of the great staircase, gazing down with proud disdain at Nazi soldiers who were commandeering the family estate.

"Everything is being attended to, sir," she said with chilly formality.

Mary darted a look at Haman Stone and his trio, wondering if they felt the woman's hauteur and resentment, but none of them appeared to notice anything out of the ordinary. Yet in her bones Mary knew that Annelise hated Haman Stone, despised him more than anyone here despised him, but he did not seem to know it.

"Very good," he said, and suddenly flicked his eyes up and down Annelise in a regard that couldn't be classified as anything except blatantly sexual.

So he did know! Now she saw that he not only knew, he thrived on that hatred.

"Annelise is the château's concierge," Stone was saying. "I trust her with everything. If you have any problems whatsoever, Dr. Smith, please do not hesitate to call her."

Like a homesick child, Mary stood hugging her bag. Without a word Annelise turned and opened the door and fixed her with another of her chilly looks and held out her hand in an invitation to follow.

Confused about whether she should tell Haman Stone that she was pleased to be in the country, or to be working for him, Mary realized that he had dismissed them both and was pressing buttons on his telephone.

"This way, please, *fräulein*," Annelise said, and ushered her out and shut the door.

"Please, call me Mary," she mumbled, trailing after her.

Her rooms, Mary discovered, were in one of the turrets she had viewed from the limousine. To get there, one took the elevator, or the lift, as Annelise called it—one of the old cantankerous ones with a sliding metallic door outside a cage that crept up and down between the floors with the pace of a spider.

The operator was off duty, and when it came slowly to rest, Annelise drew the metal door aside. "This way, please."

The corridor of stone-flagged floors and paneled walls made a half dozen twisting turns before reaching her apartment. The unsettling performance in Haman Stone's office had her imagination spinning crazily; she envisioned medieval assignations having taken place within the tower, forbidden meetings between lovers who were then executed for treason.

"I'm sure you'll be comfortable here," Annelise said as she searched through her keys for one in particular.

A blinding fatigue suddenly overtook Mary, and she wondered if she could manage to stagger to bed before she fell asleep. "I know I will be."

"It helps to have stayed here before, of course. You already know about the plumbing and steam heat."

She had almost forgotten! With her deception listing badly, she said as casually as possible, "There've been a lot of changes since then."

"Yes."

"How long have you been here, Annelise? At the château?"

Behind the woman's mask Mary caught the flash of an unspeakable hatred. "I only just came. My father was here."

So her father had been one of Haman Stone's casualties. Her bitterness was understandable.

Annelise pushed open the door, and they stepped into another world. Though having obviously been only a single room at one time, the area had been partitioned into two delightfully rustic sections. The sitting room was paneled in white with a medieval Turkish rug laid upon the hardwood floor and a marble fireplace set into an inside wall. The rafters had been left bare, and the aged timbers brought back memories of stories about Crusades and knights in armor.

Before the rug was arranged a Hepplewhite settee and a bergère chair, and to the left a tiny mahogany table bearing a cunning china tea service. Adjoining, and on a raised level, for it was built into the deepest curve of the tower, was an alcove where a double bed occupied most of the floor space. The outer wall was mortar, cracking in places but neatly patched. A folding screen sectioned off the bath, which consisted of a shower drain and a curtain, plus an aging sink and a toilet with an antiquated brass pull chain. The windows were arched, and the drapes were pulled wide. The crimson of the sunset sliced through the open blinds.

Mary's breath caught as she gazed down at clouds floating daintily below.

"It's like the giant's castle in *Jack and the Beanstalk*," she exclaimed, and looked over her shoulder. Quickly she added, as she saw Annelise's shuttered face, "Exactly as I remember it, of course."

"I'll see about getting you a dinner tray." Shutting the blinds and closing the drapes without being instructed to, Annelise turned on a lamp.

Mary smiled. "Actually, I'd like a bit of tea and whole wheat toast, if you don't mind. No marmalade or sugar, please. And if you have it, herb tea."

The request elicited no surprise. "Very well," she said with a polite bow. "Room service will be up right away."

Glancing about a final time to make sure everything was in order, Annelise turned to leave but stopped at the door and raised a slender finger, as if an item had just come to mind. "Did he speak to you about the doctor?"

Shrugging, Mary tried not to answer. Voicing opinions around this place might well have serious repercussions.

Annelise spoke as if reading from a prepared text. "The policies of the new administration are that business will be conducted only with and through approved channels and personnel. Vanessa's nutritional products, whose brand name you are undoubtedly familiar with, are endorsed by the hotel. All the Nautilus and Eagle equipment, as well. The athletic coaches are all certified in their fields and paid by the hotel. And you, naturally, will be on salary. The doctor is strictly on a free-lance basis. If his services are needed, each patient is responsible for his or her bill.''

Not understanding exactly how much of the treatise was Annelise's own private opinion, Mary nodded and joked, ''Why the aversion to the doctor? What did he do, kill someone?''

''Yes.''

Mary's jaw dropped as the young woman bowed quite properly and opened the door, hesitating in its portal like a goddess who is allowed but a short time among mortals.

''If there's anything I can do for you, *fräulein*,'' she said with a lift of her eyes that Mary saw now were stunningly sad, ''you have but to ring.''

Hardly was the door shut than Mary stumbled toward the bathroom, peeling clothes as she did. Annelise and her chilly mystery could wait. If she didn't get some sleep, she would be a basket case.

After adjusting the brass fixtures so that an anemic spray of hot water finally drizzled through the shower head, she soaped herself and sighed. She needed a game plan. She needed to figure out what it all meant and how to make the best of the hornet's nest she'd walked into.

Walked into? Hardly.

Drying off, she belted a robe about herself and the baby, drew on a pair of knee-high argyle socks, made a fire and watched the kindling catch. Laying on a log, she pulled her chair close and drew her feet alongside her in the chair. She never heard room service when it tapped on her door, then left her tray outside.

Sometime later, she had no conception of how long, she sat bolt upright in her chair.

Chapter Three

For misplaced seconds, Mary was lost in the landscape of her room.

Blinking, she wondered if she had slept. Her legs, when she moved them, felt as if they were attached to her body with safety pins. Her back could have been that of the Hunchback of Notre Dame. If she didn't have a crick in her neck the next day, she would certainly suffer from malnutrition, for her stomach was making noises like some caged creature prepared to fight to the death for a crust of bread.

She remembered where she was—St. Murren, Austria. Upon the hearth, ashes lay white and cold. The turret, swathed in darkness, wasn't relieved by so much as a sprinkle of stardust between the tightly drawn blinds.

She cocked her head, listening hard. Had some sound awakened her? Some knock at the door? Had jet lag thrown her inner clock so out of sync that her body believed it was time to get up?

"Yes?" she called in a sleep-velvet voice. "Who is it? Room service? Who's there?"

No one spoke, no one called her name. Shivering, she said to the baby "What a web we weave, hmm, kiddo?"

The strange surroundings and Haman Stone, to say nothing of Annelise's chilling performance, obviously had the skeletons in her closet tap dancing again.

Smiling, she yawned and rose to give her hamstrings a slow, thorough stretch. The tie of her robe loosened so that the sides fell gracefully away, and her limbs were a flash of silky white.

With a tug of her knee socks, she thoughtfully smoothed her palms over the convex of her naked middle. No one except another woman would know what it cost to keep a pregnant body facile and resilient and unscarred—the discipline, the exercise. Not for her were lemon meringues and mushroom pizza. Or even the proverbial pickle.

"But I would sell my soul for a plain old banana this very minute," she said, giggling.

Weighing her breasts in her palms, she looked down at her tautened nipples. Amazing how for the past weeks simple touches had made her come alive in ways she had not imagined, alarming, erotic needs, despite John's snide remarks about the Ice Queen.

"To hell with John J." She patted her abdomen in apology. "Sorry, sweetie, I know he's your father and all that."

With her robe swirling with cloudlike negligence, slender as a sylph, she moved toward the raised alcove, meaning to spend what few hours remained of the night in a prone position. Loosed from its knot, her dark hair floated down her back. She anchored a lock behind her ear.

From the table near the bed, a tiny clock ticked its serenade. Smiling, she groped her way toward it, then stopped stone-still, rooted to the spot as if a shaft of silver had pierced through her center and riveted her there.

He was in the room! She had neither heard him nor seen him, but *he* was what had awakened her—*his* being, *his* force. She knew it the way a wild animal knows when a hunter is in the forest.

A shiver jerked her spine and went to her shoulder blades. She strained to see through the layers of three-dimensional shadows, and her sense of observation seemed honed. She possessed cat's eyes, capable of seeing in the dark.

But they saw nothing. With no warning then, an arm shot out from behind and snagged her waist, reeling her back while the other looped terrifyingly about her neck.

"Well, hello there," a voice murmured huskily into the mad swirl of her hair.

Petrified, Mary abruptly found herself crushed to a man's body that was the texture of iron—a lean, pulsing, driving form, arms that were clad in leather and smelled of wood smoke, legs that might well have been carved from granite.

For a disbelieving second her reflexes were completely disconnected. She pictured a panorama of violent scenarios, and she discarded them all for a special effects gambit in a movie—time being locked, a second taking the space of a day, one frozen frame juxtaposed with another. She had lived this scene before. She and this man had rehearsed for a play and their roles were determined, preplanned, not real at all. It came as an almost weightless relief that she was participating in a drama. In that one out-of-focus moment they were neither moving nor breathing, but simply regarding each other.

Then her breath rushed in a painful spurt, and she came to life as when wind snaps a sail and the race begins. Now she didn't think at all, but reacted on instinct alone. Stabbing her elbow into his ribs with all her strength, she kicked at his shin with her heel. Whimpering, she bucked and wriggled and pounded and thrashed and flailed and tried to slither through the vise of his arms to the floor.

But his muscles were incredibly strong, and she succeeded only in grinding herself more potently against the strain of his thighs. Their scuffle had made him very hard.

She wailed a primitive, inhuman sound.

"Ho! Hey, hey..." Laughing, he nuzzled the back of her neck. "That's not very sportsmanlike, dear."

Crazed, desperate, she tried reaching backward over her head to grasp a handful of his hair, but he bound her more tightly than ever to his chest, his voice as sandpapery as a lion's purr.

"I have to tell you, Mary darlin'," he said as his chin pressed the crown of her head, "you don't inspire a great deal of self-confidence in a man."

Mary? *Mary?*

She had been prepared for his fist alongside her head. Or a gun in her ribs. Even a knife pressed to her throat. But her name? Moaning as she realized she could not escape, she collapsed against him in defeat.

She hardly recognized her own voice. "What do you want?" she croaked. "Please, please don't hurt me."

"There you go." His attack astonishingly took the form of an embrace as his mouth foraged through her hair in search of her ear. "Your kink has gotten even kinkier, sweetheart. For a minute I almost believed you."

When his teeth closed electrifyingly upon her lobe, Mary felt strangled by a dozen appalling sensations at once, feelings that ricocheted to the top of her scalp and the ends of her toes, to her nipples and the deep primal center of herself. His scent overpowered her nostrils—the smell of a gentleman but not of a sissy: spicy, tasteful, expensive, leathery, virile. The odor of fear was not on him.

It didn't make any sense. Who was he? Someone Haman Stone had sent? Someone Annelise had sent?

John! *John has hired this man to kill me, just like the man on* Sixty Minutes! *He will rape me, then dispose of me, and no one will ever suspect him. My mother will think I simply ceased to care. My sisters will always wonder. Eve and John will think I disappeared with their grandchild.*

Their breaths had grown raspy and distorted. His hand about her jaws forced her head still and turned it toward him in the darkness.

"Absence does make the heart grow fonder, doesn't it, darling?" he murmured.

"Please. You don't understand. Please let me go."

With her head tipped back, her throat a vulnerable arch, with his lips finding its column and branding her with a claim she had no conception of, Mary groaned like some tortured creature being dragged from the safety of its lair.

Her response seemed to trigger some urgency buried inside him. "Were you faithful to me, sweet Mary?" His voice was passion-thick as his kisses melted into her shoulder. "I was faithful. Hell, I was a monk."

With rapacious decadence he explored her ear with his tongue. Wave after wave of tremors raced over her. He was shaping a palm about her breast now, horrifying her but at the same time turning her to liquid inside.

Mary's life swept past in an instantaneous blur of millions of tiny sins. She wished that she'd been nicer to the sales clerk at the department store. She wished she hadn't snapped at the water man when he read the meter wrong. She wished she'd been kinder to her family, even to Eve and John. Dotty, oh Dotty. He was turning her face toward him.

"You don't have to do this," she appealed to him one last time as her hands groped in the darkness to connect with anything. "You can have whatever you want. Take anything, but—"

"Now that you mention it, darling..."

In the periphery of Mary's vision, as dark as it was, she glimpsed winged black brows and wide-set, half-lidded eyes, a head of spiky black hair, teeth startlingly white and lips that were fuller on the bottom than the top. She attempted to crack his head with her own.

He laughed. "Bad move," he said as his mouth chased hers. "Never lead with your chin, love."

In less time than it took her heart to beat, he had found her lips. But even more surprising than the thrill of his kiss was his hesitation—abrupt, startled, like that of a person about to speak but who has changed his mind.

In some perfectly logical portion of her brain, Mary knew a mistake had been made. Whoever he was, he had not come to do her harm.

Say something! Now!

But in one of the few truly insane acts of her life, an impulse she supposed she would never, ever understand, she said nothing. Her eyes snapped traitorously closed.

Drawing in a long breath of defeat, her back melted to his chest and she offered him what he was already taking—a backhanded surrender, more an accident than anything else. Yet he knew; in a mercilessly sensual way he gathered her hips to his, reaping her like sun-ripened wheat, and filled her mouth with his taste.

"God, you taste good," he muttered, and kissed her more deeply. "I'd forgotten. You've gone to my head, woman. I'm not sure I like it."

The bizarre thing was that the eroticism was increased tenfold because she wasn't allowed to face him. At least then she could have deluded herself that she controlled something.

He reached between them, and before Mary could consider his intentions, he was letting her know the hard, hot dimensions of his desire. His hands were searching for the source of her woman's heat. Part of her wanted insanely to move the tiny amount that would allow him to find her. He would know, in a way that John had never known, exactly where to touch. She could press his hand there, and he would make it happen very quickly.

But the feral instinct to protect her child brought her crashing to earth. Hurling herself forward, she fell facedown upon the bed and made a delirious attempt to scramble off the opposite side and crawl under it, around it, anywhere!

With a stunned curse, he fell as she fell. She battled to wriggle from beneath him, almost succeeding, but he grabbed her robe and hauled her back as her naked limbs flashed.

She screamed. "Let me go! I haven't done anything!" She struck to free herself of the silk that was holding her imprisoned. "If you came here to kill me, get done with it!"

"Kill you?" His merry laughter filled the enclosure. "That's playing a little rough, isn't it, darling? Even for you?"

What did he keep talking about? Nothing made sense with this man, nothing was relevant!

"Damn you!" she whimpered.

"Your wish was granted long 'ere you thought it, my sweet." Stretching full-length upon her back, he crushed her into the mattress, his legs tangling with hers as he insinuated a thigh meaningfully between her legs. "Sheathe your claws, Mary love. You've worn me out. Come on, turn around. Be nice."

"You're not nice," she choked, and couldn't believe she was debating with a madman.

"At least I'm trying." A haphazard kiss landed upon her elbow. "Which is more than I can say for some around here. Maybe I'm just going to have to fall in love with you for real, Mary Smith."

He laughed as if he had just discovered the ninth wonder of the world and began drawing her into the hot, waiting nest of his legs.

The moment the front of Mary's body touched the whole of his, he flinched—the way a man would start who has been expecting a smile and has been faced instead with the business end of a gun.

"*Wha-at?*" His breath came with a dazed wonder as he swiftly shaped the firm roundness at her waist.

How long had it taken? From beginning to end it had consumed what? Less than a minute? Forty seconds? Fifty for her life to change its course?

"Sweet *Christ!*" he yelled as he leaped from the bed.

There was an agitated fumbling with the lamp and another furiously muttered oath. Light rudely flooded the room.

Blinded, Mary fumbled for the robe that seemed everywhere but on her body. By the time her eyes adjusted and she could squint through the parted curtain of her hair, he was looming with his fists braced on his sides, glaring at her pregnant middle, then at her head drooping behind its veil of hair.

Grasping a coil of her hair and tightening, he forced up her head. Mary peered into the stunned, golden-irised eyes of a stranger, but she saw, not completely to her surprise, that he was looking at a stranger, too.

The color of his sweater was ivory, she noted distractedly, and over that a leather bomber jacket. His slacks were gray, and they were tucked into high-strapped cavalry boots. He was lean and very fit, not stunningly handsome as far as facial features went but one of the most arresting men she'd ever seen.

"Who are you?" he demanded, his voice raspy with incredulity. "And where is Mary Smith?"

Chapter Four

As Jed Kilpatrick, M.D., stared down at the rope of burnished, russet hair coiled about his hand, he guessed he was running pretty true to form.

When he had come to Austria three years ago, the old staff of St. Murren had come to tolerate the downside of his personality, mainly because his work was good and, even more importantly, cheap. The new staff, though they had never actually said it to his face, referred to him as "the son of a bitch." Rarely did he fail to meet their expectations.

This time, though, he'd outdone himself. Confused, hotly embarrassed, he stepped back from the woman and watched the tiny pulse in her throat running away with itself. She had every right to be afraid. Another two minutes and he would have been...

He didn't want to think about what he would have been doing. Her nostrils, fine and small and patrician, were pinched colorless. Anger had darkened her eyes to the same rich, molasses shade of her hair, and they glittered with unshed tears while her hair, thrown back from her face in a mass of thick tangles, was a storm cloud a man could lose his way in.

Her robe drooped low upon one shoulder. With slender, shaking fingers, she clutched it. Her skin was incredibly clear, possessing a translucence so pale that the bluish veins could be seen in the rising swell of her breasts. Except for the outrage that literally radiated from her, her expression was impossible to read. And the mouth he had just kissed—wide, ripely curved, trembling at the corners and tempting him to press it with his fingertips—could have cursed him and been well within its rights.

Shrinking against a bedpost, she was a furious, magnificent knot of womanhood.

"Ahh..." Grinning, he swiped awkwardly at his jaws and shrugged. "Look, I feel like a five-star jerk."

"You should, you idiot!" she snapped in a stinging cloud of affront. "Do you know you scared me half to death? Who are you? And how did you get in here?"

Feeling a trickle of sweat sliding down his spine, Jed frowned and started to say that she didn't have to rub it in. It had been a perfectly honest mistake.

"Well, you didn't do me any too good either, lady," he growled. "How was I to know you'd be in Mary's room?"

"Are you blind as well as demented? Couldn't you tell I wasn't... whoever you thought?"

He arranged one of his nicer "son of a bitch" expressions and sardonically inclined his head. "Perhaps your dazzling virtues blinded me, madam. I have a rather reticent sense of grandeur."

"Don't be ridiculous."

"I'm afraid I've already been that. Actually," he looked distractedly around the familiar apartment, "you kind of resemble her. You even sound like her. Where is she, anyway?"

"There's obviously been some kind of mix-up." Her chin lifted a hostile notch. "If you don't mind, I'd like you to leave now."

Jed drew himself to his full height and let out a slow stream of breath. She was searching for a toughness that obviously wasn't in her nature.

"Sorry, can't do that," he said, beginning to rather like her.

Not expecting a refusal, she squared her shoulders with a valiance he found strangely endearing.

"If you don't," she warned, her hands fidgeting with the closure of her robe and her chin not quite able to decide on its angle, "I'll . . . I'll be forced to call the house detective."

"The house detective? Jerry?" He grinned. "And tell him what? That you don't like the color of my eyes?"

A momentary confusion flitted across her features. She leaned slightly forward, peering more closely into his eyes. Straightening, she cleared her throat and said sternly, "That you attacked me, you . . . breaker and enterer!"

Before he thought, Jed tipped back his head in a burst of laughter, the absolute worst thing he could have done. Her jaw dropped, then snapped murderously shut. Coming to her feet, she threw back her head and folded her arms with a total ignorance of how vivid a portrait her robe was painting of the luscious curves beneath.

As if she were a samurai warrior sizing up an opponent before lopping off his head, she settled her weight equally upon both feet.

With effort, Jed sobered and arranged a more fitting expression. Leaning forward, nose to nose, just so she would know who was who and what was what, he said, "And just to keep the record straight, dear, I didn't break in here."

"Well, you sure as blazes entered!"

"How did *you* get in?" He stabbed an accusing finger.

"How did I—" She stopped, then said slowly, "I live here."

"Here?" Incredulous, Jed threw out his hand to include the whole room. "As in *here* here?"

"No, silly, Hollywood, California." She smirked. "Of course, here."

Then he had to have misunderstood the switchboard operator, Jed thought, when she'd told him that the nutritionist, Mary Smith, had taken up residence in the east turret. He'd be lucky if this woman didn't file charges with the police!

He waved a hand to clear the air. "Back it up, back it up. Look, I came here to see Mary Smith. And don't smirk at me like that. They told me—never mind what they told me. What they *didn't* tell me was that someone was staying with her. I agree, you have every right to be upset. Now, if you'll be so kind, just tell me where she is, and I'll get out of your hair. And while you're at it—" he gave her his most innocent expression so as not to look as much like a heel as he felt "—you can tell me who *you* are so I'll know whose name to call as I hurl myself off the nearest Alp. That way you'll get credit, you see."

A smile almost caught her unawares, but she was on her toes and quickly pressed it away. She frowned fiercely. "Are you insane? For all I know, you could be the Boston Strangler."

Boston? Yes, Jed thought wryly, from one of the best families. But strangler?

Well, that depended upon how you looked at it. Thirty-nine years ago, he'd been born, if not with the traditional sterling silver spoon in his mouth, at least with a superior silverplate. He thought nothing of the family albums that spilled photographs of his grandmother and her friend, Caroline Wine. There were shots of Betty, his mother, traveling in Europe with senators' wives Helen Erwin and Alicia Wolcott. His father's publicity stills were mounted from when Josh had served a stint as mayor before his heart attack.

Morris, the youngest son, had become a professor at Princeton. At twenty-nine, Dub had his own business in aerodynamics. It came as no surprise to anyone that he, Jed, brilliantly educated, had made such a meteoric rise at Johns Hopkins.

By the age of thirty, he had blazed startling new trails in orthopedic surgery. From all over the world people began bringing him mangled bodies to be put back together again. When Hank Damian's plane went down over the Appalachians after a rock concert, the youth was brought with his body broken in twenty places and half his face missing. Jed performed nine operations on the young star. Four years later Damian was back on the concert stage. After that, most of his clientele seemed to have their names in lights before the tragic fact, or were there shortly after.

For a time, it appeared that he held the world in his hands. What a joke! The only hours he spent out of the operating room were to eat or sleep.

"What I want to know," some declared when considering the prestigious Carrolton family he had married into, "is how Jed Kilpatrick has managed to actually impregnate his wife. Twice."

"I'm worried about Jed. Don't you think he seems rather frazzled lately?"

"Save your worry for Ann, darling. She's having a flaming love affair."

There were times when Jed thought he had subconsciously wanted Roger Pike to happen. In Roger Pike, his life came to a crashing halt when, at 12:30 p.m., one November 28, Jed stood helplessly over the operating table and knew that the all-star hero of the Atlanta Braves was dead.

All because a nurse had made a small mistake on a medical report, and he hadn't caught it.

The press did their duty admirably. "Pike Family Wins Suit for Thirty Million Dollars," headlines blared from coast to coast.

People tried to console him, telling him that patients died every so often. Not with Jed Kilpatrick, they didn't. What hurt the most was the pain it brought his family. People could only stand so much grief until they began to try to outrun it.

He finally crawled into a bottle and Jack Danielsed his way into hell and didn't come back for six months. After a bitter divorce suit, Ann took Thomas and Beth, now aged six and four, and moved back to Pennsylvania to live with the Carroltons.

When Scutter Brown found him a job in Austria at the Château St. Murren where he was coaching Olympic ski hopefuls, Jed didn't hesitate to take it. He dried out. Still feeling like Han Solo incarnate dropped into a bath of carbonate and preserved—not dead but not alive—he built up a safe general practice. Miracle of miracles, he'd made a few friends.

One of whom would obviously *not* be this most interesting young woman.

"Look," he said, detesting having to explain himself, "Mary and I—the woman they told me was here—well, I knew her before. We...sort of played a game."

For a second, Mary didn't move, but blinked at the man in disbelief. He knew Mary Smith? The *other* Mary Smith? Lord, have mercy!

Oh, it had occurred to her, all right, when she was rushing around in preparation to come. Someone on the new staff might have known the other Mary, if she did indeed exist, but the chances of her crossing paths with any such person seemed unlikely. Leave it to her to instantly attract the one person who had not only known Mary but had been on intimate terms!

Now what? Should she play it straight and hope that this man was decent enough not to betray her? Should she try to come to an arrangement?

That would only make her look guilty. And she really wasn't. Stupid yes, but not guilty. The less said, the better.

Making sure she was modestly covered, she extended her hand like a true Calvert and said cordially, "I happen to be Mary Smith. I'm the new nutritionist here at the château. I'm very glad to meet you."

The bones appeared to tighten beneath the planes of his jaws. He looked her up and down and nibbled his lip speculatively for a moment. "You're pulling my leg. Right?"

Mary swallowed down the hysteria that bubbled in her throat. "I wouldn't touch your leg, sir."

His bark of laughter made short work of her poise. "Well," he drawled, "I would certainly touch yours, babe."

Babe? *Babe!* Mary felt the sides of her mouth setting in a vise. "Look here—"

He pulled a solemn, deadpan gravity. "Sorry, the fun of the moment just swept me away."

"You seem to get swept away quite easily," she snapped hotly. "Now, if you don't mind, since you've turned my hair gray, would you please leave?"

Before he could reply, she swept into the sitting room. Feeling like a chastened schoolboy, Jed trailed glumly after her, fascinated by the way her slim hips moved beneath the shimmery folds of the robe. There had to be something seriously wrong with a man who could think of sex at a time like this, yet her whimper in that one, silvery moment continued to echo in his ears. He could still feel her heat from when she had dropped her head back to his shoulder and let her bones melt into his. Where, he wondered, was the father of her baby? Dead? Divorced? Had someone actually been fool enough to let this woman get away?

He really wasn't certain why he gave a hang. She wasn't even beautiful in the true sense of the word, though she was quite pretty with her classical bones and tall, healthy slimness. Her elegance was her true beauty—not the elegance of Ann who had gone to enormous lengths to enhance it, but more of a dignity that was deliberately underplayed. Bone deep. Modest. *That* was the word he sought. Mary Smith was modest, and modest women were always a problem. A man was invariably one step behind a modest woman, never knowing where he stood but unable to turn and walk away.

Did Haman Stone know that he'd hired a pregnant woman and brought her halfway around the world? There would be hell to pay with the insurance company if he did.

"Okay," he said, his eyes glued to the delicious backs of her knees, "you say you're Mary Smith, I accept that. I don't understand it, but I accept it. And I'm sorry for frightening you."

She turned her face the barest amount so that its quarter profile revealed a hint of softening. With her left hand, she drew back her hair. No rings, Jed noticed with a strange relief.

"There's no need to apologize," she said more congenially. "I'm sure it was an honest mistake. It's not an ordinary situation."

"You could write a book about that."

At the door, she stopped and treated him with an honest-to-goodness smile, one that reversed his conclusion that she was merely pretty; she was stunning!

"Despite my precautions against jet lag," she admitted with a shrug and a contagious yawn, "I'm afraid I've got a really awful case. I'm going to have to ask you to excuse me, Mr. uh..."

Stifling his own yawn, Jed pondered the door. She was right. He should walk to it and out of it. He should try and locate *his* Mary Smith, then he should forget *this* Mary Smith even existed.

Without answering, he zipped up his bomber jacket and reached for the doorknob. *Leave, Kilpatrick, blast you!*

I can't.

Then you deserve yourself.

Returning, he extended his hand. "I'm afraid in the confusion, I forgot to introduce myself. Jed. Jed Kilpatrick, house physician."

The name, when he said it so easily, caught in the back of Mary's throat like scalding coffee. Seized with a compulsive need to swallow, she took a step backward and, wide-eyed, placed her fist to her mouth while her thoughts raced.

This man, this doctor, was Haman Stone's nemesis? This man who was so blatantly "off limits" was the same man who knew the other Mary Smith?

Dear Gussie, what a mess! He had killed a man, Annelise had said. Maybe the death had been euthanasia. Or an accident. Negligence, more than likely. She wished she had questioned the concierge more thoroughly.

He wasn't like any doctor she had ever seen before, and she'd met dozens. He was young—forty, if that. And only a couple of inches taller than she was herself, five-foot-eleven or so. His hair was as black as Oklahoma crude oil and about as manageable. His nose wasn't spectacular, either, but it seemed to suit his ruggedly tanned face.

He could have been a race car driver, yes. Or a sky diver. But not a doctor. Not with those muscles that were the product of weight lifting and running and swimming. Not with his hostility index or his quickness to jump at shadows, like the victim of a hit-and-run who didn't dare let down his guard, always looking over his shoulder for the unexpected.

"You're the doctor," she whispered in amazement, and blinked at his extended hand.

When she looked up, his smile had disappeared. He icily withdrew his hand.

"Well," he caustically retorted, "there was a brief time in the second grade when I was Spider Man. But other than that..."

"Oh—" Mary flushed "—I didn't mean—"

"Yes you did." He turned, ramming his fists sullenly into his pockets and hunching as if to fend off a chill.

If someone had offered her a thousand dollars, Mary couldn't have kept from staring at the explicit way his trousers were pulled across his lean, muscular buttocks. Nor at the taper of his parted thighs as his legs fit precisely into his boots.

"I, uh..." She nervously felt her face for her glasses and realized she didn't have them on. "Annelise did mention your arrangement with the château, actually, but she didn't go into any detail."

"Good old Annelise." His laugh was decidedly unpleasant. "You never answered my question. Where's Mary? Not you, the other one."

Mary's nerves tightened about her bones. They were back where they began—her half-naked in his arms and him making her do and say things she never intended.

She lifted her shoulders and said, "I'm sorry, I haven't the slightest idea.

Desperate now to escape his steel-trap mind, she snatched up her leather bag from the floor and strode impulsively across the room, turning on lights as she went until the room gleamed like a carnival midway. She plopped the bag upon the armoire beside the window and, finding her glasses, poked them upon her face. He had walked back into the room and had slowly begun to move about it, as a hungry wolf might do when getting the feel of a strange new hunting ground before a kill.

Her pulse jumped. He pointed to her reflection in the mirror from which she furtively watched him.

"Good Lord," he exclaimed softly, amazed, "they think you're *her*, don't they?" As if exchanging a hilarious joke with the light fixture, he angled a look upward and laughed. "And she's accusing me of foul play?" Dispensing with the tease, he closed the distance between them and warned, "Look, lady—"

"Mary," she choked, shivering and wishing she were back in her very own bed in John's old house.

"All right, Mary." He towered over her. "I don't know exactly how much you know about Haman Stone, but when he finds out that you've duped him, do you know what he's going to do?" He aimed a finger at her nose.

"Duped? Don't be silly." Mary jerked up her hairbrush and began to rake it distractedly through the tangles of her hair. "I didn't dupe anyone." Tears of pain collected in her eyes as she created more tangles than she removed. "I was invited here."

"Really?" He shot a vinegary smile at the mirror. "Forgive me for saying so, darling, but aside from having taken a job under false pretenses, you're suffering from an acute case of pregnancy. Did you think we wouldn't notice?"

What was the point in arguing? Mary thought miserably, slumping. He'd seen more than enough, had touched almost everything.

"If you'll just go—" she lowered the brush and tried to capture the breaths that eluded her "—we'll call this a bad first impression and be done with it."

"My, my." His sooty brows arched high. "You're a very generous lady."

Stymied, Mary hurled the brush to the floor, with a raucous clatter, and stood gaping at it in disbelief. Who was this man that he had her behaving in such a way? She didn't have a violent bone in her body, but from the first second he'd had her kissing a stranger and actually enjoying it. He had her scuffling. Now he had her resorting to violence.

His lazy smile was as reassuring as a submachine gun.

"Why does it bring you so much pleasure to do this to me?" she railed. "What did I ever do to you?"

He pinched his bottom lip as if imagining ways to make her life more miserable. He studied her face, the too-quick rhythm of her breaths, her socks that had begun to droop. She thought if he didn't stop dissecting her, she would burst into tears.

"All right," he said presently, no hint of a smile upon his wide mouth. "I'll go. But before I do, you're going to do one thing, Mary Smith."

What could she do except whisper, "What's that?"

"You're going to tell me who put you up to this."

Beneath her feet, her deception shifted like quicksand, and Mary began immediately to sink.

"Who put me up..." She shook her head in confusion. She opened her mouth, closed it again.

"This is some kind of fiendish scheme to blackmail me?" His gritty words flayed her raw. "To catch me in a compromising position?" His teeth were bared in a bitter smile. "Some paternal thing, is it? Annelise told you to do this? Haman Stone?"

Trembling, defeated, Mary taxed all the dignity she had ever known. Keeping her head high and her shoulders proud, she walked around him to the door and reached for the knob only to have it slip through her fingers. Finally she got the wretched thing open, and her voice came with great effort.

"Dr. Kilpatrick, I don't owe you any explanations, and I certainly don't owe you my hospitality."

The smile that curved Jed's lips had nothing to do with pleasure. On the contrary, it felt more like an obscenity, for he wished he could take everything back from the beginning. She had to be the first woman he'd been so intensely attracted to since his life went up in smoke, yet inner demons were forcing him to do everything possible to make her despise him.

He was hardly aware of stepping through the open portal and waiting here, half in, half out.

"Before you leave,"she said hoarsely, "could I ask how you got into this room?"

"Of course."

She waited for him to go on, but Jed merely turned and flicked a final inspection from her head to her feet. Like a beautiful, regal iceberg, nine-tenths of her was below the surface. Too bad, she was one hell of a woman.

"Well?" she demanded as a nervous twitch marred the porcelain smoothness of her cheek.

Reaching into his pocket, he produced a key.

Her eyes widened in amazement as she stared at the tiny object. She choked, *"Give me that!"*

Lunging for it, Mary realized too late that she'd fallen for the oldest ploy in the world. She stumbled into Jed Kilpatrick's arms, and he caught her close, his hand wrapping about her waist so that the robe was twisted again and she was practically naked against him. Even worse, because her secret had given him a weapon, he held the key out of reach over her head.

"Uh, uh, uh," he teased, and, laughing, released her to slip the key into the watch pocket of his slacks. He gave it a come-and-get-it-if-you-dare pat. "Any more questions before I go?" he drawled wickedly. "Little mother?"

Oh, she hated him for that! "Yes!" she hissed. "How long will it take you to get out that door?"

To show that she had already dismissed such a hateful person, she clumped miserably across the room and began shoving things haphazardly into bureau drawers from her suitcase.

"Just so you understand, pretty lady," he called to her back, "you won't get one red cent out of me. Nothing personal, you understand. A small matter of blood and turnips."

Mary slammed the drawer shut with such violence, the vase shuddered on the table. She wished she could make him feel one inch high. She wished she could bring him to his knees!

"I was warned about you, you know," she declared, spinning about.

His smile went for her bones. "Annelise?"

"Just so *you* understand, Doctor, I don't need your money, and I don't need a father for this baby. I'm here at the château on legitimate business, not monkey business, and I've come a long way. I'm obviously not the Mary Smith you were expecting, and that's a long story, but in case you have any idea about taking up the same relationship that you had with my predecessor, kindly stuff it into one of your ears. Even if I *were* interested—"

Unexpectedly, the floor moved beneath Mary's feet, and nausea boiled up from the pit of her stomach. She stumbled, groping dizzily, and pressed her hand over her mouth.

Hardly had she weaved than the door slammed shut, and Jed Kilpatrick was beside her again, taking her into his arms and pulling her into his side so that their bodies were more one than two.

"I'm sorry," he murmured. "I'm a cad and a scoundrel and a thousand other things. Easy, now. Easy does it. Over here, not too fast."

Moving her luggage to the floor, he deposited her upon the settee and took charge without being asked, pressing her back upon the cushions and seeking her pulse. Mary attempted feebly to push him away, but he fit his hip to a small section of cushion and briefly timed her heartbeat.

"I'm all right," she protested.

"Sure you are."

"Once I eat . . ."

"Tell me, Mary—" his eyes were glued to the second hand of his watch "—is there a Mr. Mary Smith in all this?"

"What does that have to do with anything?"

"Because if there isn't—" finished, he lowered her hand to his lap and felt her forehead "—we have a serious problem on our hands."

She blinked at his large hand wrapped around her wrist, at the sprawling wonder of his length. "If you must know," she said on an incredulous sigh, "Mr. Smith will be arriving later."

The tick of the clock was the only sound in the room. *Liar, liar, liar* it said. *Fool, fool, fool.*

Rising, he walked to the telephone and dialed. "Room service, please." He paused, then identified himself. Mary heard a voice speaking as if from another planet, and he turned to smile absently at her. "You did? How'd it go?" A pause, then, "Not even a nightcap? Well, didn't I tell you that would happen? Next time do exactly... Ahh, look, Brewski, do me a favor and send a tray up to the east turret. Yeah, I know what time it is. I want hot soup, some whole wheat toast, some juice and fresh fruit. Well, find some. And don't pawn any of that junk off on me, either, no chemicals or preservatives. Read the labels, Brewski. You've got ten minutes. *Ciao*."

When he returned, he positioned himself upon the arm of the settee and crossed his legs as he if were prepared to stay indefinitely. Stretching his arm along the back of the cushion, he plucked an errant wisp of hair from her cheek, his voice the gentlest of rebukes.

"Was that necessary?" he asked.

Mary didn't want to see understanding on his face. She didn't want anything he had to offer.

She turned aside. "You don't understand anything about why I came here, so please don't give me advice."

"Look at me, Mary."

No! She wouldn't. But if she didn't, he would be able to see into her soul with X-ray vision.

Turning her head, she saw, as she had not seen before, that he was a man no different from her and the rest of the human race. He had been hurt. He was still bleeding. Why did she have to be afraid of him? A puzzling impulse came over her to reach up and smooth his ridiculous stubbly hair into place and press the troubled lines from his face, to just . . . touch him.

But tears had blurred the lenses of her glasses, and she pulled them off, rubbed them on her robe a few times and replaced them. "I'm divorced. Or at least, I should be by now."

"No disgrace in that."

"I don't want to explain any of this to you," she said as bloodless memories ripped her apart at the seams. "All right?"

He idly touched the shoulder seam of her robe. "What you have to understand, Mary, is that we're sort of in a mess. Resorts are like gossipy little Peyton Places, you know? The grapevine here is more efficient than a party-line telephone. It just so happens that there're a few people left who, ah...well, they once had the crazy idea..." He laughed for effect, the joke at himself. "Heaven only knows how they got it. They assumed that your predecessor and I had a love affair."

Where had they gone? Mary asked herself in horror as she leaned forward upon her knees. All the good, logical reasons she had for coming?

Heaving to his feet, he paced the floor briefly. Stopping, he spread a hand across his waist, as if he were fending off a blow.

"As it happens," he said, pointing a thumb at his chest, "I'm the one on the spot. I was the one who recommended to Haman Stone that he rehire you, Mary. I beg your pardon, rehire the woman I *thought* you were. You wouldn't even be in Austria if it weren't for me."

Looking up, Mary pulled a disparaging face. "Am I supposed to thank you or hit you?"

"Which leaves me," he said, ignoring her sarcasm, "in a unique position. Besides being responsible for you, you understand."

As the baby gave her a stout kick in the ribs, Mary's senses went on red alert. Intuitively, her hand rested at her waist. "No one is responsible for me."

"The problem is, Mary, that even if people don't know you're wearing the wrong face, they'll know you're Mary Smith. Put two and two together, and you've got a few people assuming that *your* baby is *my* baby. If we ignore each other, I'm shafted because I've deserted you. If we don't ignore each other, I'm shafted because I don't accept responsibility for your dilemma. Either way, I'm getting it right up to the old tonsils, wouldn't you say?"

Chapter Five

How was it that some words had the ring of truth even as the dust of past mistakes clung to them?

What Jed was saying was the stuff of storytellers and poets. Somehow, while she had been planning and scheming to save her child and he had been escaping his past, the paths of their lives had entwined: night tracks in the snow, proof to be stared at in the cold light of dawn.

She lifted her hands to her face. "This isn't what I thought would happen." She shook her head. "It's unbelievable."

"Believe it," he said with a tone that had already accepted fate's immunity to defeat. "It's happened."

Between the bars of her fingers, Mary watched him shrug off his jacket and toss it aside with vagabond negligence. He could have been her lover for years, so deeply was he in her life. She braced to resist his magnetism, for to admit the synergy between them with a tone or even with a subliminal thought would be to yield control of her life to a phantom.

Guardedly, she said, "Haman Stone didn't list any specific requirements in his letter. It came. I was available. More than available. Even if I'd wanted to find the right Mary Smith, how could I have in a city the size of Annapolis?"

When he did not reply, she guessed he didn't believe her. "It so happens," she said as she came unsteadily to her feet and, turning, weaved briefly back and forth, "that I'm quite good at what I do."

"I'm sure you are."

"I'm probably better qualified than anyone around here." She combed her hair with her fingers. "I should think St. Murren would be so glad to have someone who can actually do what they were hired for, they wouldn't worry whether she was going to have a baby or not."

"You're going to tell that to Haman Stone?"

"I wasn't planning to tell him anything."

"Ah, I get it." He flashed her a tongue-in-cheek smile. "You were hoping for the old miracle. You thought he might be struck blind at the appropriate moment."

Mary thought that if she'd had a stick in her hand, she would have thrown it at him.

"Well, look at me," she exclaimed and spun around, her arms outstretched. She didn't look all *that* pregnant, for pity's sake!

"Darling—" appreciation glowed warmly in his eyes "—I've been trying to do nothing else since the lights came on. You haven't exactly been making it easy."

She sucked in a resentful breath. "I meant—"

"I know what you meant." Coins jingled in his pockets as he circumvented her until they faced again.

"Okay," he said, turning down the sides of his mouth in a contemplative pucker, "I'll play your game. What was the question again? Ah, yes...how do I think you look? As on a one-to-ten?"

He was too quick by half. "Forget I said anything, all right?"

"Too late, I'm in my judgmental mode. Now you must be still, dear," he said, and took her by the shoulders as if to nail her permanently to the floor. "Or I won't be able to be objective about this."

It took all the moral stamina Mary possessed to endure the scrutiny that somehow had managed to transform itself from the rhetorical glance she intended into a thorough physical profile. He did everything but run a CAT-scan.

"We-ll," he drawled as he maddeningly tapped his jaw and shook his head, "I don't know, Mary, I just don't know."

She could smell, horrifyingly, her own heat as he stepped lazily forward and lifted a tress of her hair back from her face.

Through her teeth, she said as nastily as possible, "Don't blow it, Doctor."

"Jed. And we always want to look our best, don't we?" His smile was grounds for first-degree murder as he arranged her hair and straightened the lapels of her robe.

Slapping at his hands, Mary slammed her foot petulantly on the floor. "I knew you'd blow it."

But now the nausea that had only flirted with her earlier returned to betray her altogether. As their looks collided, Mary clapped a hand over her mouth and stumbled toward the raised alcove with its tiny toilet behind the screen. *Please don't follow me this time,* she prayed. *Please go away.*

"Haven't I humiliated myself before you enough for one night?" she wailed as his clipped steps sounded in her ear and he found her draped over the porcelain bowl. "Go away."

"Oh, don't be stupid," he said cheerfully, and turned on the tap. "After all we've been through together, humiliation is a moral imperative."

She groaned. "Stupidity's in my genes. Go away."

"You'll get no argument from me on that score."

Chuckling as he wet a washcloth while she continued to gag on an empty stomach, he knelt beside her and removed her glasses with ease, hooking them onto the sweater's ribbing at his neck while he held her head. He gently blotted her lips and crooned, "That's my good girl."

Mortified, Mary held to his arm for support as she rose unsteadily and refused to meet the amusement twinkling in his eyes. "Thank you."

"You're just full of little surprises, aren't you? When did you last eat, Mary Mary?"

"On the plane." She let him draw her into his side and walk her out of the bath. "Fruit, I think. I can't remember. I couldn't eat that processed junk they served."

"Gad." Laughing, he dipped his head so that his nose grazed her cheek and his breath was warm and sweet on her face. "I'm having a baby with a purist."

With an accusing look of censure, Mary snatched the washcloth from his hand and wiped her own face. "That isn't funny, Jed Kilpatrick."

"If I'm going to be the daddy, you've got to be the mommy and get used to these little inconveniences."

"Little inconveniences, my foot."

"A very nice foot, by the way, even if it does seem to spend an inordinate amount of time in your mouth. Now, come lie down. I'll make the bed. It seems to be torn up something fierce. One would think that lovers lived in this room."

"I'll take a chair," she said dourly. "And not in this bedroom, thank you very much."

"You sure don't obey orders very well."

"So I've been told."

Moving past him, she sought the settee and scrunched into its corner. To her dismay, Jed didn't sit down but moved through the room and dimmed the lights. She heard him putting away her cases and making order. The thought of him touching her intimate things was like a hot needle against her nerves.

Before he returned, a soft click sounded and strains of Mozart from the radio presently filled the room. When he fetched the comforter from the bed and tucked it about her legs, she tried to think of something safe and impersonal to say.

But little about their encounter had been impersonal, and absolutely *nothing* was safe!

A tap sounded discreetly at the door, and Mary started. As if he had answered room service for this room dozens of times before—and he undoubtedly had, she must never forget that—he walked to the door.

Hinges creaked and money changed hands. The door closed. Wrapping the comforter more tightly about her, Mary twisted to see.

To her astonishment, an elegant table, whose circular ivory cloth reached the floor with starched perfection, had been rolled into the room. Upon its top were trembling candles and gleaming silver, crisp napery and real china. The stemware sparkled and the cunning teapot, as fat as a cuddly Buddha, sent steam curling seductively from its spout.

"Wow, have you got clout!" she exclaimed, and came carefully to her feet, comforter and all. Hurrying toward it, she lifted a cover as he pushed. She inhaled the heavenly aroma of soup and freshly sliced fruit.

"Would you look at this fruit?" Greedily, she popped a sliver of orange into her mouth and closed her eyes, sighing with contented bliss as she chewed.

"Delicious!" she said with her mouth full.

Another bite. And another until juice trickled down her chin in a golden rivulet. She blotted it with the back of her hand and dunked a crunchy piece of toast into the soup and sucked on it, stuffing another into her mouth and washing it down with a scalding sip of tea.

"Sheer heaven!" Making sounds of earthy satisfaction, she laughed and looked up in grateful expectation of finding his smile.

The raw, naked hunger engraving his face as he watched stunned her—his loneliness was so consuming and wordlessly painful, it stole the breath from her body. It wasn't an emotion that should have been exposed to human scrutiny.

Oh, Jed, she thought with a rush of guilt as she blindly groped on the table for the napkin, her own hunger forgotten. Not finding it, she blotted her lips on her sleeve.

"Jed?" she breathed. "Please, won't...won't you..." She helplessly indicated the food. "Won't you share this with me?"

If she had been any other woman, Jed guessed he would have given her his best cavalier smile and accepted the invitation. He would have sat across the table and enjoyed an early morning flirtation until it sated his starved heart.

But she wasn't any other woman, and it didn't have to make sense. If he stayed here any longer, he wouldn't leave at all. He figured, considering her present circumstances, her presence in a strange country, her nervousness and need of someone tó care, that he could have eventually broken her down. And he didn't want to risk losing... losing what? What could he possibly lose? He had nothing with her, nor she with him.

Before he could think about it or change his mind, he grabbed his jacket in a fist and strode briskly to the door.

"It's getting late, Mary," he said with a voice bordering on rudeness. "I'd better be going and let you get some rest."

Dazed, Mary followed him to the door and blurted the first thing that came to mind. "How much did this cost? I have to pay you back."

At the door he wheeled hard about, and Mary stopped, fearing to go farther. Hazardous lines grooved his face. He was all high-tensile steel, and she wasn't capable of holding her own.

"Pay me for what?" He shrugged into this jacket. "Attacking you?"

Her protest was a whisper. "You didn't attack me."

"Hell, Mary. I wanted you bad enough to..."

Trembling, she forced herself to accept the totality of what he was—a man who had come so close to destruction that his instincts for survival were primal. Her words came with great effort.

"I'm not afraid of you, Jed Kilpatrick."

He was suddenly gripping her shoulders, and she writhed at the unwitting pain he brought her.

"You should be," he muttered roughly, giving her a shake. "You should be terrified. I destroy everything in my path. Haven't you heard about me? No? Well stick around, honey. You will."

Releasing her so suddenly that she stumbled against the wall of the cramped corridor, he raked his fingers distractedly through his hair and scoured his face, messing up his brows. The veins of his neck were knotted channels carrying his grief all over his body.

Softly, Mary said, "I never meant to complicate anyone's life, Jed. Certainly not yours."

He attempted a dour smile, but failed miserably. "It's not you. Forget what I said." He rubbed briefly at his eyes. "Seeing you...I don't know, seeing you makes me miss my children."

Mary thought if she didn't do something quickly, she would shatter into a million pieces. Swiftly, before logic could take the place of her woman's compulsion, she stepped forward and took his hand and placed it gently upon the swell at her waist. She watched, not the large masculine palm covering her baby's nesting place, but the surprise that touched his face and gradually transformed it.

"They never kick when you want them to," she shyly admitted with a laugh, having never done this except with her sisters. "You have to be patient." To her abdomen, she said, "Are you awake? Come on, you've got company."

To Mary's surprise, the baby obliged by choosing this moment to make its presence felt; it rolled so that a tiny heel poked its impression against Jed's hand.

To Mary, the look upon Jed's face in that instant was worth all the grief and insults she had suffered from John and his family. Yet, it made her remember all the anger and bitterness she'd felt in the beginning. Tears sprang unexpectedly to her eyes and she wanted, more than anything, to tell the baby she was sorry. She wanted to tell Jed.

Perhaps he knew already. As if he meant to drain the moment of every last pleasure, he smilingly moved his fingers over the tiny foot, shaping it with awe. He placed both hands upon her abdomen and, laughing softly, got a bearing on the way it was curled inside, sleeping, trusting.

His look lifted to hers. They were caught in a moment of poetry—two pretty, laughing children who had stumbled upon a most wonderful buried treasure.

"Ahh, Mary," he said. "It's so fine, so fine."

"Thank you," she whispered as tears drizzled slowly into her mouth.

"How many months?"

"A little over seven now."

"Mercy, woman, where are you carrying it? In a hollow leg?"

She laughed tearily, and he laughed because she did. Gradually their smiles disappeared, along with their pleasure that had been stolen out from under the nose of a distracted fate. Their return to earth was sure and certain, but this time they had reached too far across the distance of the past and even into the future.

In slow motion, frame by gentle frame, they moved irrevocably closer.

Neither spoke, neither looked away.

Without apology, he cupped a hand about her jaw and probed her for answers to questions that had no voice. Watching his own hands, as if to stop them should they go too far, he placed them upon her hair and moved them down the long, creamy column of her neck and over the planes of her shoulders, the tops of her ripened breasts.

"Stop me," he pleaded softly. "Don't let me—"

Trembling, Mary wet her lips and tried futilely to smile. "I . . . can't."

The scent and leathery sounds of his jacket were heady, erotic. Mary heard the sultry rustle of her robe beneath his inquisitive fingers. His parted lips grazed her cheek, and he stepped the remaining inches into her body.

"God," he moaned softly as he folded her into his arms, "I don't know what I'm doing. I've lost my mind."

"Yes," she said, flicking her tongue at the salty tears.

As delicately as a summer breeze, he sought her lips. His breath was incredibly, incredibly sweet in her mouth. All the angles of her body were fitting to his now, and Mary no longer resented the tight stricture of her pregnant waist. She opened her eyes and watched his own as they closed so tenderly. He was frowning, and he frowned deeper as he moved his lips upon hers as if he must now find a balm for the unhealed wounds of his life.

Rising on her toes, meeting his kiss, Mary placed her hands upon the back of his head.

"Hold me for a little while, Jed," she begged. "Stay and hold me."

She would never know, Jed thought, how much he wanted to. He desired her almost beyond his ability to control, and when she slipped her hands beneath his shirt and pressed her palms upon his chest, he took her hand and moved it over his side and over his thigh to the raging part of himself. Never had he known a woman to bare her soul as she was doing, but everything he had touched in his life had turned into a tragedy. He couldn't, he *wouldn't* add another statistic to that list.

Very quickly, very hard, with a savage hold on his own will, he kissed her lips and stepped back.

With bitter clarity, he said, "You're not a one-night stand, Mary. I'm not saying I couldn't carry you to that bed this very minute, because God knows I could. But you don't want that, and I don't have anything else to offer a woman. I wish to heaven I did."

His words cut to the quick of Mary's soul. Shrinking, not believing she had broken the one inviolate rule of her life by asking him, she clutched her robe as if it could hide her thoughts as well as her own need.

She couldn't face him. "I don't want you to worry about what people will say. I'll find a way to spare you any embarrassment. Just behave to me as you would anyone else. I'm very sorry for getting you mixed up in this. If you'll give me a little time..."

Before he could protest, she left him standing in her door. She touched the light switch and slipped into the shadows where she could slump against the wall in misery without dread of being seen.

She had hurt him, but he had hurt her, too. He was groping through his thoughts in search of an answer, and whether or not he found that answer she would never know, for the sound of the closing door reached her.

As if a blade had passed through her, she leaned forward, holding her breasts and the ache that was couched so treacherously beneath them, holding the urgency that was buried lower. And much deeper. She pressed hard against that urgency, and she moaned, she wept.

Jed barely made it to the elevator before the backlash of what he'd done hit him. How? How, in the name of sweet sanity, had it happened? He'd arranged his exile meticulously, as painstakingly as a bride would plan the details of her wedding. He'd spared no effort to protect his wounds from being reopened. How was it that he was bleeding because he'd let a total stranger with alive brown eyes and a winsome smile come from behind and invade him?

He couldn't even blame it on Mary. He had it coming. Boy oh boy, did he have it coming. *He* was the one who had gone to her room. *He* was the one who'd put his hands where they didn't belong, *he* had tasted the honey of her kiss and thought for one trembling moment that it was possible to turn back the clock and pick up his life again.

Wincing as the elevator deposited him at ground level, he strode through the silent corridor to the infirmary and unlocked it. Stepping inside, he put on insulated ski togs. After checking to make sure that his cap and gloves were in a pocket, he locked up and walked morosely through the deserted lobby.

"Doctor?" The night clerk looked up in surprise from his magazine of women dressed in fishnet stockings and little else.

Jed inclined his head curtly as he passed. "How're you doin', Walther?"

Grimacing, the clerk ducked his head into his magazine again. He was curious what the doctor was doing in the hotel so early in the morning, but he was even more protective of his job.

With the clerk's unasked questions sticking into his back like sharp little darts, Jed hesitated at the pay telephone before going outside. He consulted his wristwatch. Was it fair to call his children, to remind them of their past?

Discarding the idea, he zipped his parka high beneath his chin and removed his gloves from the pockets. He shivered as he stepped into the purple night and worked on the gloves, lifting his face to the sea of clouds above his head.

St. Murren was at the top of the world. Everywhere lay a dreamscape of powdery snow and swirling mists. Above the château were passionate mountains of rock and cliff, deserted, groomed slopes that would by tomorrow be dotted with skiers as bright as flyaway scraps of yarn.

He didn't ski, at least not as people here skied. Until tonight he had thought the challenge of the Alps was the most intimidating force he'd ever known. He'd been wrong.

The ski lift, as foully cantankerous as his frame of mind, was shut down for the night, but the luminescent bloom of the lights along its spindly system stretched high into the spaces, flickering like the eyes of invading aliens.

He got the cable moving and jumped nimbly into one of the passing baskets. The gondola carried him upward past one concrete tower after another. At the top of the peak, he bounded to the ground and was met by a streak of bounding, rust-colored fur.

"Down, Adolf," he commanded when the huge animal jumped up to his chest with the force of a ten-ton locomotive. Jed staggered, laughing, as the dog whined his affection and licked at his face. "I missed you, too. Now cease and desist."

Obediently, Adolf trotted alongside him and dropped to his haunches beside the door of the humble log cabin, cocking his intelligent head as he watched the man remove a shiny key and stand still, staring at it for long, silent moments before he slipped it in the lock and turned it. Then he slithered deftly inside and dropped down beside the door as he had been trained to do and covered his nose with his paws.

From a curtained partition inside, Scutter growled as the door shut. "That you, Jeddo?"

"No, it's the abominable snowman."

"Sam Hill." Rousing, Scutter fumbled for the clock upon the table between two twin beds. "What time is it?"

"Go back to sleep."

"Three o'clock!" bellowed the trainer. "In the *morning*?"

The rasp of a match.

Gradually, the interior of the one-room cabin came into view—rough and masculine but comfortable, and lighted by the oil lamp Jed held above his head. The bare floor was worn smooth by salt and sand and was covered with a bright plush rug before the hearth of the stone fireplace. The bed opposite Scutter's was unmade and burdened with crumpled pants and sweaters and socks and clean, unfolded laundry.

Unlike the bedroom, however, the kitchen off in a corner was immaculate. The water supply was a metal container with a spigot, and the sideboard bore a pan for washing dishes. The stove was fueled by bottled gas, and the storage shelves provided evidence of Jed's own penchant for cooking when he was upset: glass canisters containing fancy pastas and a gourmet spice rack, natural grains and dried fruits.

Off the kitchen was another door to the outside, which opened onto an ingeniously fashioned bathroom that was generally subzero temperature—still better than the old-fashioned john, Jed thought as he stepped inside it, keeping the visit as brief as possible.

Though he hadn't eaten since lunch, Jed had no appetite. When he returned to the warmth, he stoked the fire and extinguished the lamp. Scutter heaved himself up to sit and came to his feet by degrees. After going to the bathroom, too, he bustled back in and hopped and skipped on the warm hearth.

"You're getting in awful late," he complained congenially, yawning.

Jed considered the garish fireworks on his friend's outlandish pajamas. "You don't mean to tell me you actually sleep in those things?"

"Wise guy," Scutter mumbled, and climbed back into bed. "Where've you been?"

Leaning back in the creaking Boston rocker, Jed closed his eyes. He didn't want to talk about it, as if by putting words to magic, he and this new Mary Smith would cease to be. What was she doing now? Was she sleeping? Was she lying awake, thinking about him?

He imagined them together—here in the cabin with lightning stuttering outside like a bad connection, the tattoo of rain upon the slanted tin roof. He saw her nakedness electrified in the blue light and saw her eyelids fluttering down like wings as he stroked her. He heard her soft moans as she took him in her hand and guided him to the source of all his rampant agony.

Pinching the bridge of his nose, he sighed. He should be sleeping, but getting to sleep was the most dreaded part of his existence, ever eluding him.

"The nutritionist arrived today," Scutter volunteered.

"Come on, boy," Jed called to Adolf with a snap of his fingers. Adolf whined sympathetically as he laid down beside the chair to have his ears scratched. To Scutter, Jed said, "I know she did."

"What's going on? I walked up and was about to grab 'er when she turned around. I nearly swallowed my teeth."

Jed laughed mirthlessly and closed his eyes.

"But she's fine." Scutter whistled softly to himself, and Adolf looked up, whining. "Man, is she fine."

Eyes snapping sharply open in surprise, Jed curtly ordered, "You keep away from her."

Scutter bridled. "Oh-oh. What's this I hear? Ladies and gentlemen, do I sense a drop of human emotion in the old snowman himself?"

Jed flushed angrily. "All I meant was that she's about seven months pregnant. You dig, Romeo?"

"You're kidding." Pounding his pillow, Scutter propped himself up on it and scrubbed at his stubble. "St. Murren's insurance company may take a dim view of that, Bones."

"Yes, well . . . they're not the only one."

"You gonna tell me about it?"

"About what?"

"Hells bells, man. How Mary Smith is not Mary Smith. And how you know about it. To say nothing of the little matter of pregnancy. Are you sure about that? She didn't look—"

"She is."

In as few words as possible, Jed told Scutter about Mary Smith's deception, intentional or otherwise.

The trainer thought for a moment, then said, "Seeing as how Mary Smith is . . . *was*, well, you know what I mean. Seeing as how she's Vanessa's number one girl, I think it would be fitting if we paused for a moment of silent prayer, Jeddo, in the hope that Miss Universe doesn't come calling this year."

Jed rubbed his bleary eyes. If Vanessa made one of her glittering, whirlwind stops at St. Murren, complete with press and an entourage that royalty could envy, there would be hell to pay. If she found another Mary Smith upon the premises, that is, who was not Mary Smith.

Mind-boggling. "I thought of that," he said grimly. "And I also pictured another scene."

"If the first Mary Smith turned up."

"Not a very appetizing thought, is it?"

Personally, Jed had never been exactly certain *what* Mary did for Vanessa, except to attend seminars and stand up and swear by Vanessa's products on the graves of children that didn't exist. But Vanessa took care of her own; Mary had been paid well to approve. Then Mary had fallen from grace, had taken the money and run.

Water under the bridge? Possibly, But, then . . .

Stretching, he rose and walked to the empty twin bed and flung himself facedown without undressing. Dragging a pile of clean laundry upon his back, he covered his head with the pillow and tried to force out the world.

He came up for air. "I heard you and Stone had another run-in today," he said to Scutter.

"That bastard." Scutter's voice was heavy with sleep. "Such a jerkola. I was tryin' to explain that the village is on the verge of burning him in effigy. Merely tryin' to do him a favor."

"And?"

"Euphemistically speaking, he told me to perform an unnatural act."

"Keep away from that man. He's dangerous."

"He's stupid."

"Like I said, he's stupid. Keep away from him. I'd hate to have to get in there and use my karate to defend you."

"Me and the Karate Kid."

"Part Two."

Jed covered his head again and tried to shut out the sound of Scutter's soft snore. He lay very still. He would give a year out of his life to be able to drift off like that. He thought about this new Mary—strange, how he could hardly remember the first Mary now—and he mused about a dark silk robe clinging to sweet, aroused nipples and a lovely curved belly and long, clean-smelling hair. He thought about his own mouth kissing hers and how soft her breasts were and how right her hands felt threading through his own hair and drawing him closer. He saw himself entering her gently, very gently.

For the first time in three years, he went quickly and painlessly to sleep.

Chapter Six

Juggling was one thing, balancing on a high wire without a net was quite another.

During the next week Mary's involvement with Jed Kilpatrick was limited to a professional, albeit tense, brushing of shoulders—unexpected encounters in the restaurant as they stole stealthy looks while pretending not to watch, nerve-racking meetings in crowded elevators where they electrified each other with brushing shoulders and bumped elbows, startled glimpses caught across the lobby and gradually slow, long-distance inspections and a repertoire of wordless communication.

How's the baby?

Very good. How're you?

Pretty good. You're looking wonderful.

A blush.

A smile.

You're looking wonderful, too, Jed.

Sure, sure. I think about you a lot.
So do I.
A sigh.
A goodbye.

The only time Mary truly spent alone with Jed was during the inevitable late-night fantasizing in her lonely room. "Get over it," she brutally ordered herself at least a dozen times a day. "It's a no-win situation, and you're a fool if you think otherwise."

So she placed her promised phone calls back to the States and wrote ridiculously upbeat letters to her sisters and her mother, telling them how utterly "fantastic" she was, that the scenery was "absolutely gorgeous," that everyone was "simply marvelous, and that they must *not*, on pain of a gruesome death, disclose her exact address to anyone lest John find her.

Then she made a thorough search of the files in her predecessor's office. To her surprise, she found ample evidence of a Mary Smith having been at St. Murren, followed by a woman named Patricia Prince who had been killed in a plane crash. But there was not one shred of personal information about Mary Smith herself. The files had been stripped clean.

She stopped by Annelise's office as the concierge was on her way to see about a business affair planned for Haman Stone's power broker friends from the States. When she asked if she might see her own file and said that some items might possibly need correcting, Annelise didn't blink either of her cool, aloof eyes.

"You will excuse me, though, won't you?" Annelise said with ever-perfect decorum.

Mary smiled politely. "I'll leave it on your desk when I'm finished."

In the file was a copy of the letter Haman Stone had sent to Annapolis and some personal notes of Annelise's and her own reply. "Worked season before last," Annelise noted. "Possibly located through U.S. accreditation. Several telephone numbers were scribbled on the paper and her years with the Harvard Public Health people. Plus her own mailing address.

Feeling as if she'd just been pronounced innocent of a crime, Mary squeaked softly to herself. It was nothing more complicated than a good old human error! They had obviously lost track of the original Mary Smith and thought they were tracking her down through published credentials, which had turned out to be her own. The letter *had* been meant for her!

She immediately fired off a note to her editor at *Foods for Life*. "There's no problem in meeting my deadline," she promised happily. "This place is a writer's heaven!"

Mary was surprised when she received a personal note from Mavis Duvall, hand delivered by one of the Incredible Hulks, demanding a personal consultation.

A bit put off, for she was busy learning the ropes of her job, she stepped out of the elevator toward a second-floor suite of ten rooms and rapped briskly upon the door of the holy of holies, fully prepared to place Miss Duvall in the same category as escargots and chocolate-covered grasshoppers.

Instead, she found the actress in the very ordinary process of making up her face. With one eye accentuated with mascara and the other comically normal, her hair in dishabille and her famous body clad in a faded robe and slippers, Mavis looked more like Mary's sister than anything else.

"It's really not fair, you know," she complained over the hysterical yipping of the terriers in the next room.

She waved Mary absentmindedly inside, and returned to her dressing table with its ruthless mirror and lights. "You simply must help me. If I gain so much as a pound, I'll look like Elmer Fudd, and the studio will make all these threats about getting Meryl Streep to replace me."

She paused to light a cigarette and flutteringly blew smoke at the ceiling. She finally met Mary's look woman-to-woman. "One sip of alcohol, and I swell out to here. Fruit breaks me out in hives, and cheese makes me sneeze. The only thing I can consume without a guilty conscience is water, and if I start looking gaunt, the tabloids start whispering that I'm anorexic or on drugs or have a social disease."

Mary laughed and slapped her own fanny. "I know exactly what you mean."

Thumping ash onto the floor, Mavis said, "I might as well kill myself and get done with it. What do you suggest?"

Mary couldn't help liking the actress. She grinned. "Guns are too messy, Miss Duvall, and hanging would wreck your hair."

Mavis gurgled, and Mary made a quick reconnoiter to see if the bodyguards were on duty or if she should expect to be attacked by the terriers. The only thing worth noting in the suite were a dozen outfits flung untidily over the furniture and the dressing table that spilled Angela Cummings diamonds as if they were so much costume paste.

Mary said, "Let me work on your diet and the allergies, Miss Duvall, and see what I can come up with."

"Call me Mavis. My real name is Judy, but I answer to anything." She finished with the mascara on her other eye. "And these..." After another deep drag on her cigarette, she dipped into various jars and compacts, adding subtleties to her cheeks and nose and jaws with darker shades and shadows. "Well, you see how weak I am? As for the allergies, you think I haven't spoken to that *divine* Dr. Kilpatrick about those? Talk about smiling Irish eyes!"

At the unexpected mention of Jed's name, an acrid taste filled Mary's mouth. She knew more about Jed Kilpatrick's eyes than this woman.

She briskly removed her pen from the pocket of her lab coat and snapped it several times as if ready to begin writing. "I see."

Mavis Duvall's laughter was like dark French perfume—irresistible. She brandished a sable brush and sang an impression of Stevie Wonder: "Isn't he lov-e-ly?" She grimaced. "You realize, of course, that the little Yankee weasel who runs this place is trying to force him to leave. Kilpatrick and that coach friend of his are the most interesting men here, unless you count the jocks, but they're just babies, aren't they? On second thought, Mary—may I call you Mary?—send me a fruit plate for lunch with lots of strawberries. I think it's high time for a good case of hives, don't you!"

While Mavis drifted off into giggles over her own joke, Mary wondered why she wanted to inform the beautiful actress that she and Jed shared an intimacy.

But she'd boxed herself in where Jed was concerned, and that was the way she wanted it. That's the way it should be.

Moistening her lips a final time and running her fingers through her flaming hair, Mavis lifted her arms and twirled like a child showing off in her mother's dress.

"*Voilà!* What d'you think, Mary?"

Incredulously, Mavis Duvall could have been someone else entirely. Mary could hardly believe the uncanny
transformation—the cheekbones, the chin, the spacing
of the eyes. If it hadn't been such a miracle, it would have
been sinister. She could, Mary suspected, make herself
pass for any kind of woman she wanted to be.

"You're an artist, Miss Duvall," she said honestly,
enthralled.

"Tricks, darling," laughed the actress. "And do call
me Mavis. People see in me what they want to see, not
what I really am. It's in the wrist, Mary, all in the wrist."

The United States had made an extremely poor showing at the previous Olympic Winter Games. There were,
so the experts declared, far too many non-finishes
chalked up to America's credit—injuries and unfortunate accidents, broken legs, fractured fibulas, even a
broken hip. Desperate, some competitors had resorted to
drugs and steroids and the illegal practice of blood-
packing where one's blood was removed, then trans-
fused back into the athlete's system prior to a grueling
event.

Scutter Brown was under the gun. The amateur skiing
programs were an opportunity to increase America's
chances in the 1992 Games in Albertville, France. So he
placed his hopes upon the students he could train for the
next four years.

If Scutter was under the gun, Jed was into preventive
medicine, a field he could heartily support. He was also
a medical policeman. Each student was to be given bi-
weekly physicals and drug tests, but more crucial than
that was to teach the youths how to make nutrition and
safety a way of life.

Since each competitor was a law unto himself, Mary found her desk in a constant state of chaos. Not only must she oversee the diets, she must conduct classes. Each student was represented by a bloated file.

On Thursday, as she walked into her office, her arms spilling charts and graphs and folders, the phone was ringing. Pinching the receiver beneath her chin, she inched sideways and dumped her baggage onto the tiny red sofa that was a consolation prize for having no window.

"Hello," she said, and caught sight of a note clipped inside the top folder of the new stack on her desk.

A strange voice sounded in her ear, "Hello?"

"This is Mary Smith," she said as she pulled the card free of the paper clip and turned it over.

"My name is Dane, Mary Smith."

"My *dear* Ms. Smith," Jed had attached to Percy Dunhaven's file. Percy was a taciturn, blond, twenty-year-old downhill racer from Ann Arbor, Michigan.

Please see that this athlete gets only sixty-five grams of carbohydrate per day. Religiously. And do yourself a favor, dear, and check your own calcium intake. Would you like me to prescribe something? I make house calls.

Yours, Jed.

Before she could turn back the pages of her memory and relive Jed's kiss for the thousandth time, Mary jerked her mind back to the phone. "Dane? How may I help you, Dane?"

A disturbing silence followed.

Mary was puzzled. She imagined Jed writing the note—his hands, his fingers, his neat, blunt nails. She aimlessly jiggled the switch. "Hello."

"This is Dane," the voice said again.

Confused, Mary repeated, "If you'll tell me what you want, Dane, I'll be glad to help—"

Click.

Baffled, taking her seat before the desk, Mary stared at the receiver and hung up. A wrong number, but how rude! What had the man thought she would do? Bite his hand through the wire?

On Ellie Anderson's folder—Ellie was from Terre Haute and despite her unbecoming wet-look hair and locker-room tongue, she showed excellent promise in the slalom event—Jed had attached a more formal note: a card with violins and trumpets on the outside.

Mary,
This student could have a possible diabetic condition. No sugar, please, not even in fresh fruits.

Jed

P. S. The more sugar Ellie eats, the dirtier her mouth becomes! Be kind to us all.

Jed

P. P. S. Have you made any decision where the Big Event will take place? I'm very good at BEs. Love and kisses.

Love and kisses, indeed! The rogue would steal her heart if she wasn't careful. Smiling, Mary penned back, "I think you've forgotten our arrangement, Doctor. Do you want everyone calling you Daddy?"

* * *

"I'm also very good at daddying," his retort came the next day. "Oh, yes. I like your hair up. I actually mistook you for Jane Seymour stepping out of the elevator yesterday morning."

Mary felt as if she'd missed a step. It wasn't over, was it? Despite their distance, it was just as dangerously there as ever. They were pussyfooting around the trap, like curious little mice, having heard the snap of its killing jaws but unable to resist the delicious smell of cheese.

On impulse she spent five dollars at the gift shop for a box of notes. "Don't be ridiculous," she penned, then added as she imagined him smiling, "And thank you. You looked rather Kevin Costner-ish yourself."

She didn't sleep well that night. She dreamed that Jed came to her turret door and knocked, but when she opened the door, Kevin Costner was looking at her with those brooding, Gary Cooper eyes and shook his head in pity.

"Where is he?" she asked, meaning Jed, and he pointed cryptically to a door down the corridor. Yet when she hurried to open it, no one was there. Up and down the halls she flew, opening and slamming doors in a frenzy, searching for Jed but finding nothing.

Weary and gritty-eyed, she found Jed's note the next day on Juliet Haney's chart.

Please be a good girl, Mary, and see that Juliet gets Vanessa's supplements six times a day, and nothing else. Close tabs on this one. It's a pain, I know, but Miss Universe keeps the wheels of the old machine well-oiled and working. I wouldn't put off the BE decision, if I were you.

Attached was a small envelope the size of a half-dollar with a teddy bear embossed upon it. Atrociously typed was, "Do nnot open till . . . 'til Christmmmas . . . Xmas."

From the beginning, Mary had admitted to several very real reservations about Vanessa and International's health and beauty products. Since they apparently made the difference between red and black on St. Murren's books, however, she kept her mouth shut, yet, for her own peace of mind, she had immediately sent a sample of Juliet Haney's supplements to her chemist friend, Guy Rhodes at Fields Laboratories.

From the outset, Juliet had made it crystal clear to Mary that she wished to be called only by her first name. "Like Cher," she'd said with more self-confidence than Mary would amass in a lifetime. "Or Vanessa. One day I will be more famous than either of them."

Besides being an Olympic contender, Juliet was also a human scientific experiment. On a highly specialized diet that Vanessa had developed and packaged in tear-open envelopes, the girl required meticulous records for her food and drink and every other item she put into her body. Once a month, critical nude photographs were taken from every angle. After five years, a reassessment would be made of every inch of Juliet's body, proving to the world—so Vanessa claimed—that Vanessa had truly discovered the legendary fountain of youth.

Swiveling in her chair, Mary fingered Jed's tiny present as she scanned the pictures of Vanessa that were tacked, taped and mounted all over the walls of her office—pictures of Vanessa wearing her Miss Universe crown and a bathing suit, smiling blowups of Vanessa's perfect blond face and frame, Vanessa in a lavender leotard, Vanessa in a bathing suit, Vanessa accepting awards and autographing her three best-selling books, Vanessa on television, Vanessa dancing with a glamorous play-boy half her age. Vanessa claimed she was forty years old, but she didn't look a day over thirty.

And now she wanted Juliet to win an Olympic gold medal. "Talk about publicity gimmicks," Mary mumbled wryly, as she lifted the flap of the packet and emptied its contents upon the desk.

Out spilled a circlet of gold so fragile, so intricate, so delicate that only the tiniest baby finger could wear it.

Oh! Mary lost track of how long she simply sat and stared at it, unable to think of anything except the planning that had to have gone into its selection. Had Jed bent over a glass-topped counter, looking up with consternation as he entered into a grave discussion with the jeweler? Had he argued with himself as she had done? *She will think I'm a fool. I am a fool.*

Of course he had. He had placed the tiny thing into the cup of his big man's hand and had imagined, not the baby who would wear it but the mother's smile when she opened the packet.

"What are you doing to my heart, Jed Kilpatrick?" she whispered, trembling. "What other keys do you have in that pocket of yours?"

Lifting out one of the crisp, parchment notes she had bought and pushing back the clutter of her desk, she considered how to go about finding a way of escape from the ultimatum she had given him that night.

But her ultimatum had been based on Jed's statement about getting shafted. That situation hadn't changed. If they had dinner, it would fuel hotel gossip. If they met for a drink, it would be construed by Haman Stone as a direct violation of his "house policy." To have Jed to her room, of course, was unthinkable.

Removing her glasses and pressing her eyelids, she replaced her expensive paper and took out a plain sheet.

"I'm very concerned that I don't know the composition of Vanessa's products, Jed," she scribbled with businesslike brevity. "Don't you think it's a bit dangerous for Juliet to consume nothing else? I really don't believe I can conscientiously do it. Couldn't you run tests? Oh yes, thank you for the ring. It's the most touching thing that's happened to me in months. She'll adore it."

The next day, with her heart in her throat, she waited for interoffice mail.

Nothing came. Disappointed, she had a terrible day. Tomorrow, perhaps, she thought.

Nothing.

Nor did anything come the day after when the mailboy brought an armful. On and on the pattern repeated itself until four days had passed.

Mary hated herself for coming unglued. She was sick of walking into a corridor and listening for Jed's voice, or entering a room and having her radar home in. Anger finally saved her. The baby's ring hadn't been a means of winning her affection, anyway; it had been an apology, a bribe. The message had been all too loud and clear.

So be it. You want off the hook, Jed Kilpatrick? Boy, are you off!

From the airport in Vienna, Jed postponed going immediately to the University Medical School where one of his oldest and dearest friends—Uri Stempke—was on staff. For years he had known this moment had to come, and now that he faced it, was prepared to take a step from which there would be no turning back, he felt compelled to understand why the old familiar eagerness churned in his stomach again.

"Hotel Am Stephansplatz," he said to the driver as he tossed his nylon duffle into the back seat of the smoking Mercedes.

Sinking back into leather seats that smelled of worn leather and stale tobacco smoke, he closed his eyes and smiled. There was an old adage, "If you really must fall sick, then do it in Vienna." The Viennese had one doctor for every three hundred inhabitants. One of those was Uri, and during the year of Jed's own doctorate that he'd spent in the city, he'd accepted a lot of favors from his mentor. One of them had just been called in.

Ordinarily, he would have refused. Why not now? He glanced at his watch and pictured where Mary would be in her routine of the day. He should have told her he would be gone for a few days. But that would have presumed she wanted to know. What evidence did he have of that?

Not until Mary did he truly understand just how much of his life he'd spent alone. There was medical training and the books. Even Ann had possessed only a small portion of his time. He had loved Ann and he certainly loved his children, but he'd never felt that surge in his veins the way he did now. Just imagining Mary, the secrets of her and the discovery, was like coming alive.

He had begun to begrudge the moments when he couldn't dream about her. He could imagine, as the taxi carried him through the graceful old city, that he could turn his head and find her beside him with her slim legs crossed and her chin at that challenging little angle. He could reach across the distance and touch her hand, could place that hand upon his knee and feel a . . . a safeness.

The taxi came to a screeching halt. He was thrown forward. Glancing at the meter, he fumbled for his

money and took hold of his luggage, opening the door
before the driver could do it.

"*Danke,*" the driver said.

Jed gave him a tiny salute. Stepping outside into the
hazy evening as lights twinkled in the dusk, he drew in a
breathy resolve and gazed at the familiar sight of St. Ste-
phen's Cathedral. Nervous, he strode briskly into the
hotel and headed for the telephones. He would place a
call to St. Murren and at least leave a message for Mary.

Once he was fitted into the paneled niche, however, his
nerve failed him. Would he be able to bear a rejection
from her?

An unexpectedly keen pain slashed across him. Staring at his hands, which had ended the life of Roger Pike,
he cursed himself, dropped the coins into the slots and
dialed. As it rang, he turned and watched the lobby that
bustled with bellboys and the hotel florist carrying an
elaborate bouquet. An assistant manager was seated self-
importantly at his desk as business picked up at the reservations counter. Ranks of airport limousines and taxis
had just discharged a bevy of passengers.

"Hello?" answered a deep, chocolate-rich voice in
German.

Years fell away from Jed. "Uri," he said hoarsely as a
violent, unbearable loneliness welled in him, "I just got
into the city."

"Ah, Jedediah. How wonderful to hear your voice
again."

Jed wished fervently that Uri wouldn't persist in calling him Jedediah. "I'm about to check in, Uri. How are
things?"

"As we expected, the girl has improved. We can do the
surgery very soon now."

"I'm not sure I can take up a knife."

"Then be my eyes."

"As long as you understand I'm in this for consultation only."

"Tell me, what made you change your mind? A week ago—"

Across Jed's mind, memory spattered a collage of unfocused images: *God, you taste good... I'm getting it right up to the old tonsils... Stupidity's in my genes, go away... Delicious... Sheer heaven... Stay and hold me... So fine, so fine... Be afraid, I destroy everything in my path... Stop me... I can't...*

"Shall I come there?" he said more gruffly than he intended.

The sigh at the other end of the line was an acceptance of the locked doors still within him.

"That will be perfect, my friend," Uri said, understanding.

Catching a ride on an antiquated ski lift was like hopping a freight train—a monumental test of faith, in Mary's opinion. One of the attendants showed her how to grab hold and swing up into the basket, then hang on for dear life. Two other lifts serviced the resort—new ones—but they didn't go to Devil's Elbow.

A new layer of snow had fallen the previous night. For skiers, weather conditions couldn't be better—cold, bright and bracing. But Mary wouldn't have looked forward to talking with Scutter Brown had heaven descended.

She found him on the top of the peak with a group of students, one of whom was Juliet Haney.

"Mary!" he shouted, waving when he saw her trudging through the snow in her ski outfit, which had been easy to hide in. A long low wolf whistle met her halfway.

"On a pass-fail basis, lady, you get tops marks for your digs if nothing else."

For that, of course, Mary was compelled to stop where she was and imitate a model's slouch. "Should I have called first, dahling?"

"Anytime I, Scutter E. Brown, can't stop for a pretty woman," he announced with mock gravity, "I quit." Over his shoulder he yelled, "Hey, Zeke, be back in a sec. Carry on."

Mary's concern about Scutter's suspicions of why she'd come had been wasted. He happily bought them hot chocolate at the concession and offered her a bite of his beef energy bar. They kept to the ruts of the trails as he took her on a short tour of the slope.

Tearing the jerky with her teeth, Mary inched into a discussion about Juliet's fitness program.

"Actually," he said as if it were a confidence, "I try not to have any kind of opinion about that girl. Her diet? Sure, I'm always on the lookout for steroids and drugs, to the point of paranoia sometimes. Places like this attract smugglers, and we certainly get our share, but Vanessa's a pro. She's been peddling health products for a long time now, and she has that mega-publishing business and contests with six-hundred-thousand-dollar winner cups. Besides, Jed keeps close tabs on all these kids. And he's really who you came to talk about, isn't he?"

Mary suddenly strangled on her hot chocolate and bent double, coughing and sputtering while Scutter thumped her gingerly on the back.

"Dear, dear," he mused. "Was it something I said?"

"I'm going to have to hurt you for that, Scutter," she gasped when she could get her mouth open.

Laughter gurgled out of him. "Forgive me. I've got a sordid imagination. I thought you wanted to know where he'd gone."

Mary's lungs refused to operate as she tearily gaped at the man. As he patiently waited, merriment bursting from his seams, she retrieved enough control of her voice to wheeze, "Has Jed been gone?"

The tug-of-war was no contest. She was a miserable player, and he was a worse winner. They entered into a delicious conspiracy with Jed the object of both. "He's the best friend I've ever had," Scutter said. "If I can't have you, I wish him the best of luck. You know where he goes on those trips, don't you?"

"He has another life as a spy?"

"He does free surgeries all over Europe. Small things mostly, plus consultation on some very big cases. He's a pioneer in his field, you know. A brilliant surgeon. There's no way to estimate the lives Jeddo's saved, but he can't heal up from the one he took. The way I see it, he's as real a tragedy as Roger Pike."

Shading her eyes, squinting, Mary pretended to watch Percy streaking down the slope and Ellie fretting with a ski clip. "I know he's special, Scutter."

"Too bad he doesn't. Oh, he knows, he's just not ready to accept it."

"How can you be sure he will?"

"Go back into surgery? Have you ever watched the way he protects his hands?"

She didn't know him that well, Mary wanted to say, but she turned her back to the sun and cupped her hot drink, breathing in the curl of steam. "I know Dr. Kilpatrick is very conscientious. I—"

Without warning, Scutter tipped up her chin with a gloved finger. The facades were hopelessly stripped away, the pretenses pushed back into the hole they'd crawled from.

"Give it a chance, Mary," he said. "Give *him* a chance. He's worth it. You won't be sorry."

There, in the depths of Scutter's green eyes, Mary saw the truth. "You know all about me, don't you?"

Releasing her face, he sucked his upper lip into his mouth and thoughtfully mauled it. At length, he said, "I know that you're as special as he is. Listen, Mary, there's something I've been meaning to tell you about Vanessa..."

He didn't go on, and she didn't know what to ask for. She laid her hand upon his arm.

With a shake of his head, he closed the door he had just opened. "Nothing, don't mind me. I just don't want you to worry about Juliet, that's all. Vanessa's quite fond of Jed, you know. If it weren't for her, he might still be making his home in a bottle."

But she did mind, and she recognized a warning when she heard one. She extended her hand in thanks, which Scutter took but did not shake, lifting it instead to his lips.

"Please," he said in parting, "if there's any trouble, don't be brave. Come to me. Promise?"

The moment was decidedly unnerving. Retrieving her hand, Mary smiled thinly. "I promise. Ahh, I suppose I have to ride the lift back down?"

"Unless you want to have that baby—oops!"

He clapped a facetious hand over his mouth, and laughing, she punched him none-too-gently in the chest. "I don't know who gets it first, you or Jed."

"Meet me in the restaurant tonight, and I'll let you reform me."

Mary wasn't at all certain as she left, smiling to herself, that Scutter's loyalty to Jed wouldn't slip a notch where a woman was concerned.

Staff meetings at St. Murren were conducted every Tuesday evening in one of the resort's bars that was, for that one night, closed to the public. Mary's frame of mind the last days had progressed from irritation at Jed to a black resentment.

To make matters worse, she was late for the meeting. And Jed had absolutely nothing to do with the fact that she changed clothes three times. Or that she had finally selected something she was certain wouldn't appeal to him, or to any man on the planet—an ankle-length skirt and an aging blouse worn on the outside, belted with its tails flapping about her hips.

In a deepening funk, she pulled on the everlasting lab coat that had the bad taste to be shorter than her shirt. She scowled fiercely at her reflection in the mirror and gathered her hair with both hands and made a face.

Aghh! Arranging the heavy mass about her face, she swiftly attacked it with a teasing comb, then brushed that until her eyes watered.

"To hell with it!"

In disgust, she plaited her hair in a French braid and dropped it morosely down her back, jammed her glasses onto her face, raced for the elevator and ran down the main floor corridor to open the door.

"Fräulein!" a voice accosted her from behind.

Mary turned, her hand upon the knob, as a valet hurried toward her, a folded paper in his hand. "Yes?"

"I tried to catch you when you got off the elevator," he explained, and proffered the paper.

"Thank you." Belatedly, Mary remembered his tip and fumbled in the pocket of her coat for money. Had Jed sent her another of his famous memos?

"Danke," he said gratefully, and scuttled away.

With an odd excitement, Mary opened the note and read, in a spidery handwriting, "I want what you have." It was unsigned.

Confused, she turned the paper over, thinking she had missed something. Jed? Jed wouldn't write a note like this. Perhaps it was from one of the trainees. If it was a sexual proposition, not only was the person barking up the wrong tree, he wasn't even in the right forest! And she had wasted a perfectly good tip.

Wadding the paper and tossing it into an ashtray, she slipped through the door.

The bar was a hysterically overdone baroque room. Filled with gold-trimmed mirrors and flourishes of tedious filigree and velvet and statuettes, it looked like a box of fancy bonbons for a mistress. Most of the people present she recognized—Haman Stone and Annelise, a few of the floor supervisors, the house detective, the assistant general manager, chief engineer, head of maintenance, the chefs, several of the ski instructors, the physical fitness administrator, head of transportation, and—her heart stopped—Jed.

Life tripped her like the edge of a loose rug. She lifted her hands shakily to the plainness of her braid. Why hadn't she made herself prettier? Why hadn't she availed herself of Mavis Duvall's clever makeup tricks? Worn something nicer? Added some jewelry—anything to make her seem less of what she really was?

He was sitting with his profile toward her, his chin cupped in a large hand, his brows furrowed and his face a map of concern. For the first time, he came close to looking what he was—his hair freshly trimmed, bristling about the backs of his ears with a stubby military neatness. His suit was an expensive Austin Reed, and he wore a sweater over his shirt, one of the fabulous Ungaro knits a shopper could find in Europe. Lest he give too much of an establishment impression, however, chukka boots peeked from beneath his cuffs, and he sported a Swiss Raymond Weil wristwatch and no other jewelry.

He sprawled low on his spine, fiddling with a key—her key?—turning it end over end as Haman Stone fenced with Scutter. Unwittingly, she imagined those beautiful hands undressing her and touching her with knowledge, touching her baby, those long, agile legs tangled with her own, his eyes closing, his...

Ever so casually, she took off her glasses and slipped them into her pocket. She bit her lips and took a deep breath to keep her heart from leaping through her lab coat.

"What Jochen Weingarten's policy *used* to be is no longer viable here," Stone was declaring, punching his words. "This is *now*. St Murren is catering to a *different* clientele. Our policy is that evening social functions sponsored by the resort will be *off limits* to students and day laborers. That is not to say that private parties won't be welcome. Indeed, they will be encouraged."

Haman Stone was conducting the meeting from the center of a white-clothed table upon which had been set a portable rostrum. Beside him was Annelise, who took notes. The light overhead glanced off his shiny face. He spread his hand upon his vest as a woman would touch her bosom...

Mary guiltily glanced about her end of the room. Over the din of the room's buzz, Scutter Brown shot back his retort with a brandishing of his rolled-up magazine.

"Hell, we're supposed to take that seriously? You're telling me that my students can't go to a stupid dance?"

The tension of Haman Stone's mouth caused it to all but disappear. "As you said, Mr. Brown, they're students."

"I'll be damned." Scutter Brown hurled the magazine to the tabletop, knocking over a glass of water in the process. The entire room gaped at him in astonishment, and he stared at the droplets clinging to his hand as if they would eat away the flesh and devour the bone.

Leaving the water to spatter upon the floor, Scutter angrily elbowed his way through the room, muttering to himself.

The silence of the staff had a crust to it that grew thicker with every flick of Haman Stone's eyes searching for defectors.

"If there is no additional discussion," he declared tersely as he drew in his mouth and locked it tightly, his fingernail clicking sharply upon the table, "we'll proceed to Miss Duvall's complaint—that of room service being tardy."

"If you'll wait up just a moment . . . sir," drawled a deep voice that made Mary start.

All eyes veered to Jed Kilpatrick, Mary's most of all.

"If a student is going to be discriminated against," Jed said with a flashing smile that was only a step shy of insolence, "I think he should be given a discount on room and board."

Titters of sympathetic laughter rippled through the room. They stopped abruptly as Haman Stone's small dark eyes hardened.

"I'm sure you don't expect me to take that remark seriously, Dr. Kilpatrick," he snapped. "The Château St. Murren does not discriminate."

"Is that a fact?" Smiling, Jed slid lower upon his spine and gave an idle, percussive thrum with his fingertips upon the tabletop. "You could've fooled me."

The titters hushed altogether. The room grew still. The bartender ceased cleaning glasses. Coffee cups echoed in their saucers, and the people who put them down could have been staring at a hand grenade on the table with its pin pulled.

There was in Jed's manner an unquestioned authority that Mary supposed came from his having lost so many of the material things the world deemed necessary. He was a man without a boss or a deadline to meet, therefore he was not vulnerable to men like Stone.

The silence had run its limits. No one said a word in Jed's behalf.

Stone said, with a fragile flick of his eyes and anger serrating his voice, "May I remind you, Doctor, that you are not a staff member of this hotel. You are at this meeting because I allow you to be. You have no right to an opinion regarding policy."

"And may I remind you that students have come to these Alps for years to train for the Olympic games. Before you or I did, actually. A very demoralizing discontent has permeated this institution, sir. As well as the village."

Rage reddened Stone's cheeks. "That is not my problem," he snapped, and took a breath to say something more.

Jed cut him off. "You damn sure better make it your problem. We're getting the reputation of being capitalists. Of course, Americans have always had that, haven't they? But now it's worse. Find out for yourself. Spend some time in the village. Listen to what's being said. You'll see what I'm talking about."

Stone leaned forward across the table. "It occurs to me to wonder how you know so much about what's being said, Doctor. Could it be that you're doing a bit of the saying? Hmm?"

People's nervousness was evident in the shuffle of their feet and the scrape of their chairs. Mary's own hands were sweating. She wanted to scream at Jed to be quiet. *St. Murren will not thank you, Jed!*

Annelise was watching the encounter with an expression devoid of emotion, but Mary wondered if she weren't hoping that Haman Stone would be humiliated.

"It isn't to my advantage to sully your reputation any more than it already is, Stone," Jed countered tightly.

Stone's face was red with rage, and a pulse worked wildly on his forehead. In another time, another less civilized age, as master of the château he would have had Jed flogged. With the veins standing out on his neck, he fixed Jed in his sights, fully intending to bring him down with one shot.

"Don't you think," he said acidly, "that you would do well to leave the matter of reputations to those who have a better track record?"

The insult would have been painful under any circumstance. At that precise moment, as Jed swung sharply around, his neck stained a dull crimson, the lines of his face deeply etched and his mouth curved in a tight, angry smile, his eyes met Mary's. Theirs was no collision of forces, but rather one of coming together while all the external influences ceased to be or faded into insignificance.

His stare changed and widened. In full view of the room, he came to his feet—a graceful, troubled knight with his dark head erect and unbowed. Never had Mary felt so proud of knowing another human being as when he walked with princely dignity to the door.

Enough! What kind of person was she that she could let a fear of disgrace keep her from standing on the side of decency? That she could fail to champion him because he hadn't told her he was going away?

She drew in her breath to step forward and speak to Haman Stone. "May I—"

Jed's hand shot out and grasped her wrist as he passed with a force that half-blinded her.

"Don't be stupid," he hissed. "It won't change anything. Stay put." With a crush of her bones, he released her and moved past.

As the door shut behind him, Mary waited precious seconds with her lips parted and could almost smell her own blood pounding in her veins. She waited too long. And then it was too late. The moment could never be regained. The meeting moved on to other matters. Jed had taken the licks alone. She was, more than at any time in her life, deeply ashamed.

Chapter Seven

The instant the meeting was over, Mary was the first one out the door. Her conscience came hard after, kicking and screaming.

Guessing that she looked like a snowplow with her head lowered and her legs chugging, she pushed her glasses onto her face and dodged athletes who had just come from the gym on their way to an early bed. When a group of reveling guests entered one of the back doors en masse, rather than face them, she bleakly headed for the stairwell. Groping in her pocket for her glasses, she pushed them onto her face.

Wallowing in self-pity wasn't like her. She was too smart to keep torturing herself with Jed Kilpatrick, and much too disciplined. The man had his own life and did what he had to do. She had hers, and there were enough problems in it without a love affair.

Love affair! Would you listen to her? Her, the ultimate old-fashioned girl? She didn't have love affairs, she *married* her mistakes!

And it *was* a tad presumptuous, wasn't it? After all, he'd not only gone away without a word, he'd returned the same way. Gad, but she was an idiot!

She threw her weight against the door and let her head thump miserably against it. Which was the reason she didn't see the tall shadow detaching from the wall, nor the long arm as it reached over her head and braced upon the door.

"Easy, Wile E. Coyote," he murmured, chuckling as the hinges creaked and she stumbled, gasping with shock, through the opening. "You're exceeding the speed limit."

They tumbled down into the stairwell together—Mary, with her hands splayed wide as she attempted to right herself, and Jed twirling her around in a neat pirouette and folding her deftly into his arms.

Jed thought, as she clung to him, that human beings had to be the most stupid of all creatures. Why were they constantly inventing roles and playing games? Why did they let life numb them so they forgot the wonder and delicious shock of engaging in something so right as this?

"And baby makes three," he said, chuckling as her middle pressed intimately into his.

She gave a tiny whimper of dismay.

"Shh, do us both a favor," he whispered into her hair, laughing as he spread a hand upon the sweet maternal curve. "Don't make a public announcement about this."

The door clicked shut. The darkness was a friend now. The emptiness was filled with the gentle scuffs of their shoes and the whisper of their breaths and their murmured words.

"You're crazy," she said, sighing dizzily as the sides of his suit coat closed about her head. "What d'you think you're doing?"

Jed wondered if he truly knew. "The last I heard, sweetheart," he drawled as he found her temple with the tip of his nose and nibbled his way to the shell of her ear, "it was called kissing."

Far back in a private place of Mary's brain her alter ego taunted her. *Didn't I tell you, didn't I tell you?*

"Do you remember the first time we did this?" he asked.

The violence of that memory was both paralyzing and thrilling. "I remember fighting off a crazy man."

"The only crazy thing I did that night was not stay for breakfast when I was invited."

"Don't be sorry." She appalled herself by giggling. "It wasn't all that good."

"Maybe I should take a rain check."

"Rain checks are for laundry detergent and serious competitive sports, Jed."

"I think, my darling, that this is about as serious as it gets."

Serious?

Abruptly, the door burst open. They were captured in silhouette by two laughing guests stumbling into the stairwell. Like guilty children, she and Jed jerked from each other.

"S-sorry," a young man mumbled, chagrined. "We didn't mean to interrupt a party." Turning the ruddy shade of his ski boots, he said to his companion, "Let's get out of here."

Their laughter rippled gleefully away, and the door snapped closed, leaving Mary shivering with the realization all over again of how unfortunate it could be for both Jed and herself if they were seen by the wrong people. Haman Stone would not only take great pleasure in dismissing her, he would crucify Jed.

She recovered from her temporary insanity and attempted to keep Jed at bay with outstretched hands. "I was on my way upstairs." Nervousness put a tic in her throat, and she coughed into her fist. "But I admire what you did in there tonight. Very much."

"Did you, now?"

"It isn't right, what's happening to this town, and no one but you had the nerve to say so."

"Yeah, I'm a real hero, all right."

He was studying her gravely, as if to rearrange the molecules of her body. The edge of his upper lip was caught between his teeth, and his brows couldn't decide if they wanted to be irritated or mocking.

Scattered in the fringes of her mind were images of this ending very badly. "Anyway, I thought you were... quite..." She huffed a more honest sigh and shifted her feet. "Would you excuse me, Jed? It's been a real bummer of a day. I'll talk to you later, all right?"

Feeling like a flashing neon idiot, she began stomping up the stairs.

"Wait a minute." His words clambered after her. "I'll walk you to the elevator. You don't need to be climbing these."

"I want the exercise. Really. It's okay."

Mary kept her eyes fixed tenaciously upon her shoes as they swiftly took the steps. She hoped he would not follow; she prayed he wouldn't, yet part of her, the hungry, feminine part, thought she would die if he didn't.

The heavier tread of his step underscored the vast differences between them. Higher and higher they climbed, farther from the world and the safety of reality. The baby kicked, and she paused to rest. Sensing her limits, he caught up and took her arm, looping it through his own, bearing her weight.

"My, my," his tease rumbled deep in his chest, "this is an emotionally charged moment."

Mary's difficulty was in making her retort convincingly flippant. "I dare say I could give *you* a run for the money."

He chuckled. "I don't doubt it for a minute. How have you been, anyway? You look good enough to eat."

Blistering him with a glare, Mary felt her nerves reaching the shattering point as they climbed. *One step, two steps, three.* "Fine," she said at length. "Perfectly fine. Great, actually. Just... great."

Jed wondered what she would do if he simply caught her up in his arms and kissed her—now, breathlessly, the way he had wanted to do for weeks so that she couldn't think of anything except the melting sweetness. He imagined them making love on the stairs, the tiny whimpers she would make, her hands upon his face as he pulled her to the floor and buried his hard, aching flesh deep within the perfection of hers.

An ache began to ferment in his groin. He tried to think of something else. "That's good," he said, and noticed the paint was peeling on the walls in green, oblong strips.

She doggedly kept her head bent. "I suppose *you've* been all right?"

"Oh, yes. Fine," he said, "fine. Just fine."

"That's good."

"I just got back, actually."

"Really?"

"Yeah. I, uh... I had to go to Vienna."

"Vienna."

"It was . . . it had to do with business."

"There's no need to explain."

From deep in his throat, he made a growl of exasperation. "I may have to hurt you, Mary, if you don't stop getting so personal."

Expecting at least a flicker of amusement from her, Jed stopped shy of the landing. Sighing, he placed his hands upon her shoulders and closed them upon her bones that felt to him as fragile as porcelain but were, he knew, as strong as steel.

"Well, hell." Pulling her glasses down the bridge of her nose, he leaned forward, squinting with playful ferocity. "You might as well spit it out and get done with it, Mary. If you don't, you're going to pop, and that would make an awful mess here on the stairs."

Mary didn't move. Hadn't she wanted this confrontation more than anything? Now that he was going for it, she couldn't explain how she really felt—how the ache inside her was worse than any physical pain she'd ever known, and how there was a need so great, the whole world couldn't fill it. She had never been so unhappy in her life as she had since meeting him.

But what did he care? Business in Vienna! Hah!

Sidestepping, she snatched off her glasses to clumsily clean off his fingerprints with the hem of her lab coat. Replacing them, she gave him the back of her head. "I don't have the slightest idea what you're talking about."

"Oh, brother." An exasperated breath whistled through his teeth. "I had hoped, my prickly pear, that we had progressed in our relationship—"

"Relationship!" Mary hoped that the look she hurled over her shoulder adequately reflected her exasperation.

"I had *hoped*," he repeated, giving her braid a mischievous yank, "that we could get beyond this to something much more...what shall we say? Pertinent and meaningful?"

Mary made a resentful grab for her braid. "What could you possibly know, Jed Kilpatrick—" she tossed her head "—that would be pertinent and meaningful?"

"Well, let's see now." He clicked his tongue thoughtfully against the roof of his mouth. "Necking for the rest of the night, maybe? Or—this is just a suggestion, you understand—letting me explain to you just how much the tip of your delectable little nose turns me on? Maybe we could spend the whole night just staring at each other and discussing how your walk has to be one of the most profound experiences known to man."

Mary wanted to hit him. Did he think this was a joke? She had been doing some major, major suffering the past week. But, of course, he was much too busy in Vienna to know that.

She stomped dejectedly up the last three steps and headed for her rooms, the bow of her back telling him not to push one inch farther.

Refusing to follow, he anchored his boots and hooked his thumbs beneath his belt. "I'm having one of those profound experiences again."

Aggh! Spinning around, her braid slapping her across the cheek, Mary knew what his stance would be—that eternal macho pose, the arrogant crotch, the straining thighs, flat belly, big virile hands and beautifully shaped fingers. She would have bartered with the devil himself to be able to storm away in a magnificent huff, but his sensuality was a puppet master's string that kept her a prisoner.

"You *want* to fight, don't you?" she accused him. "You've been wanting this from the beginning."

❧ IT'S A ❧

SILHOUETTE HONEYMOON

A SWEETHEART

OF A FREE OFFER!

FOUR NEW SILHOUETTE SPECIAL EDITION® NOVELS—FREE!

Take a "Silhouette Honeymoon" with four exciting romances— yours FREE from Silhouette Special Edition®. Each of these hot-off-the-press novels brings you all the passion and tenderness of today's greatest love stories . . . your free passport to a bright new world of love and adventure! But wait . . . there's even more to this great offer!

A LOVELY BRACELET WATCH— ABSOLUTELY FREE!

You'll love your elegant bracelet watch—this classic LCD quartz watch is a perfect expression of your style and good taste—and it's yours free as an added thanks for giving our Reader Service a try!

AN EXCITING MYSTERY BONUS—FREE!

With this offer, you'll also receive a special mystery bonus. You'll be thrilled with this surprise gift. It will be the source of many compliments as well as a useful and attractive addition to your home.

PLUS

SPECIAL EXTRAS—FREE!

When you join the Silhouette Reader Service, you'll get your free monthly newsletter, packed with news of your favorite authors and upcoming books.

MONEY-SAVING HOME DELIVERY!

Send for your Silhouette Special Edition® novels and enjoy the convenience of previewing 6 new books every month, delivered right to your home. If you decide to keep them, pay just $2.74* per book—21¢ less than the cover price with no additional charges for home delivery. And you may cancel at any time, for any reason, just by sending us a note or a shipping statement marked "cancel" or by returning an unopened shipment to us at our expense. Either way the free books and gifts are yours to keep! Great savings plus total convenience add up to a sweetheart of a deal for you!

START YOUR SILHOUETTE HONEYMOON TODAY— JUST COMPLETE, DETACH & MAIL YOUR FREE OFFER CARD!

SILHOUETTE SPECIAL EDITION®

FREE OFFER CARD

FILL OUT THIS POSTPAID CARD AND MAIL TODAY!

4 FREE BOOKS

FREE HOME DELIVERY!

PLACE HEART STICKER HERE

FREE BRACELET WATCH

FREE FACT-FILLED NEWSLETTER!

PLUS AN EXTRA BONUS MYSTERY GIFT!

YES! Please send my 4 SILHOUETTE SPECIAL EDITION® novels, free, along with my free Bracelet Watch and Mystery Gift! Then send me 6 SILHOUETTE SPECIAL EDITION® novels every month and bill me just $2.74* per book—21¢ less than the cover price with no additional charges for shipping and handling. If I'm not completely satisfied I can cancel at any time as outlined on the opposite page. The free books, Bracelet Watch and Mystery Gift remain mine to keep!   235 CIS R1X5

NAME _____
                          (please print)
ADDRESS _____ APT _____

CITY _____

STATE _____ ZIP _____

CLIP AND MAIL THIS POSTPAID CARD TODAY!

BUSINESS REPLY CARD

First Class   Permit No. 717   Buffalo, NY

Postage will be paid by addressee

Silhouette Books
901 Fuhrmann Blvd.
P.O. Box 1867
Buffalo, NY 14240-9952

NO POSTAGE
NECESSARY
IF MAILED
IN THE
UNITED STATES

"What's wrong with a good, old-fashioned brawl with a lovely lady?"

"Well, come on, then." Matching his brashness with one she guessed would probably fail her at the last minute, she jutted her chin and waved him up the steps. "Give me your best shot, Doctor Dolittle."

"Gee..." His Groucho Marx ogle as he climbed two steps was more ludicrous than his grin or the finger he wagged back and forth before her nose. "Just as I suspected. You missed me, Mary Mary."

Leaning down to his step until her nose all but touched his, Mary purred with malicious sweetness, "Why, Jed Kilpatrick, have you been gone? I do declare, it seems only yesterday you were sending me notes and clever little propositions through interoffice mail. You all but asked to have breakfast in bed, as I recall."

His eyes were gold in the shadows, and no amusement glinted in them as his smile slowly faded. "I *did* ask."

The silence told too many secrets, and Mary wanted to throw up her hands and dash into the corridor and hide.

"Oh, that's good, Jed," she pretended to sneer. "I, on the other hand, being born a fool, mistook all that carrying on to mean that we were—"

She couldn't finish. And he, if he knew how, refused to bail her out. Only the telepathy between them arced like an electrical spark threatening to burn them both.

"Friends?" he eventually supplied.

Mary shifted her weight and tried to look away, but he drew her back with the force of his will. She wilted. "Look, Jed—"

Catching her hand, he made her alarm even greater as he pried open her fingers and pondered her palm as a mystic would seek the meaning of life. With mesmerizing slow motion he traced the lines and furrows.

"Friends? I dunno." A mild shake of his head caused sprigs of his hair to stick up with endearing untidiness. "I'm looking here for friends, Mary, but I don't see friends. I see... Ahh!" He traced the line on her palm and met her eyes as if he knew a delicious conspiracy.

From behind drooping lashes, Mary said, "You're certifiable, Jed Kilpatrick."

"I'm an acquired taste. Do I have to show you everything? Look, stubborn one. It says right here...see? This line?" With a solemnity that Mary found achingly irresistible, he turned her palm to the pale light. "This is your love line. 'Jed,' it says, plain as day. And here...'Mary.' No?"

Wetting his thumb, he scrubbed the line, then wiped her palm on his leg and peered at it again. He shook his head in a woeful way. "Tsk, tsk. I'm sorry, Mary. I wish I could lie to you, but I'd burn in hell if I didn't tell you the truth. I'm afraid we're stuck with it. We have to be lovers." He grinned. "Kismet."

His suggestion didn't offend Mary, but his cockiness did. How many days had she wrestled with her feelings and been torn because the timing was all wrong. She was still dripping blood from John, and there were people who wanted to take her baby. She'd miscalculated Haman Stone, who could damage her future, and the only place she had to go back to if she got fired was to her mother's.

And Jed was cracking jokes!

The stairwell was suddenly awash with light when she opened the door. As she stood poised in the stabbing shaft, Jed glimpsed the dewy half-moons of her lashes and the glistening heaviness of her hair. He could remember her naked loveliness of that first night—her smooth, sleek skin and her breasts ripe with child, the softer inside of her thighs and the curls protecting the hollowed furrows of femininity.

Had any woman had such a quick and compound effect upon his life? It was a paradox. She irked him no end. She made him question everything he'd taken for granted. She was stubborn and so set in her ways that she would argue a point to death if it suited her. She took pride to extremes and was as opinionated as a schoolmarm. Everything about her was tightly under lock and key.

But she was in his blood like some virus, damn it, and he'd promised that he would not do the very thing he was doing. In Vienna he'd resolved to find out where he stood before leaving himself open to pain again. So why was he standing here shackled at the ankles? Why was he full of aching currents?

Following her, he stood framed by the doorway. "You know you've set a hook in my mouth, don't you?" he said bitterly.

She opened her mouth as if to speak, her cheeks darkened with stain. Turning, she swiftly walked along the corridor to her door. Then, frustrated, she fished repeatedly through her bag for the key.

Stepping into her, he took her face lovingly into his hands, his nostrils flaring as he savored her scent.

"Listen carefully," he said on the raw, bitter flange of desperation, "because I don't think I can say this but once. I've come a long way to get this close to you, Mary. I've taken some hard looks at myself, and I've repaired a few bridges I didn't think I'd ever have the courage to face again. I know you're scarred. *I'm* scarred. You're afraid, but you don't have to be. I can keep you safe if you'll let me. I can take care of you. I *want* to take care of you. You need someone just now, sweetheart. You need me. Can't you even admit that much, that you need me?''

Stepping away, she stood incredibly still, so still that he could have leaned over and licked the diamond drops that glittered in the corners of her eye. Her braid was unplaiting and presently, with an impatient move, she reached behind and wrenched off the clasp. Over and over she turned the ornament in her fingers, staring as if it possessed some magical formula to restore things to the way they had been.

"That's quite a switch from being shafted up to your tonsils, wouldn't you say, Doctor?''

Jed didn't answer her. He couldn't. With the outrage of a man who has invested everything into a machine that stubbornly refuses to run, he swept her up in his arms and, with a vicious kick, connected his foot with the door.

It slammed back with a thundering crash. The blinds of the apartment had been left open. Jed and Mary stood trapped in the flash point of confusion, harshly etched by shadows of the room, their breaths audible and the tension having a sharp, painful aftersting. They were two routed fighters in two different worlds, able to see and to call across the boundary, but incapable of crossing into the reality of the other.

The truth rose to the surface of Mary's stagnant excuses. She knew why nothing seemed to fit anymore. She knew why her world was out of kilter and off its axis. She loved this man. But what did that make her, an expert in matters of the heart?

"Put me down," she said quietly.

Letting her slide slowly to the floor, he stepped back, his hands extended wide. "You're down."

His smile didn't match the burning gravity of his golden eyes. How did he do it? she wondered. How did he make her remember the fragile girlish dreams of being wooed? Dreams of a fairy princess in her tower waiting for her knight and being seduced, ever so tenderly, into the ageless ritual of mating? She'd forgotten things that other women took for granted—how it was to simply be held, the muscular solidity of a chest beneath your cheek, a man's thighs and his body warmth, his symmetry.

Gesturing distractedly, she whispered with a shake of her head, "You can't...I don't know how you think you can just come in here and..."

The room felt much too warm. She shrugged out of her lab coat and tossed it negligently upon the table. Exhaustion rode heavily upon her shoulders. He had worn her out, and she wished he would go.

But she could almost feel the powerful surge of blood through his body where he stood. In his eyes were reflected two twin slivers of moon. His breath was rough at the edges, harsh with unexpressed longing. Her awareness of their opposites approached the quickness of a torn fingernail.

She folded the edge of her coat into straight lines and smoothed the wrinkles, then smoothed imaginary wrinkles—smoothing, smoothing, smoothing as he watched her in the shadows.

"I didn't get the divorce," she admitted at length, the words coming with effort. "I forced John to get it. Partly out of anger, I guess, making it harder for him because I could do it. But partly because I didn't think I could bear to be one of those millions who'd made a mess of it." Tortured, she focused upon the past. "Some people say they don't care what people think, Jed, but I do care. I care what *I* think. I have to conduct my life with as few mistakes as possible. I just can't have an affair that goes nowhere, I can't. No more than I could get a divorce one week and marry the next. I'm a rule follower, Jed. There has to be a . . . a rightness to life. There has to be . . .''

She sighed heavily. From faraway came the throb of music. Somewhere, she thought, some people were living normal lives. Some people were actually happy.

When Jed stood before her, she wanted very much to touch him. But what if he pulled away? What if he told her not to touch him?

When he reached out and touched the top button of her blouse, she caught at his hands with a jerky panic.

"Please don't," she begged.

"Why not?"

"I told you."

"No one's here to see if we break the rules, Mary."

"Then, I . . . don't want you to."

"I don't believe that."

"You don't understand."

"Make me understand."

"I'm . . . I'm . . ." Mary's pride foundered in the mire of her memories. "Damn you, Jed Kilpatrick. I'm not pretty now!"

He took a moment to digest the words of such a plea. A slow smile of understanding formed, and with an exquisitely tender intimacy, he lifted a wisp of hair as if it were a strand of silver from the moon.

"He told you that? John?"

With trembling fingers, she clutched her blouse closed and gave him her shoulder. "Forget I said that."

"My God." His words came on a breath of relief. They touched the gauntness framing his mouth, softening it. "Is that it? Do you have to be told, sweetheart? Don't your instincts make you know how special you are? You *have* to know, Mary, that you're one of the most beautiful, most elegant, intelligent, special women I've ever met. But it wouldn't matter if you were ugly, because what I love about you isn't on the outside. It's here, my darling."

When he closed his hands gently upon her shoulders and turned her, tipping her face up beneath his own, tears knotted viciously in Mary's throat, threatening to strangle her. She began to tremble violently, and she feared he would hear her bones clattering as she shook apart.

"Don't say those things," she breathed.

"What things, love?"

"Endearments. Sweet words. I'm not used to them. They...undo me, Jed. I wish you wouldn't do it. Please."

"Undo you? Ahh." Smiling, he caught her up in his arms like a child so that her skirt billowed and furled about his hips. Her legs dangled across his arm. One of her shoes came off.

"I'm sorry, darling—" he laughed unrepentantly "—I didn't know. I wouldn't undo you for the world. My baby's shy? My love is a soft, shy kitten."

Before she could protest his zaniness, before she could laugh or cry or declare he was a womanizer of the lowest order, his face was suddenly dipping toward hers, and Mary's head snapped back against his shoulder like that of a rag doll. For one crazed second she attempted to turn back the force of the wave before it was too late. But his kisses melted, one into another, and she was suddenly starved for what he could give her. If she could have done it, she would have climbed into his skin.

Yet part of her could not come entirely from behind her armor. "Jed," she protested, struggling as he walked with her to the bed.

"It's okay," he whispered hoarsely into her mouth. "I just want to hold you, sweetheart, nothing more."

As he sat with her upon the bed, Mary closed her eyes, content to let herself drift in a stream of sensuality, moving her hands over his chest and his arms as he rocked her and said her name.

Jed thought he was drowning. At the beginning, when he had not known who she was, and she had, in that fragment of need, reached out for him, he'd had a warning of her complex passions. But she'd hidden them well inside her shell. Now she was twisting off his lap and rising onto her knees and was strewing molten kisses upon his shoulders and beneath his jaws and on the lids of his eyes.

Falling back to the pillows, pulling her on top of him, claiming her lips with a sigh of hunger, he molded her to the torment between his legs—pressing, pulsing, grinding until he feared he could no longer hold back the spasms that threatened to course through him.

Over and over she whispered his name into his mouth. "Jed, Jed."

He swore to heaven he tried to ignore the mad dogs snapping at his heels. He placed her on her back and, with trembling fingers, unfastened her blouse and her bra. He took her nipple into his mouth and found the most exquisite pleasure in the way she cradled the back of his head. He wanted to say that he loved her, but he feared she wouldn't believe him. He kissed the baby through her skirt. He kissed the V of her legs, her sides and her stockinged feet. He kissed her eyes and her cheeks and her nose and her throat. He kissed her until neither of them could remember the past, until she was straining for more.

Yet, when he peeled out of his jacket and hurled it to the floor, keeping her mouth a prisoner as he reached beneath her skirt and stripped off her stockings to send them sailing after the suit, her instincts of survival erupted through the flames.

He slipped between her legs and parted them, the crash of his heart deafening him to her sounds of alarm. She tried to tell him in a dozen ways that he had gone too far, but he refused to listen. Ponderous heat was strangling him, and pain knifed his temples. He was determined, in the fury of his desire, to have her.

She snatched her lips from his and struck wildly with her fists.

"No," her plea came ringing through the chambers of his lust-drugged brain. "You promised."

In disbelief, Jed gazed down at what he was doing. She was pushing from him into a tiny, shuddering knot, and the ache inside him was deeper than any real pain, terrifying in its size.

His arms went around her gently and humbly, for he understood now a thing he had not known with Ann: when a man loves passionately enough, he lays his whole character on the line with all the despicable things about himself naked for the viewing. And he sees in his beloved all the bad soon enough. A frightening thing, love.

Flipping onto his back until he could breathe again, he drew her protectively against his chest.

"I didn't know this happened anymore," he grimly confessed when his voice returned. "I feel like some kid out of the fifties in the back seat of his father's car."

"I'm sorry."

"Don't be. It was my fault."

"No, it wasn't. I asked for it."

"No, you didn't."

"Yes, I did."

"Am I going to have to drag you down to the floor and break both your legs before you listen to me, Mary Smith?"

They were surprised to discover that they could still laugh. The world was still intact, was still turning. They were sizzling, their desire sharper than ever, but it was like playing some tantalizing and irresistible game. They would play it again. The combustible forces between them would not go away. That knowledge was sweet.

The silence, then, was at peace with itself. When they began to talk, it was as if life had turned wrong side out and they must work in reverse to get back to the beginning. Suddenly they had more to say than the world could contain. For hours they talked and talked and talked—until they were hoarse and the moon had disappeared. Mary thought if all she had ever explained about herself had been collected into one lump, it would not equal what she had just told Jed Kilpatrick in the darkness.

"Your father," she said. "What kind of a man was he?"

He lay on his back, idly combing her hair with his fingers. "My father?" A smiled edged into his mouth. "My father is the perennial crisis man, the most humane man I ever knew, sound as a rock, someone to cling to in a storm. You'll like my father."

"My father was a dreamer. I inherited the worst of him, I think."

He chuckled. "No argument here."

Mary's laughter turned into a yawn. It was contagious. He yawned, and she sighed as he leaned across her to squint at the clock. "It's one o'clock, little owl."

Again she yawned. "We've talked for four hours."

She turned so that her back was pressed into him like a spoon molded perfectly to its mate in a drawer. The music was silenced now. Only the ticking of the clock kept them company. He was absently tracing the shape of the baby—around and around and around. Mary had lost count of how many times and in how many ways he had touched her.

But there was one special thing they had not talked about, and she had not asked. That one part of him was locked in a steel safe, impervious to man. Didn't she have a right to ask?

"What did you think, Jed?" She told herself that if he hesitated, even for a second, she would pull back and never ask again. "When it happened?"

As first she thought he would refuse to open that last door. He drew in a deep, controlled breath and his hand stopped moving upon her, remaining where it lay in quiet possession of her child.

"I once told my mother that watching the monitor of Roger Pike's heartbeat was the most horrifying thing that had ever happened to me." His voice took on a tight, lost timbre. "It *was* horrifying. I don't think I've had a dream since that night when I haven't woken up in a cold sweat hearing that buzzer go on and on and on."

The boundaries of Mary's soul blurred and interwove with his. His pain became her pain.

"But that wasn't the most horrifying." The past took on a life of its own. "It was the walk from the operating room to the waiting room where his parents were. I've often wondered if a man on death row dreads his walk any more than I dreaded that one. I was ill. I was catatonic. In the operating room, you see, I had my colleagues around me, and they understood. But out there, out there were his parents. They were simple black peo-

ple, having sat there for hours, trusting in me to make
everything all right. His mother was wearing a plain
brown coat, and . . .'' His poise broke, and he battled for
it. ''Her shoes needed new heels. I think I must have
looked at those heels all the eternity that I stood there. I
never was able to meet their eyes.''

Her hair flowed about their shoulders, a weightless
cloud of silk that shut out the world. Mary lovingly
traced the planes of his face and the outline of his bones
that lay beneath his skin, the cragginess of his nose. She
smiled as she arranged his tousled hair and drew the back
of her hand along his dark stubble of beard.

Jed, dear Jed. He had stolen her heart when she had
sworn it wasn't for the taking. When he lifted a tress and
laid it across his face, she thought he was hiding from the
memories and, spellbound, she lowered her lips to kiss
him, expecting him to meet her in tender absolution.

But he dragged an arm across his eyes. Thinking they
were past the point of barriers, she started to speak, but
when his nerves snapped taut, she grew still. A great
shudder swept through her heart like a wind blowing it
clean and ridding it of all the debris that John had placed
there. Tenderly she lifted his arm and saw the tears that
ran in salty rivulets into his mouth.

''Oh, Jed,'' she whispered, and she gathered him to her
heart as a mother would comfort a hurt child.

She cradled him to her breast, which was capable, at
that moment, of bearing the grief of the whole world. His
tears upon her neck were hot and her fingers were wet.
''My darling man, my darling Jed.''

''I killed a man.'' His confession was ripped from him
as by a giant hand that reached into his soul and pulled
it out by the roots. His face contorted with the killing
weight. ''A man is dead because of me. I wanted to die,

but I couldn't even die. God, Mary, I couldn't do anything. Nothing, nothing.''

"It's all right, Jed," she whispered, weeping with him.
"It's all right to cry. Life ends, but life begins."

He clung to her with the ferocity that only damned
souls know, and Mary had never had a man cling to her.
In her memories, she wasn't sure anyone had. Part of her,
the best part, belonged to Jed now. With a sense of her
own humanity, she knelt beside him and, whispering his
name and shielding her fears with her hair, she unfastened his clothes. She kissed his brimming eyes and his
lips and the curls upon his chest and, with trembling fingers, searched for him. Passion was gone, but she made
it return until, with a sound that was the consensus of his
frustrated desire, he pulled her across his waist.

Yet as she was preparing to obliterate the final distance that stretched between them, he caught her hands.

"No," he groaned with a desperate expenditure of will,
"not like this."

Horror etched her features. Holding her tightly, he
shushed her apologies before she could make them.

"No man will ever love you as much as I can love you,
my sweetest girl," he said, and lay wearily back, cra-
dling her. "But there'll be time enough. The rightness will
be there. I'll make it be there. No regrets, Mary. No pen-
ance for this. I love you for it. Hold me. I won't let you
go."

Except for his daughter, Jed had never seen anyone cry
himself to sleep. Perhaps the paternal instinct had made
him do what he had done; it was too much for him to
analyze.

For a long time he cradled her in his arms, stroking and
soothing, and not until he heard the sweet, steady rhythm

of her breath did he let the tension seep from his own soul.

Pulling himself against the headboard so that she lay upon his chest, her hand clutching his thumb and making him smile, he studied her. God, he loved her. He had thought this would never come again. It was a miracle.

In slumber, she looked like a child. Afraid that he would wake her, he held his breath and traced the path of one long swirl of hair where it followed the curve of her shoulder. She murmured in her sleep. What was the matter with him? Why hadn't he made love to her when he had the chance? Who was to say the time would ever come again?

He stared at her face until he could see her small, fine nostrils pinching infinitesimally as she breathed. Gently opening her hand and removing his thumb, he rose and repaired his clothes in the darkness. Then horror overwhelmed him as he walked to the door and realized that life could have so easily made a mistake and that she would never have come to this place and he would never have found her.

Chapter Eight

The lightning was a garish yellow as it shot through the sky from the bow of some capricious god. Thunder, sounding the promise of snow, rumbled through the valley in its wake.

The staff meeting ended, Annelise Weingarten hurried across the parking lot in a belted raincoat, her four-inch spike heels clattering an erratic code on the tarmac. She climbed into a black, older model Jaguar and roared out of the parking lot to speed down the switchback turns to the village of St. Murren, a road she knew as well as the contours of her own beautifully troubled face.

Rain was pelting the windshield by the time she arrived, and her headlights slashed across the grain. Rolling down the window, she let the cold wind sting her cheeks. With agitated fingers she clawed the pins from the bun at her nape and shook the golden strands free so they caught the wind and swirled about her head in a daring, wild torrent. The rhythmic snap of the wind-shield wipers set up a hypnotic chant.

Once she reached the cobbled street she sought, she edged into a narrow alley and, with a savage downshift, skidded to a stop behind the bistro owned by her cousin, Orso Reuther. Disdaining to lock the car, she skirted garbage cans and the alley cat who inveterately panhandled anyone near the door.

"Scat!"

The door creaked sorely on its hinges, and she entered the noisy bar that was blue with the haze of smoke and discontent.

The club was filled with wall-to-wall people. American rock music pounded her eardrums and talk followed her as she elbowed her way through—bragging that was too much on the desperate side and brave, bawdy stories.

She made a point to speak to the waiters and waitresses and kitchen helpers of the château. When a waitress from the bar asked what she was drinking, she smiled.

"Anything," she said, and slipped into the seat beside Stepan.

Two other men besides Stepan were in the booth, Paddy and Ian Gregov. Leaning over, Stepan kissed her upon the mouth.

"How did the meeting go?" he asked in German.

She replied in the same German. "Exactly as I told you it would." She exchanged dour looks with the two brothers who had once worked for Jochen Weingarten at the château. "There is nothing left for us on the mountain anymore. The Americans have left us the scraps. We can either take them or go somewhere else."

Ian sighed gravely. "Perhaps if we talked to Haman Stone again."

Shrugging, Annelise thrust money at the waitress when a glass of gin and tonic was placed on the table. She lifted it in grim salute to the men, and with an irony that contradicted the cool, demure image she exuded at the château, she tossed it down her throat as a man would do.

"Talk?" she challenged, banging the glass down upon the table. "Tonight Stone enforced a policy that will keep villagers from attending the social events. That's only one step away from barring us from the staff meetings. And then we won't have any say at all."

"Our profit sharing is gone." Paddy was older than the rest and able to remember more of the glory of Christmases past. "All our investments, our futures. My ancestors built the château. My family has worked there for generations. Where will my sons work?"

"My father was a casualty of this man," Annelise snapped impatiently. "He is destroyed. And my mother was buried by the lies of Haman Stone. My father sits in his chair, day after day. Do you see me sitting with my hands folded in my lap? I refuse to rest until this man and his Judas silver are gone."

"You say you kiss Stone's behind because you plan to get even." Stepan lit an American cigarette, blew smoke at the ceiling to join the rest of the blue haze and announced, "Some of us have been wondering if you don't just enjoy kissing his behind."

The crack of Annelise's palm connecting viciously to the side of Stepan's face carried over the throb of the music.

For a split second everything stopped and heads craned to see, mouths muttering "Oh, well..." when the onlookers realized it was only Annelise again on one of her endless campaigns.

Lunging hysterically to her feet, Annelise cried passionately, ''What will it take to make you believe in yourselves? If everyone would unite, we could bring the man down.''

Snatching up her raincoat and not bothering to conceal her disgust for them all, she stormed out. By the time she returned to the château, the rain had stopped and the threatening folds of mist had dissipated. A pale moon had begun its rise in the ragged sky, and the air grew sharply cold.

She didn't take the elevator to her room, but walked down a carpeted corridor to a wing where Haman Stone had a suite to himself. From a key on her chain, she unlocked the door and stepped into the muted light.

Haman had a phobia about total darkness. Even when he slept, the lights were on somewhere. Entering his bedroom, she found him awake, as she knew she would. Haman had a thing about sleeping, too, and he rarely slumbered more than three hours at a stretch.

He was completely naked in bed, his body smooth and boyish. No words passed between them. They weren't necessary. He knew his power over her. And she, better than anyone, knew his ravenous greed for more and more power.

The role she would now play was little different from the one she had rehearsed with him from the beginning. She would arouse him and then she would disconnect her mind from her body. That body would accept the blows he dealt when the scene was done. When he could not know was that in accepting his brutal substitute for passion, she was the one who wielded the power.

The dawn crept into Mary's room with cold, inquisitive fingers. Outside, nibbling capriciously at the eaves and teasing the windows until they chattered, a north wind was steadily pushing the mercury down. It sneaked down the chimney and stirred the ashes on the hearth so that the smell of them was in the room along with the smell of cold.

Mary opened her eyes and closed them again, a languid, dreamy smile on her face that she slowly became aware of. With a drowsy purr, she snuggled deeper into the warmth and slid her hand along the sheet in search of Jed's lean thigh. A dozen things to say were in her mind, but for now she wanted only to remember last night and savor the fine, muscular length of him, to rest her cheek upon his waist and be reassured by the strong rise and fall of it that she was not alone.

Deep inside, desire whispered to take him into her hands and learn with her body and her eyes and her breath and her mouth everything there was to know about Jed Kilpatrick. All her talk of rightness...what could be more right?

"Jed?" Rolling over, silky with passion, she opened her arms.

But he was gone.

Somewhere in stone was chiseled a law that said when a person went out in public feeling like a tomato blight, he would meet everyone who could and would give him a hard time.

At six o'clock in the morning, Jed stared into the mirror in the men's locker room at the gym. When he'd left Mary's the wind had already been hurtling down from the north. He had slept in his office and awakened stiff and out of sorts. An hour later, he'd done everything he knew of to come to grips with the other pain, the one low in his groin that no one could see.

After having worked out until he could hardly breathe, and having stood beneath the scalding blast of a hot shower until he was charbroiled, then taking vitamins and conversely swigging coffee and running laps and staring morosely out the window, he still ached from having desired her so futilely. Just imagining her legs locked around his waist could start the whole miserable process all over again.

When he looked into the mirror, he saw nothing but tomato blight staring back at him. "Damn!"

He toweled his hair dry and tried to comb it—a task as futile as extinguishing the fire that burned inside. He walked through the mirrored room where the weights and mats and punching bags were. With a final check of his wristwatch, he considered the telephones beside the entrance of the gym.

Seven hours difference in the time between the U.S. and Europe. He couldn't help it. Approaching one, he dialed the operator.

"Yes, I'd like to place a call to the United States, please."

Several early risers staggered sleepily into the gym while the ringing on the other end of the line stopped and a voice he had not heard in nearly a year sounded wistfully in his ear.

"Hello, Mother?" he said, his own voice quivering so that he had to swallow.

"Jed? *Darling?*" The woman's voice caught. "Is that you?"

Before Jed could stop them, hot tears stung his eyelids. He could picture the gauzy, lace-trimmed nightgown his mother would be wearing and could smell the familiar fragrance that was her.

"I wanted to hear your voice," he said, which meant, *I never meant to hurt you. I love you.*

He was certain that he heard her weep, and she whispered roughly aside. "Wake up, Joshua, it's Jed." Returning, sounding more like his mother, she said, "You sound different, darling. What's happened? Is something wrong? Are you all right?"

Squinching his eyes shut and gritting his teeth, feeling as wired as he had three decades ago when he'd stood on the high board for the first time and leaped into death-defying space from which he knew he would never return, Jed plunged.

"Nothing's wrong, Mother." He made a clean arch and sliced superbly through the brilliant blue water. "Actually, something's very right. I've met someone."

There was a short, questioning pause on the other end of the line. A breathless woman's sigh. "Yes. I can tell. I hear healing in your voice. It's serious with this someone you've met?"

Laughing, Jed let the back of his head thump against the wall in relief. He pictured himself striding like a Viking warrior into Mary's rooms with his arms recklessly full of her. Healing? Yes. Because of Mary and a miracle he didn't understand, he was able to accept, at last, the pain of his failure.

"Yes, Mother," he said, and remembered with startling clarity Mary's smile and her wonderful shining hair. "It's very serious."

At first Mary thought she imagined it. The morning was, after all, unreal because her love was new and she wasn't altogether certain who she was. But she knew who she wasn't. No woman of the eighties went around demanding that a man as sophisticated as Jed wait a "decent interval."

And she had had the gall to speak of rules! What rules? There were countless rules, unspoken or otherwise, about conducting affairs and getting out of bad ones. There were rules of how to protect oneself and what to do when one slipped up. Marriage had rules, and divorce and children. But where were the rules about waiting for sex until it was "right?"

She huffed a sigh as she stepped out of her morning shower and danced around in the cold. "I hope you're more sure about this relationship than I am, Jed Kilpatrick," she gasped.

It was as she was hastily fumbling with a garter belt— panty hose were uncomfortable now—and was yanking on her stockings, shimmying into her trumpet skirt and pulling on an angora sweater that dropped below her knees, that she first had the feeling that something wasn't right.

For long moments she stood before the bureau in the alcove and studied its comfortably cluttered top. "Did I leave it like that?" she mused, half aloud.

Slowly rotating, she ran her eyes expertly over the room and smiled briefly as she passed along the rumpled bed, the floor, her clothing spilled over the arm of the chair.

The chair. Had it always been so close to the wall?

Frowning and pulling on her boots, zipping them, she stood with her hair wadded into a clump and noticed the arrangement of her cleansing cream and perfume and hairspray and talc upon the bureau. She always staggered the bottles with the tallest at the back and the fat jar of cream to one side, their labels turned out—a scientist's manic penchant for detail.

"You're jumping at shadows," she said. "Suffering from paranoia because you vowed you wouldn't do this." She rearranged the bottles. "No one has searched anything. Jed probably smelled your perfume before he left. What are you complaining about? It's romantic."

Smiling, she brushed out her hair and dabbed some Obsession beneath it and on her wrists, imagining Jed finding it. She opened the drawer that contained her small stash of jewelry and swiftly examined the boxes, taking the time to open each one with a snap. Nothing was missing. Yet...

"When did I wear the bracelets last?" The day before. And she always made sure that they were kept separate from her porcelain necklace for fear the porcelain would get chipped. "I must've been in a hurry."

But she was never in *that* much of a hurry.

A heavy, viscous sensation spread through her chest. She moved through the apartment, sensing rather than looking, letting her invisible antennae guide her in the ways in which thing were not as she had left them. If she had a maid, it would have been explainable, but the hotel cleaning woman came once a week. The rest of the time she did her own cleaning.

"Someone has been here," she said, and wasn't even certain if she should believe herself.

How could she remember precisely how things had been the day before? After Jed had kissed her, the night was a blur.

Good grief, she would be late for her nutrition class!

"Now that we've learned about our livers," Mary said later as she smiled at Scutter's young athletes ranging in age from fifteen to eighteen, "is there anyone who doesn't know what carbo loading is?"

Teenage faces were sprinkled around the dining tables of a room that had been designated for them. They were dressed in various combinations of gym clothes; they would go straight from breakfast to a daily warm-up session with Scutter. Hungry, they slumped on their elbows and sprawled over the tables with 7:00 a.m. rust still in their eyes.

"Carbo loading is like using high-octane gasoline," Mary explained, and gestured to the buffet island at one side of the room. "For the next three days, seventy percent of your calories will be protein. You will eat five small meals a day, and I want you to stay within the calorie guidelines that Dr. Kilpatrick established at the beginning of your training. Then, for three days, you will eat the same seventy percent in carbohydrates. After that, of course, Coach Brown will have scheduled you in a grueling event, and we'll see how well you hold up."

Percy Dunhaven raised his hand, his blue eyes squinched as he drawled, "Is this more or less dangerous than shooting heroin, Dr. Smith?"

Everyone laughed, and Mary retorted, "At least you won't go to jail for doing it, Percy." As the laughter subsided, she added soberly, "Continued use of it could be dangerous, though."

"How dangerous?" asked Mark Cogdill from Stockton, California.

Mary shrugged. "Kidney failure, heart disease. As in everything else, abuse produces bad results. What we want you to do is to empty your system of glycogens with the protein diet and exercise until you're exhausted. Then, when you go onto the carbohydrate diet and get a maximum of rest, your muscles will soak up glycogens like a sponge. This will give you the energy you need for an exhausting competition like cross-country skiing.

You're in the most taxing sport there is, you know. We want you to come out of it healthy and not resort to practices that can literally kill you."

"Steroids," one said.

"Blood doping."

"I would never do anything like that."

"Hell, no. And blow our one big chance?"

How young and idealistic they were, Mary thought. They couldn't yet conceive of their own capabilities for hurting themselves, and not until that Olympic gold medal dangled before their noses would they be driven, in desperation, to do almost anything to win it.

"That's why," she said gently, "we want you to know a better way."

Juliet Haney lifted her chin to a perfected angle of disinterest. "Does Vanessa know about this?"

Mary shrugged, her smile tensely intact. "I don't know, Juliet. We'll keep special tabs on you. You'll go for a checkup at the end of every day."

Everyone knew that Juliet was a special case, and her built-in edge didn't set well, especially with some of the boys.

Aloofly, Juliet said, "I'll have to consult with Vanessa before I begin any program as drastic as this. I really think if it were all that important, she would've told me."

Little Miss Smart Britches! Mary scooped up her student charts, clipped her pen smartly into the pocket of her lab coat and indicated that they were free to begin serving themselves breakfast.

"That's up to you, Juliet," she said tightly. "Let Dr. Kilpatrick know what you decide. In any case, make a record of what you eat."

"It isn't necessary to remind me—" she made an insincere sound of respect "—Doctor."

Keeping her temper on a tight leash, Mary left them to their breakfast. She marched briskly to her office, made some notes about Juliet and tried to reach Jed by phone, but was told that he was setting a broken leg at the hospital in St. Murren. Threading a fresh page of paper into her typewriter, she looked over her half-finished feature for *Foods for Life*.

She considered the fitness craze and, on a brainstorm, edited the entire feature, slanting it to modern sports science. Immediately after her noon duties in the kitchen were finished, she returned and edited it again and worked until dinner.

Once dinner was done, she returned to her office with a thermos of apple juice and typed a final draft.

"I'll be darned," she said aloud when it was done, "it's good." Giving it a final read-through, she clipped the pages together, placed them into an envelope addressed to the States and experienced the most keen longing to hear Jed's voice.

On impulse, she slipped in a note to her editor. "Harry, do you think there's a book in this? And if there is, would you be interested in hearing some ideas? Say along the lines of the athlete of the future? Olympics, 1992?"

She consulted her watch. Unbelievable. It was eight o'clock. The day was gone.

Her attention rested upon Juliet's file. She still didn't know what to do with the girl. Jed would have gone to the cabin by now, she guessed, but she had one very legitimate reason for seeing him.

Not in a mood to let a good thing go to waste, she swept up her shoulder bag and walked to his office just to make sure he wasn't there and found a note taped to the door. *Gone to gym.*

The complex surrounding St. Murren was much larger than it appeared to be. Beside the château and the grounds and the two ski lifts and a chair lift, the resort operated a cable train that had originally been built for the workers. Several spas were housed alongside the main building, along with three tennis courts, one of them indoors. A large indoor swimming pool took up one wing with a handsome gymnasium on the other, plus a nightclub and three restaurants in various areas of the grounds.

Stepping out into the night and onto a sidewalk that had been freshly shoveled, Mary pulled on a soft cap and shrank deeply into her coat. If she had the sense of a penguin, she would return to her room, take a hot bath and plan the no-sodium, low-calorie hors d'oeuvre for Haman Stone's guests from the States.

Anton, one of the maintenance men, was trudging to the dumpster, pulling a cart loaded with garbage bags. When he spotted her, he stopped, his ruddy, windburned face breaking into a smile. *"Fräulein,"* he said, "you iss going to get a frostbite on dat pretty nose."

Mary drew her coat beneath her chin in a friendly way. "Then maybe that'll keep me from poking it where it doesn't belong, Anton."

He made a buffoon's face. "Vat a boring life vit'out a morsel now and again, eh?"

"Anton, am I to believe that you would stoop to gossip?" She dropped her jaw in mock horror.

"Me?" He fished a half-smoked cigar from his pocket and, gripping it in his teeth, popped a match on his thumbnail. "Naww. But a great disappointment it vas, I tell you, da telephone company inventing private lines. But da really goot stuff vorks its vay to da garbage dump, given time." He chuckled at his own irony.

Leaning forward, her hand cupping her ear, she whispered in conspiracy, "Okay, what's the latest, Anton? You can't start a story without finishing it. You know it won't go any further."

His pale eyes danced delightedly. "All I know iss," he chortled, "dat big doin's iss planned for da big man. Rooms getting ready all over—VIP, mail goin' out, comin' in, phones ringin'. From da States, too. New York City. Oh, oh, oh. Not very pleased vit da big man, dey say." He shook his head. "Not very pleased."

Haman Stone? Having fallen upon hard times with his Wall Street backers? Jed would be very interested, to say nothing of Scutter. *And* Annelise, if there was any truth to it.

Stamping her boots and blowing on her fingers, she said, "You wouldn't happen to have seen Dr. Kilpatrick, would you, Anton?"

With too-knowing brows, he inclined his head toward the gymnasium and started heaving his cart again.

"Thanks, Anton." She walked backward to wave at him.

"Gott bless."

Mary hurried along the sidewalk and turned a corner while anticipation bloomed, unbidden, in the pit of her stomach. She would see him. They would smile and remember, and coals would be fanned to life.

Already she burned inside. Snowcapped boughs licked at her coat as she brushed against them. Echoing her steps with fluttery whispers against her cheeks, the ends of her hair soaked up the cold.

A welcome blast of warm air embraced her when she pushed open the door.

"Good evening," the receptionist greeted from behind his desk in the center of the carpeted lobby. "Would you sign in, please?"

Feeling like a visitor to a prison, Mary signed her name and ran her finger down the list to find something illegible beginning with a K scrawled in Jed's hand.

Tingling, and not in a mood to chitchat, she strolled alongside the ranks of racquetball courts and weight rooms and paused briefly to watch a few lingerers slamming balls with ear-splitting quickness. Hardly had she gotten twenty feet than she was spotted by Scutter, who had packed up and was ambling toward the lobby with a bag slung over his shoulder.

Sweats drooping about his ankles, he zipped a down-filled parka beneath his chin. "Hey, beautiful!" he called, grinning and wiggling his sandy brows with an unabashed proposition. "How's it goin'?"

"You ask me that every time you see me, Scutter," she complained playfully, to disguise her irritation.

"That's because every time you tell me the same damn thing."

"That's because I lead a dull, boring life."

He winked. "I'm doin' everything I can to change that, but you just won't say yes."

When she blushed—it was impossible to remain piqued with the man—he cleared his throat and pretended to be apologetic.

"He's in there. Doin' that damned kung fu stuff. I keep tellin' him he's gonna ruin his hands someday, but he won't listen. Maybe he wants to."

Mouthing something about it being late, Mary moved toward one of two arched doorways and slipped through.

The room had no windows. Mirrors covered all four walls. The heating was kept low even though it was cold outside. Jed was not alone. With him, standing opposite, was an older man, a small-framed Asian whose loose-fitting cotton trousers were caught about his waist with a drawstring. His chest was sleek, and the hair on his head nearly white. He was clean shaven, and his black eyes were set into a beautifully serene face the texture of parchment.

Tiang-Si, she knew, though she had never seen the man. The château flew him in once a week to give specialized instruction to some of the more glamorous clientele. So deeply was Jed immersed in the man's soft monosyllables, his whole body was in a pose of reception, and he seemed not to notice that she had entered.

"The body must be tensed," the man said, "including the throat and esophagus, forcing the air out of the abdomen. Use all your strength. Give and snap back."

Jed wasn't wearing cotton trousers but tight black briefs that gripped below his navel and stretched over his crotch and across his buttocks with such precision, he could have been stark naked. Sweat streaked his tanned sides and the ribboned stripes of his ribs, diagramming his naked back into a sensual pattern of muscle and bone. He wore no shoes, and the soft, midnight curls upon his chest were glistening with droplets, as was the line of hair that divided his body in two. He had to be the most sexy, appealing man she had ever seen.

The bow between the two men was controlled and formal, the room so still that Mary felt her pulse throbbing its tense cadence to her toes. She was an intruder, her reflection watched from all the mirrors, but she could not leave.

With his left leg off the floor, Jed swung around backward in a balletic step and kicked with such a sudden speed, head high, that she was incapable of following it through. But Tiang-Si countered his student, and Jed was forced quickly to retreat.

In a series of precise, whirling turns in the air, extraordinarily beautiful and controlled only by his feet, Jed proceeded again and again to execute the same move and was each time countered by his master. Their slams upon the floor were loud and aggressive. Their heavy breaths filled the room, as did the smell of healthy exertion. On and on the lesson went. Then, as a final instruction, Tiang-Si spoke to Jed in his low, whispery voice, and Jed altered his body to resist, unwinding his stance as easily, as effortlessly, as a serpent would uncoil.

Like lightning, the older man kicked. Such ferocity in a man so small took Mary's breath, and with a crash Jed landed flat on his back.

Dear God! she thought in horror, having to cover her mouth to keep from screaming.

Before she could blink, Jed was on his feet again, crouching, positioning himself, the tips of his fingers stiffened and slightly curved, his concentration radiating with a power that was chilling.

Not your hands! Mary wanted to shriek, but she didn't dare make a sound.

Again Jed attacked, and again he landed on his back. She heard words she didn't understand. *Kansetsu-waza, ate-waza, shime-waza, osae-waza.* Each time Jed took the brunt of the instructor's feet, but on the final approach he skimmed the floor in a long, gliding stride and launched himself high into the air, his right heel leading.

Tiang-Si was thrown back, and the bout was abruptly over.

With a surprising bow of courtesy and respect, the men exchanged a few brief words, bowed again and parted. Hardly had Mary gotten her bearings than Tiang-Si slipped through an opening at the opposite end of the room and magically disappeared.

Without a word, Jed walked to a wall, flipped a switch that killed the brutal lights and, hesitating a moment to adjust to the darkness, walked straight toward her, as magnificent as a naked savage.

Mary's heard plummeted, and she couldn't move, nor could she think of anything to say. A leg of his brief had ridden too high into his groin, cutting him, and he hooked a finger beneath the band and absentmindedly dragged it lower.

Was it really happening? Were her feelings true? Had they always been meant for each other but were just now discovering that star-crossed fact, having come halfway around the world?

"You came to me," he said softly as he stopped only inches away, smiling, adoring her but not touching.

A pleasurable fear caused Mary's smile to crack around the edges. The crescent of light from a distant hall isolated them. From one of the courts beyond, someone shouted, and the sound of a smashed ball reverberated through the gym.

She shivered as Jed slowly bent his head and brushed his lips along the edge of her jaw. "I'm sweaty," he said.

Liquid fire pooled at the juncture of her legs. "Jed..."

"Why did you come?"

"Not to do this." Collapsing with a laugh at herself, Mary drew off her cap, crushing it with her hands. Did he have any idea of what he did to a woman? "Oh, dear."

"What, then?"

She arranged her face into a worldly-wise smile. "Oh, all right. I came here to gawk at your bod."

He spread his arms to give her a better view, chuckling vainly. "I highly recommend it."

He would, the rogue! "I really came to ask you about Juliet," she quickly amended.

"You're such a bad liar, Mary." Amusement shone in his face. "It makes me have faith in mankind again."

She mutinously tweaked a curl on his chest. "I'm going to have to break your face."

Laughing, he assumed a defense posture as when he'd faced Tiang-Si, and she bowed in immediate surrender.

"Much better." He grinned. "Now, what about Juliet? But walk with me while we talk. I'm freezing in here."

As they walked, his hand rested protectively on the small of her back. When he wasn't looking, Mary surreptitiously slipped her glasses into her bag along with her cap. He guided her deep into the entrails of the building, where the heat had collected from the furnace and lights were seductive and hazy and the rest of the world was orbiting somewhere out in space.

The heels of her boots clicked a staccato counterpoint to the whisper of his bare feet. They emerged in the men's shower, and Mary blinked at spigots lining the wall and the drains checkering the tile floor.

"Where have you brought me?" she asked with a saucy face that pretended to be offended.

"Into the lair of the dragon. Couldn't you see better with your glasses?"

He had *seen*, the devil! "I hate you, Jed Kilpatrick."

"That's why you came, isn't it?" He grinned. "To give the dragon his due?"

He was much too appealing and too clever and too much of what she had imagined the perfect man to be, and she was much too intoxicated by her own senses. With lashes heavy upon her cheeks, she deliberately tipped her head so that her hair fell, shimmering, between them.

"What dragon?" she asked softly, knowing exactly what he meant. "What due?"

"You have to look deep into his eyes and fall beneath his spell to know. You have to burn. You have to be on fire. Do you know what it's like to be on fire, Mary?"

"I may have felt nothing for John, but inside, I'm a woman just like any other."

"Oh no, love." Intensity roughened his voice. "Not like any other. Never like any other."

Mary felt as if she were two different women separated by centuries. One was completely in the eighties and unafraid, the other was locked within the staid rules made by other people. She might hate those rules, but she could not escape the restrictions they had branded upon her id long before she was old enough to prevent them.

"The rightness you spoke of," he said solemnly. "*We* are right, Mary. Vintage stuff, you and I. It's a fact you haven't accepted yet, but in your heart, you know it's true."

"Oh, Jed." With more honesty than she had let anyone else see in her, Mary pressed her temples. "Every time I think I know myself, that I've got it all worked out, you take me by surprise. Every time we're together I learn something I didn't suspect was inside me." She stared at him point-blank. "I don't even know who I am anymore."

The building was alive with its own sounds, and a rush of water rattled the pipes. Starting, she looked around them for fear of being seen. She slumped with chagrin at her skittishness.

"Guilt, Mona Lisa?" he teased.

"No! Not guilt! I told you, I'm not a prude."

He measured her with the shrewd instincts of a veteran infighter. "I can take the bad with the good. Besides, it's bad karma to take advantage of a pregnant woman."

"Aggh!" Slumping against the tiled wall, she angled her exasperation at him. "What do I have to do to convince you? Drag you to the floor?"

A growl rumbled playfully from his chest, and he braced his arms on each side of her head so meticulously, they did not touch.

He lowered his face until his lips touched her only long enough to make her want to chase them. "I've thought about you all day."

"I know."

"I've wanted you all day." His whisper fanned her blazing cheeks.

"Have you?"

"I called my mother. I told her about you."

The room was very warm, and Mary was overdressed. Beads of perspiration formed above her lip and across her brow. In a gesture so sensual that it made her feel violated, he licked the droplets.

In a small voice, she asked, "Why did you leave me last night?"

"Because it hurt to stay," he muttered as he plucked at her ear with tiny bites. "If I had stayed...damn." Straightening, he let out his breath. "I love you, Mary. Don't ask me to explain it, because I don't know why. I know you want to do the right thing. I know it bothers you that it's happened so soon after your divorce. But life doesn't obey the rules, sweetheart, it's an undertaker. I want you every way it's possible to want a woman, right or wrong. Tell me what to do. Name it and I'll do it or I'll get it.''

With her throat too clotted to speak, Mary knew he was far ahead of her. He wasn't delivering ultimatums, he wasn't proposing an affair, he wasn't hiding behind a mask. What would she feel, she wondered, if she had six months to live and had heard such words? Would she be concerned with rules then? Would committing herself to Jed Kilpatrick ''before the ink was dry'' appear foolish then?

She felt robbed of a perspective. And her own code of conduct, self-made or otherwise, was strangling her to death.

She clung, trembling, to his shoulders, which were sleek with sweat. There was no subterfuge between them now, no circumstantial smiles, no plastic facades. She was, suddenly, quite tired of herself.

''Oh,'' she said helplessly.

As if he understood, his mouth was abrupt and hot upon hers. Her arms were unexpected and urgent about his neck. It was madness, and nothing mattered, nothing existed except the ravenous hunger of their souls.

Mary felt herself being lifted, but wasn't certain if he picked her up or if she climbed him. She knew only that he was capturing parts of her as if he had laid traps for them: her hips were his, her arms, her throat in its high, arcing curve that could receive the brunt of his hunger, her breasts and even that maternal convexity that she had found so unpretty. She was in the center of herself with the apex of her body rocking upon the hard fulcrum of his.

He skimmed beneath the voluminous skirt and found her hips and the silly garters. Kissing her more deeply, he found her readiness.

"Jed." She tried to hold his hand imprisoned there, pressing and straining against it.

His breath was a grating rasp, and he was shaking when he lifted his head. "Not in this place," he said with gaunt effort, and looked around them. "We've waited this long."

Engulfed by heat, aching, Mary groaned as he lowered her gently to the floor where she slumped in his arms like a rag doll. Without recrimination or apology, he released her as suddenly as he had embraced her. As she dizzily collected the strewed pieces of herself, he walked to one of the showers and twisted on the jet. With a flick of his thumb, he stripped off his briefs and tossed them aside.

Mary saw him watching her take in the sight of him soaring rampantly out of himself.

"Don't worry about it," he said wryly as he stepped into the erupting volcano of steam. "It's never fatal. At least it never has been."

He made a comical double take, as if he weren't quite sure the normal rules applied where she was concerned. Raising his voice, he added, "I'm driving you into the village for a late dinner. Then I'm taking you up to the cabin. One way or another, my darling, tonight you're going to agree to marry me."

Chapter Nine

Mary had never felt comfortable with nakedness before. The sacrificial ritual between John and herself had always been conducted in the dark, and though she had been honest in telling Jed that she wasn't a prude, her horror of being thought ugly had taught her that a human body was highly overrated.

Modesty seemed to be totally foreign in Jed's thinking. He gave no thought to the little things of which she was so violently aware—the simple male appeal of his jeans being left unfastened below his navel after he put them on, the intrigue of the curls on his chest that sparkled with water every time he moved or took a breath, the dark line of hair that dissected his frame and disappeared into the wedge of thicker hair below.

As he strolled toward her, barefooted, jeans shifting loosely about his pelvis, she felt she was standing upon the San Andreas Fault. Any second now the earth would open up and swallow her. She glanced nervously at the ceiling, at the floor, anywhere but at his gleaming, golden eyes.

"What d'you mean, you came to talk to me about Juliet?" he asked, stopping directly before her, his hands filled with his towel and a shirt and socks, his black tufts of hair glued together in dripping arrows.

Mary struggled to clear her head. "Ahh . . . did I say that?" She stared ridiculously at the plumbing overhead, then at him. He had the most beautiful mouth she'd ever seen.

"Did you say what?"

Blinking, she looked toward the wall beside his head. "I s-said," she stammered, and fervently inspected the toes of her boots, "what you said."

"Oh. Juliet."

"Yes." A normal subject, thank God! She snatched at the microscopic particle of sanity. "It goes against my grain to dispense a concoction when I don't know anything about it, Jed."

"By concoction, you mean Vanessa's health line."

"Have you tested them?"

"They have been tested, but no, I haven't done it personally."

"That doesn't satisfy me, Jed."

"Really. What *does* satisfy you?"

His bare feet were now toe to toe with her booted ones. She stared at a scar on the side of his left instep.

"It surely is warm in here," she muttered at last, and pushed back her hair with a sigh.

"I'll be damned if it isn't."

And then he laughed one of those cockily pleased male laughs—sounding the high school jock who has just made it with the homecoming queen in the back seat of a Chevrolet convertible. Taking her swiftly by the shoulders, he placed a hard kiss upon her mouth.

"Don't ever change, Mary." He laughed. "I'll break all your bones if you change. Stay right here." He planted her on the floor. "In the words of the famous Terminator, 'I'll be back.'"

Was he mad? She couldn't have taken a step if he'd offered her the moon!

After jeans, boots, sweater and jacket had made him proper once more, he walked her through the room where he and Tiang-Si had worked. When they passed by the racquetball courts, Scutter was gone. The sidewalks were deserted—everyone was escaping from the cold and camping around the fireplaces inside, nursing welcome cups of steaming brew and pleasant, evening conversation.

"Unless you want to amputate my feet," she told him, "we have to stop by my office for a pair of socks."

"By all means." He laced his fingers through hers. "I have a foot fetish."

"Idiot."

Hugging each other for warmth, they never saw the twin shadows detach themselves from the snow-laden shrubs and follow them at a distance. The wind was lashing at the trees and flinging snow from the drifts. Exhilarated by the night's cold beauty, they laughingly ran the last few steps to the glass doors at the back of the building where the cupolas and chimneys stood watch.

At the steps, he took her into his arms and kissed her. "I want you very much," he said, then swept open the door.

Since her occupancy would last only a season, Mary had made only the most meager changes in her office, adding a brightly covered chair that she had confiscated from one of the bars and a table lamp that one of the receptionists had been in the process of scuttling.

A chill was in the room when they entered, and when Mary flipped a switch, a lamp cast a subtle glow over the freshly vacuumed carpet and the glossy leaves of the schefflera in one corner. Still trembling from her ordeal, she searched through her desk drawers for a pair of argyles.

When she glanced up, Jed had removed his jacket and tossed it to a chair and was thumbing through her manuscript pages, flipping idly at first then beginning to read in earnest.

It was an unexpected vulnerability. She realized suddenly that it was every bit as important for Jed to respect what she did as it was to him that she not think him a failure. With her heart on hold, she followed the track of his eyes.

He turned a page, then another and another. By the time he'd finished, her nerves were flayed raw, and she had plucked threads loose in her socks.

"What do you think?" she asked huskily. "Lie to me."

His smile touched her brow, her eyes, her lips, and he laid the pages upon the desk without looking to see where they went.

Their pages ruffled gently as they slid to the floor. "Don't ask me again why I love you."

Mary made no move to pick up the manuscript. "I take it back. Don't lie to me. Tell me now, Jed, if all you want is—" she gestured to her length "—this."

When he reached behind his back and felt over the door until he located the lock, the click seemed like a signal for some dreaded moment of truth Mary had known, intuitively, had to come.

"That's not the lie you're afraid of," he softly accused. "You don't doubt *me.*

She took a step backward.

"Do you want *me* enough?" he asked. "Will *your* love last?"

He didn't know how cruel he was, Mary thought. "I want you. I'm honest in saying that. You have to understand that for me to desire anyone is to love them. I never wanted John, and I never loved him. But Jed, how do I know what I'll be feeling in ten years? In twenty?"

He matched her steps with his own, the soft light creating a network of tiny grievances alongside his mouth. "How does anyone know?"

"I don't want to make a mistake."

"You think I do?"

From the posters lining the wall, Vanessa was watching them with an obscene smile upon her beautiful lips. Positioned as he was, Jed appeared to be standing lazily beside her. Mary laced her hands and twisted them until the circulation cut off. He moved closer, but still did not touch her.

Convulsively, she angled her gaze to Vanessa. "Why don't we just forget all my rash talk about rightness—all that stuff? We could . . . you know, try it out and give it some time, give *ourselves* some time to make sure."

The uncompromising smolder of his eyes didn't match the half smile of his lips. "Nothing doing. Not with you."

"But earlier you said—"

"What I said earlier does not apply. I want you for the rest of my life, Mary. I want to help you raise this baby. Now, say you'll marry me, damn it, and know that I mean until we die. If we've made a mistake, we'll live with it. That's what human beings do, Mary, is make mistakes. The fault with our generation is that we've learned to run from them. Well, by God, I've run for the last time."

A mother's love was so much simpler. One didn't divorce a child. One only divorced its father. But she *hadn't* divorced the father, the father had divorced her. She *was* capable of forever!

Mary bargained desperately with his eyes. "After dinner, you said. You promised to give me until after dinner."

"I lied."

"Jed—"

"Say, 'Yes, Jed,'" he instructed, and fit his legs to hers as he spread a hand wide upon the curve of her hip. "'Y-e-s.'"

On perfect cue, the phone rang, and Mary's brain could have been drugged with sleep. She looked at the phone, then at him and dazedly back to the phone again.

"Let it ring," he whispered as he leaned farther and farther so that she was bending back over the top of the desk like a reed before the force of a strong wind.

Mary flailed haphazardly behind herself in search of the receiver. "I have to answer it," she gasped, and knocked the instrument across the desk.

He grasped her beneath her hips and literally laid her back upon the smooth hard surface. Her coat was dragged to her waist, and its sleeves bunched at her wrists. As she freed an arm and grasped the receiver, dragging it to her ear, he forced her knees apart and slid with perfect ease into their soft wedge.

Equilibrium lost, Mary dodged his face coming down in search of her mouth.

"Hello?" a voice said from a great distance. "Hello, is anyone there?"

Jed's lips were strewing kisses upon her nose and her ear. "H-hello," she stammered the word as heat generated at the juncture where their bodies joined.

"Mary?"

"This is Mary Smith," she managed to gasp. "Who—"

"This is Guy, Mary. Guy Rhodes. I can hardly hear you. Can you hear me all right?"

"Guy!" she repeated stupidly, as she rose onto an elbow and stared in a daze of disbelief while Jed blissfully unbuttoned her blouse and discovered the tiny clip on her bra.

Unable to look away, she watched Jed's head bending. She shuddered as his breath washed hotly over her and his tongue traced the tip of her breast. Her nipple sprang impudently to life, and he drew her deeply into his mouth.

"That sample you sent me, Mary?" Guy's voice came from halfway around the world. "I've finished analyzing it. I'd stay away from that stuff if I were you."

"What?" Mary heard some strange woman asking, then heard another woman completely different groan. "No, no."

"What did you say? Are you there, Mary?"

"Yes," she said raspily, and trembled as Jed drew the life out of her body and into his. Discovering the garter belt she wished she had never worn, he amused himself with it stretchy lace. "I mean, go on, Guy."

"There's some kind of weird steroid in this stuff, Mary. Mind you, it's a subtle one. I had to run every test in the book on it, and I'm still not one hundred percent positive, but it reacts like a steroid. I'd have to run some long-term experiments with it, but I figure somebody's already done that. Its base is exceptionally good quality lactose. Are you still with me?''

With him? She no longer knew where she was or who she was. Her panties were being drawn down to her knees, and Jed was bending her legs and battling them farther apart, was touching her and finding her and placing his fingers where she was all satin and stardust and miracles.

"Are you all right, Mary?" Guy was repeating.

"Actually," Mary could hardly speak. "Actually, Guy..." She turned her head from side to side. "Actually something's...come up. Guy, I really appreciate—"

Jed's kisses to the insides of her thighs were dragging her to the edge of some killing precipice. With his tongue he traced the curves and the spaces and vacancies of her body, the line of her hip, her navel and the curve of her abdomen, the soft nest of curls. And when he kissed there, her fingers clutched great fistfuls of her coat.

"Sure thing, honey," Guy said. "Say, this is costing an arm and a leg. Get back to me if you need anything else. Okay?"

"Okay," she whispered. Jed looked up at her. He drew her into the small concentric circles of his eyes, into that black pupil and burning golden iris. "Thanks..."

"Anytime, hon."

But she didn't hear, for she was dropping the receiver and it clattered noisily against the side of the desk and bounced and swung back and forth, back and forth. Mary cupped Jed's head with her hands and wantonly guided him while her whole life pooled into one silver current whose source was him.

The click... The dial tone... It droned forever as she was wrapped in flames and lay upon the desk, groaning as she burned and burned and burned to a cinder and slowly stopped moving.

"Open your eyes," Jed whispered as he stood abruptly and laid himself upon her, bracing his weight upon the desktop with his arms.

"I can't."

He kissed her, and Mary could taste the sweet musk of herself upon him. There was no artifice about this man, and his lack of inclination to accept lies was the most devastating thing she had ever confronted. He kissed her thoroughly and waited until she had the courage to meet his eyes.

"I know I promised," he said, his own desire distorting his voice, "but I'm not sorry."

Mary thought that she would never again in her life know the thrill of recognizing love for the very first time. She had been married, and she had conceived a child. But she had never given herself unconditionally before. Not once.

This man loves you. Don't break his heart by clinging to the past and its fears. Take the chance. Give to him as freely as he is giving to you.

He replaced the receiver. Gathering her into his arms, he carried her to the tiny red sofa. He then placed her there and aligned himself upon the small portion that was left.

As he carried her, Jed thought that she seemed very small and easily hurt. But he must never let himself be deceived, for in the final accounting she was much stronger than he.

Murmuring words that meant absolutely nothing, he placed kisses upon her arms and tried to see the future. He couldn't, but he knew that nothing about it was worth a penny unless he could bring it to her and lay it at her feet.

Her knees were quivering, and a shiver took her. Goosebumps pebbled her arms and the gently rounded curve of her baby. Wanting nothing between them, he started to undress her the rest of the way. Yet she rose up, honest panic in her eyes.

"No!" she said roughly. "Please, not that."

For a moment their eyes sparred, and Jed knew she would fight him over it. John Smith had scarred her more than he knew.

The ache in his groin was almost unbearable now. He unbuttoned his jeans, and with unskilled fingers she helped him undo the buttons on his shirt.

"Tit for tat," he teased gently, leaving his clothes on but removing his boots. "There are fewer secrets between us, at any rate."

"There's nothing wrong with having a few secrets," she parried. "Why did you do that to me?"

"Because you needed it. I think you even hoped I would." With his fingers idly circumventing her breasts, he asked casually, "Who was that on the phone?"

She unthinkingly arranged his hair back from his forehead. "My chemist friend in the States. He says that Vanessa's giving Juliet a steroid."

The statement caught Jed unprepared. His hands grew still. "The hell you say."

"A very elusive steroid, to hear him tell it. I'm not sure what to do about it, but I'll certainly have to do something."

Tension riddled Jed's body. "If you have any ideas about confronting Vanessa with this thing, forget them."

She bridled, her brown eyes dark with puzzlement. "I can't do that."

"Vanessa will chew you up and spit you out, Mary. Listen to what I'm telling you."

"Then you confront her."

"Me?"

"You know her, I don't."

"It's not that simple."

Not understanding, she was weighing him in the balances of some judicial scale in her brain. Sighing, Jed blindly watched the silky valley of her cleavage as she breathed.

"There's something you don't know yet," he said.

Her legs stiffened beneath him. "What're you saying?"

"I was going to tell you before."

"What don't I know?"

"That Vanessa knows you."

"What?" She attempted to push him away and to pull herself up to sit.

"Wait a minute. She simply knows, or *will* know if she ever sees you, that you aren't the Mary Smith who was here before."

Confused, she looked at him with the same expression that a wife has when she finds a note from a lover in her husband's pocket.

She said tightly, "Just how well did you know Vanessa?"

Jed grinned. "It's nothing that concerns you, Mary."

"You slept with her, didn't you?"

He closed his eyes in defeat. "Mary..."

"I want to know about it."

"Well, I'm not going to tell you. It didn't mean anything. Have I questioned you about John?"

"You didn't have to. I thought you were faithful to your wife. You said you didn't play around."

Looking up, growling his exasperation, he heaved her onto her side. "This was after my divorce. If you're going to be jealous, little cat, be jealous about someone who matters."

Distorting her mouth, she studied him through narrowed eyes. "Miss Universe doesn't matter?"

"Vanessa isn't a particularly beautiful person inside, Mary. She's small, and she's the most selfish woman I've ever known. She's built herself an empire, and she isn't about to let anyone jeopardize that. She'll hurt you if you try to push her into a corner."

She pushed out her lip in a pout. Emphatically, she declared, "Well, I'm not going to give Juliet any more steroids, and that's that."

Jed was envisioning what kind of woman time would make her—the lines that would sculpt her—and he knew he could not have loved her had he not been able to picture her when her flesh would not be so resilient or so smooth or so slender. He trembled with a poignant memory of his grandparents growing old in their old Boston home.

"What're you thinking?" she asked, reading him well.

A blade slipped neatly between his ribs. "I was thinking that my grandfather would like you very much."

When he curled his hand behind her head, she closed her eyes in anticipation and lifted her lips to be kissed.

"God, I love the way you taste," he whispered. "I love the tightness of you."

"Jed—"

"I know," he said. "And I love that irritating logic of your brain, even that silly pride of yours that drives me up the wall. Tell me, Mary."

She took his face between her hands and kissed his mouth. He hovered at the entrance of her warmth, but then he could wait no longer and, knowing he must surely have brought her pain, he buried himself into her like a spike driven into its place. Even then he knew he was committing the rest of his life to a humiliating attempt to be all things to her. But he wasn't all things, not even now, for he had desired her for so long and so painfully, it was over before it even began. Yet she, with the ancient wisdom of womankind, understood and gathered him to her breast and held him tightly.

"I can't believe I found you," she whispered against his sweating jaw as he lay heaving upon her breast. "I love you, Jed Kilpatrick. I'll marry you, but please, don't ever hurt me."

Chapter Ten

The restaurant was off the beaten path of St. Murren's espresso bars and ice cream parlors and nightclubs. Having once been the home of the exiled duke, Gorlitz Brenner, it was a large square building, well back from the road with a front lawn of gravel and a statue standing in the middle of the huge turnaround.

To one side, a small lake was frozen solid and shivering trees were strung with lights and music was piped outside so that skaters could twirl round and round, their scarves unfurling behind their heads.

A hunter's moon had slipped from behind the clouds when she and Jed arrived, and the night had turned a biting silver. A few courageous skaters were on the lake, but Jed hurried her inside where a string quartet was interspersing western ballads with Brahms, their bows flashing to the counter-melody of German speech and the rich clink of silver upon glass.

It was sometime later that Mary hesitated and, with a bite of shrimp poised neatly between dish and mouth, spoke through a congealed smile. ''Jed, don't turn around.''

Jed paused in his boot's conquest of her shoe. ''What?'' he said.

''The man at that table is staring at me.''

''If that were a crime, my darling, I would be locked up by now.''

''Be serious.'' She lowered the shrimp to her plate and touched her lips daintily with her napkin.

He grudgingly craned his neck. ''Which man?''

''Don't stare, don't stare. Over there.'' She gestured vaguely.

''Ah. I understand.''

I hate sitting here, Mary thought as she watched Jed's hand brace upon the table, his fingers so beautifully shaped, his nails square at the top, the sparse black hair across the back. *I wish we were somewhere quiet so I could take one of those hands into my lap, so I could place it upon my breast.*

Jed felt like a mine field. He had made love to her once already, but he wanted her again. Worse than before. He wanted her white beauty, her white heat. He wanted to make her scream.

God, how beautiful she is in the candlelight, he thought. *A distant lunar beauty. Incredible, how that word doesn't even have to mean sex where she's concerned. There isn't a neurotic, narcissistic thing about her. She's the most honest, immediate, real woman I've ever known. I wish I could die inside her.*

She sighed and picked up her fork again. ''He's behind the woman dancing with the man in the red dress. I mean the woman in the red dress, not the man. Dancing. Over there.''

Jed laughed. "Darling, are you sure you know what you mean?''

With the end of her fork, she tapped on the tablecloth. "You're doing it again, Jed.''

Jed stilled the smile that came automatically every time he looked at her. "What, love?''

"Driving me up the wall. Treating me like a mechanic does a woman: 'Oh, it's supposed to sound that way, dear lady.' Then she turns her back and he rolls his eyes.''

"How do you know I roll my eyes if your back is turned?'' Grinning, he gulped a swallow of wine and reached for her hand. "Come, dance with me.''

She slid so low in her chair, he feared she would disappear beneath the table. "What?''

"It's a waltz.'' He cocked his head. "I waltz divinely. You can look up into my eyes with adoration as I spin you about the room.''

"At least you're confident.'' Her laughter rippled, but when nearby heads lifted and turned to smile, she sobered and said, "Forget it, Jed.''

"Why?''

"I can't.'' She waved his hand away and popped a shrimp into her mouth. Lifting another, she studiously inspected it. "Do you think they put sulfite on these?''

"What d'you mean, you can't?''

"I just can't, that's all.'' Now it was her turn to gulp wine. "I know they put sulfite in this wine.''

"Too strenuous? After all those exercises you do? The splits, no less?''

If he were a gentleman, Mary thought, he would drop the matter.

"I mean," she kept her head at an adamant angle, "that I can't dance, Jed. Not well enough to put myself on display in a place like this. John hated dancing. Besides, I feel . . . pregnant. Drop it, will you?"

Amazement glittered in the gold of his eyes. "Inconceivable. I couldn't have fallen in love with a woman who doesn't know how to dance. What kind of children will we have?"

"Little stubbly black-haired ones, heaven help us."

Rising, he walked around the table. Genuinely piqued, Mary slapped at his hand, but he scooted her chair out from under her, and unless she wanted to create a scene, she had no choice but to follow him to the postage-stamp dance floor.

"We'll think of a name for the baby while we dance our first waltz," he said, smiling down at her. "Then, when I teach her how to dance fifteen or so years from now, I can say, 'Now, your mother, bless her saintly heart . . .' "

She should have guessed that he would be a sublime dancer. Not to follow him was impossible, and in a moment, as she allowed herself to feel his body powerfully directing her own, she was dancing as if she'd been doing it all her life.

The walls swirled dreamily past as he rested his jaw gently against her temple. The scratchiness of his chin comforted her. He moved his hand along the hollow of her back and held her very close. Even the man she fancied was staring appeared no more menacing than one of the waitresses.

The song ended, and another began. She lost track of the time.

"If we're not going to name the baby, at least we can set a wedding date," he murmured.

Smiling, her eyelids weighted and bubbles floating around in her bloodstream, Mary thought she was dangerously close to being hypnotized. "Why are you in such a hurry?"

"I don't trust life that much. I take it when I can get it."

He would. His realism had a way of shattering her most treasured illusions. When she was with him, life seemed more precious somehow, and she wanted to press against him and take all his bodily warmth into her. But the future was frightening. She could never be complacent with Jed. She could never disassociate and hover around the edges of life or drift away, weightless, beyond the stars. He wouldn't tolerate them touching lightly upon each other's lives, like upstairs maids casually dusting family heirlooms.

Between lovers, marriage was the test of the authentic, and Jed wanted it all. Now. She loved him, yes, but it was a new love, mostly sexual for she was, at thirty, still inexperienced. She was a victim of what she didn't yet know. And he knew so much because he had been in the depths of hell itself.

Would he weary of her inexperience? Would he give her time to catch up and not begrudge her the mistakes along the way? She had never met a man she liked more or found more interesting. But she was the one who stood to gain. He was the one who would take the risks, chancing his future upon a wish without collateral.

He was making love to her with his eyes, probing into the most intimate, secret places. She felt the familiar tightness in his groin, and she wished he would drag his hand down the front of her body. She wished she had a whole night just to kiss him.

"Look," she said breathlessly, "our dinner's arrived."

Perhaps there was something to be said for Cinderella, after all, Mary thought later as she looped her arm through Jed's and matched his strides across the gravel expanse to where his modest Volvo was parked. She laughed softly as they looked over their shoulders at the skaters.

Suddenly she was starved for laughter, and she stepped from his arm to fling her arms into the night sky, her hair swirling out behind her as she twirled and chanted, "I'm happy, I'm happy, I'm happy!"

Except for the statue that stood shivering in the turn-around, the lot was deserted. Before they reached the car, Jed drew her into his arms and bent his dark head.

"I've been wanting to do this all during dinner," he said as he clasped her capped skull and captured her mouth savagely with his.

The hunger hadn't abated, it had only grown more acute. Their heads moved and slanted as if they could never taste enough, could never slake the thirst that had them gasping and their breaths coming quickly, their hips straining as their tongues argued and sparred and exchanged illicit secrets they would never share with any other human being in quite the same way.

"Get in the car," he muttered when he finally straightened, "or I swear I'll take you here in the snow."

With kiss-pinkened lips, her luminous eyes searching his, Mary met his passion without shyness. "Have you no shame?"

"Shame has nothing to do with us."

As they stepped briskly to the car, sounds materialized behind them—sounds that blended into the landscape and the distant music. When the sounds stopped as suddenly as they had begun, however, Mary's awareness registered the silence on a subliminal level, as though she were waiting for the other shoe to drop.

Turning, she realized that Jed had already looked back. He had stopped in mid-stride and was staring hard at the man who had watched them in the restaurant.

Incredible! What was he doing here? Following them? Except that now he wasn't alone. A taller companion lurked in the shadows of the poplars, and Mary felt a clutch of despair. She had known the moment was too good to last.

She reached for Jed's arm with an urgency she couldn't explain. "Jed?"

His stare remained coldly fixed upon the man whose jowls quivered as he moved nearer. When he was close enough to speak, the man pushed back a fur hat with thick fingers.

"Mary Smith?" His voice sliced clearly through the cold, ice blue night. "I've been looking for you, Mary Smith."

Stunned, Mary instantly recalled the note: *This is Dane. I want what you have.* The fear had a name now, and Mary stood perfectly still. Jed had positioned himself so that his body was between hers and those of the two men.

An unnerving silence unspooled in the night. What was happening? What had been happening all along to bring this stranger into her life?

"I beg your pardon, gentlemen?" Jed said, his voice thinned to a thread. "May I help you?"

"Jed," she whispered to the back of his shoulder, "I know this man."

His acknowledgement was a taut, visible stiffening. Not for an instant did he veer his attention from Dane.

"We want to talk to her," Dane was saying, and included the figure that lurked in the shadows.

Now Jed cursed himself that he hadn't paid attention to Mary when she'd first told him about the man. He strained to see the second through the shadows, but could distinguish nothing except that he was quite tall and, unlike his counterpart, sleek and quick.

"Who are you?" he demanded, stalling for time as he reached behind his waist to make sure that Mary remained put.

"*She* knows."

Jed willed his body to relax. He needed more information. "Look, it's getting late, and it's cold. I have to take the lady home. Why don't you go inside and have yourselves a nightcap and call it a day?"

"Step out of the way," the man ordered. "We don't have any quarrel with you. The woman behind you is Mary Smith, and she has something that belongs to us."

Before Jed could prevent her, Mary stepped from behind his shoulder and said to the man, "My room *was* searched! You searched it, didn't you?"

Surprise caused the hair to stiffen on the back of Jed's neck. With a look of incredulity, he demanded, *Are you serious? Why didn't you tell me this?*

Her shrug told him, *I thought I imagined it.*

To the man, she said, "And you called me on the telephone, didn't you? You had the bellboy bring me the note. You're Dane."

High above, the moon dangled like a gold coin over the treetops. Snow blew through the branches. The skaters twirled blissfully to the distant music. The figure in the shadows remained silent.

Instinctively, Jed arranged his body into one of passivity. Whoever these men were, they were nothing but messenger boys, gofers. Gofers weren't possessed of Einstein mentality or they wouldn't be gofers.

"What is it you want?" Mary was asking. "I don't have anything."

"You're Mary Smith, aren't you?"

"Yes, but—"

"Then you have it. You brought it here, you give it to me now. You must follow procedure. *I'll* see that it gets to her."

Mary had brought it here? Jed thought. From the States? Brought what? His questions tumbled over one another as he struggled to fill in the details. Jutting his weight to one hip, he spread his lips in a slow, mocking smile.

"You're not very bright, are you, Dane?" he drawled.

The heavy man stopped in his tracks and picked at his teeth with a fingernail as he contemplated Jed.

"And you have a smart mouth, Dr. Kilpatrick."

So, the man knew who he was. "At least you've done your homework," Jed said. "But I have to tell you that you're really hacking me off, Dane. Searching her room like that, making a nuisance of yourself. I tell you what— to hell with procedure, I'll get the stuff to her myself. Now, why don't you just get out of my face and don't let me hear of you bothering Mary again?"

As if the matter were settled after such a brash speech, one that wouldn't have fooled a five-year-old but that might just work on Dane, Jed bluffingly dismissed the man and turned to take Mary's hand.

Drawing her close into his side, he murmured, "Stay cool. Act as if nothing has happened."

Behind them, Dane was moving into the shadows to confer with his partner. By the time his voice rang out, Jed had reached the car and was feeling in his pocket for his keys.

"*You* have it?" Dane called out.

As if his patience were infinite but had been sorely taxed, Jed pretended to slump and pinch the top of his nose. "Of course I have it, Dane." He sighed. "How d'you think I'll get it to her if I don't have it?"

"Get what to whom?" whispered Mary.

"Get in the car. Quickly. Lock the doors."

Before his fingers could get the key inserted, Jed saw the shadow separate from the copse of poplars. If he had been used to physical combat as a way of life, he thought, he would've been able to predict such a move, but his mind didn't work that way. He estimated the milliseconds it would take for Mary to scramble inside the car with him climbing in after. The door would have to be shut and locked, the car started. Which could conceivably be done if the pair didn't have guns.

If they were armed, however, the incident could end very badly, depending upon whatever it was Mary was supposed to have in her possession. Which, in the light of Dane's dim-witted tenacity, had to be of considerable value and importance.

Turning, his intentions were to put off the shadow with much the same strategy as he had used with Dane, but he saw immediately that he had made two very large miscalculations. First, the shadow wasn't a man, she was the tallest, most fiercely agile woman he'd ever seen! Second, she moved with the fluid, vicious ability of a black belt. And, a third miscalculation, she was launching herself at him with the impetus of a fired torpedo—her hair black as his own and shorter, her face set with a hideous ruthlessness, her arms spread and her legs blurring.

"Oh, damn!" he cursed, and literally picked Mary up and shoved her across the hood of his car.

"Vanessa ain't going to like this!" Dane was yelling.

Vanessa?

With lightning speed, Jed's brain made the connection of Vanessa to the steroid to Mary Smith. His muscles jumped in galvanic response as the woman landed upon the hard-packed snow in front of him with a thud.

She assumed a crouched stance on one side of him while Dane darted toward him from the other, surprisingly quick for a man of his bulk. Jed assumed the martial stance Tiang-Si had taught him. Never in his wildest dreams had he envisioned himself using the skill upon a human being. He wasn't sure that he knew how.

"Hey, Dane," he called out with a more desperate bluff as his brain was racing, "if that's the way you're gonna be... hey, no need to get huffy. Geez!"

Whether or not Dane would have swallowed the bluff, no one would ever know. As the words were falling from his lips, the woman was motioning Dane forward. Following orders, the heavy man lunged toward Jed with a snarl.

The momentum carried him, and Jed swung his leg in a wide arc, the impact of which Dane caught on his jaw as he whirled.

The man's thick grunt jarred the night air as his heavy arms flew out and the blow spun him backward. He was unconscious before he struck the ground.

No sooner had Jed struck, however, than he took the powerful brunt of the woman's heel as she shot from the front of his car and struck him hard across the clavicle. Jed stumbled, rocked with pain. Then the woman was all over him, using her weight to trap him in a lock and cut off his air supply.

Knowing instinctively that he must break her hold or lose consciousness within a few seconds, Jed tried a forearm blow that Tiang-Si had taught him. The woman saw it coming and knocked his hand away as easily as if he were a child.

He had no leverage and was no match for her. Mary's scream rang in his ears, and he caught a glimpse of her stumbling toward the restaurant door.

Adrenaline poured into him. *Think!* he demanded of himself, and did the only thing he knew to do.

Using his last remaining oxygen, he roared the cry of the attacker and felt the woman prepare herself. Her face was so close that he saw the whites of her eyes grow larger, and he melted momentarily against her as if defeated. Then he thrashed out with a crazed and pointless frenzy of kicking and stomping and swinging. If her hair had been long enough, he would have pulled it out of her scalp.

She was amused and was prepared to finish him off with a clean, leisurely blow to the back of his neck. But her amusement made her careless. For one fraction-splitting instant, Jed saw the glimmer of an advantage and knew that it was the only one he would get. Slamming his foot hard upon hers, he stabbed his elbow into her rib cage just below her breast and brought the hammer of his fist sharply across her pubic bone.

Her breath of pain caught in the back of her throat, and he reeled swiftly from her reach, but not before he felt his nose erupt and blood gush into his throat.

"Agghh!" He roared with pain, but rather than protect his nose, he led with it and cracked his head with hers, taking yet another cut upon his cheek. With his surgeon's right hand, he slashed a blow that caught her squarely in the windpipe, the bones and cartilage taking the punishment.

She stumbled back on her heels, and far back in his awareness Jed heard Mary's cries as she banged upon the restaurant door and shrieked for someone to come, to please come. She ran to the lake and alerted the skaters.

The amazon took the blows Jed dealt her, but for every one he dealt, she returned four. She must have connected to every part of his body, and most of the time he was simply protecting himself and waiting for a chance, any chance to retaliate.

It came sooner than he expected. The flash of Mary's slim form was in his vision for only an instant as she returned. She had come upon the amazon from behind and had hurled the contents of her bag at the woman's face. It was stupid, hilarious. Here the amazon was, prepared for her final, cataclysmic blow, and she found herself pelted with a gold compact, keys on a ring, a bottle, a lipstick, a pen, a notepad, a wallet and an assortment of cough drops and loose change.

Stylistically speaking, his kick would never have passed Tiang-Si's critical perfection, but his heel nonetheless found the target it sought, and it connected to the soft underside of the woman's chin with all the weight and power he could place behind it. Grunting, she stumbled backward and had no time to recover before he assumed the offensive. Jed attacked her as he would have attacked Attila—one murderous kick after another as his heart throbbed in his chest as if it would burst. He flew through the air. He was Nijinsky.

She didn't make a sound as she knelt, then collapsed into the snow. Catching himself upon his hands and knees, Jed fell beside her, groaning with his own pain.

Had he broken his hand? The knuckles were swollen and split. The pain was shattering his temples.

Dozens of pairs of feet formed a circle around them. Dane still lay in the snow. Lights blazed as people bent over him.

"The police are on their way," someone said.

Another edged forward. "Are you all right?"

"We've called a doctor."

Their voices blurred. Seeking only one woman, the one pushing her way toward him with her hair swirling about her shoulders and tears of shock streaming down her face, Jed felt an exhaustion such as he had never known.

With a grip of her arm, he gratefully accepted her support and said to no one in particular as he heaved to his feet, "Get these people some help."

No one was of a mind to question him or deny him anything. Finding his car keys, Jed placed them into Mary's hand as someone gathered the contents of her bag and handed them to her.

"You drive," he said, and climbing wearily into the car, sank into the seat to close his eyes.

"Those goons said *what*?" Scutter asked in disbelief. "Run that by me one more time."

Jed recounted the incident again—callously devoid of emotion as Mary moved about the room with a blanket draped about her shoulders like a shawl. Scutter had not yet gone to bed when they had ridden the lift up the mountain and pounded on the door. As their boots dried upon the hearth, Jed sat in his stocking feet upon a footstool, staring gravely at his bandaged hand.

She tipped up his face and, for the third time, washed it with a cloth that turned the rinse water red. He removed the cloth from her hand and pressed it to his nose, holding it there.

Scutter was saying, "Mary's been concerned all along that Vanessa's products might not be entirely kosher. Are you sure that nothing was planted on you, Mary? Nothing put into your luggage that you brought over unwittingly?"

A tight knot of surprise knitted between Jed's brows. Just how many conversations had Mary had with his best friend? Why hadn't she come to him from the beginning?

"Look," he declared with more edginess than he meant to, "it is just possible that Mary—the other Mary—had her own arrangement with these goons. Don't go convicting Vanessa on circumstantial evidence."

He looked up to find Mary frowning. "You think Vanessa doesn't know about her own product?"

Shrugging, he let her take the wet rag from him and rinse it again. "I didn't say that. I said that whatever the men wanted from you might not have been the steroid that your man at Fields Laboratories isolated. They might have been two different things."

"Oh, come on," Scutter groaned.

Mary said tersely, "Dane said that Vanessa would be upset. He said her *name*, Jed. She's in this up to her neck."

The accusation in her tone was too much for Jed to cope with. Depressed, secretly angry at having laid himself so ignorantly open to attack, he snapped, "Mary will have to stay the night up here, Scutter. I don't want her to be alone."

Scutter shrugged his agreement.

"Oh, no I—" she protested.

"Either that," Jed said, "or I'm sleeping down below."

"I'll sleep in Mary's room," Scutter volunteered. "I hope someone does come. If it's true that Vanessa's been making a fool of us all, I want proof, by heaven. And when I get it, I'm gonna bring that bitch down."

"You will stay away from that bitch," warned Jed, rising to prowl like a caged lion.

Mary pondered the incredible violence that lay just beneath Jed's surface. Who knew, truly, what a man was capable of? But what frightened her more was the resistance that hardened his face every time Vanessa's name was mentioned. Had he been her lover?

Of course he'd been her lover. "Scutter's right about Vanessa, Jed," she said tightly. "And I have no choice now but to tell Juliet that she's taking a steroid." Her eyes widened as Vanessa was momentarily forgotten. "D'you think the girl knows?"

Gathering his jacket and cap and boots and gloves, Scutter swore to himself. "We'll soon find out."

Mary wondered, after Scutter had taken his leave and she had washed in a pan of soothing hot water and put on a pair of Jed's insulated underwear and a flapping, long-tailed shirt, if she should ask Jed point-blank about what he and Vanessa had shared.

Not certain she could bear the truth, she drew on a pair of heavy wool socks and twisted her hair into a single shank, wrapping it about her head and pinning it there. The firelight cast Jed's silhouette into bold relief, his bare back bronzed by the flames. He was sitting again with his knees drawn up, his arms draped thoughtfully around them. In his eyes were reflections of twin fires, and she tried to look at him as Dane and the woman must have looked at him: a human weapon with quick hands and murderous feet, deceptively lean and very lethal.

But she was also aware, tenderly and compassionately, of the circles beneath his eyes and the stubble of beard blurring his jawline. He was waiting for her to meet his unspoken questions, and when she moved beside his knee, he smiled unhappily and wrapped his arms about her hips and laid his cheek upon the baby.

"You can't stay by yourself anymore, Mary. Before, I didn't want you living alone because I wanted you with me, but now it's not safe. Marriage or no marriage, I want you with me."

"I'll be all right. They know now that I don't have what they're looking for. It's over. Anyway, we can't solve it tonight."

No sooner had she spoken than he came to his feet and pulled her into the cradle of his thighs. She drew in her breath to protest, but he sealed the words in her mouth, thrusting his tongue against hers in a challenge to deny him if she could.

He had to be hurting all over his body, she knew, yet she sank her fingers into the hard curves of his hips. Lifting her off the floor, he continued to kiss her as he moved with her to his bed and laid her down. He thrust his fingers in her hair, pulling it free of the pins, and closed his teeth upon her lower lip when she turned her head aside.

He said raspily, "I don't want to lose you, Mary."

Mary knew he loved her. She knew he wanted her and needed her. She raised her hands to his hair, clenching and unclenching her fists as he kissed her shoulders and her throat and her lips.

"Marry me now," he whispered. "You'll be safe then."

"I have to finish my job first," she heard herself say, and knew, even as the words came, that they weren't the real reason.

What she longed to ask was why did he turn away whenever Vanessa's name came up? Why did he hesitate? Why did he protect her in his heart? How much of his heart did Vanessa really possess? Did she possess some of it still?

Jed felt the door close inside her to leave him outside. Even as her face sank against his neck and she let him strip off the bottoms of the underwear, he knew she was simply allowing him to love her.

But it wasn't fair, damn it. He didn't question her about her ex-husband, did he? Why must she know every detail about Vanessa? Vanessa had come at a terrible time in his life. He'd been deaf and dumb to the world. Yes, he'd slept with the woman, but slept only; love had nothing to do with it, nor did either of them pretend it did.

Frustrated, he started to slip off her, but she threaded her fingers through his and splayed her legs. He wanted to bash his fist into something, to smash it as he had smashed Dane. She shifted and lifted her head to be kissed, and he tasted the depths of her mouth and found her with his fingers, sank them into her. He wished that he could have driven her to her knees with desire, but the door was locked, and this time he had no key.

Wounded in a way he had not thought it was possible to be wounded, feeling cheated and angry, he moved carefully within her, cautiously, watching her face with its beautiful closed eyes.

He wanted to yell that he had never loved Vanessa. But he would not demean himself with excuses. Mary either trusted him or she didn't.

He was glad when it was over. Eventually she went to sleep in his arms, sweetly, gently, and he never knew when the torture of his own soul eased with slumber.

It was very late when he felt her hair brush his face. Or had he heard her make some sound? Rousing, blinking himself awake, he raised groggily onto his elbow and realized that she was bending over him, weeping.

"I'm sorry," she whispered over and over as she touched his face and lifted his bandaged hand and kissed it, holding it to her tearstained cheeks. "I'm so sorry I hurt you."

Confused, sleep-drugged, he caught her hair and held it as one would have held gold. "No, no, Mary. Don't be sorry, sweetheart."

"I knew you were hurting, and I wanted you to hurt."

"Shh."

"I knew what you wanted from me, and I was angry because you defended her."

"I wasn't defending her, Mary. I—"

She shushed him with a kiss. "It doesn't matter. I do love you, Jed. I'll do whatever you want me to do."

And he, Jed thought, must be the world's biggest fool, for he suddenly felt as if a terrible weight had been lifted from his back. Her anxiety had caused her to move, and she trembled.

With her eyes glistening with the reflection of the firelight, she wrapped her hand around the base of him, matching the rasps of his own desperate breathing. Her mouth was like satin. He felt as if someone had taken a hot blade to the insides of his thighs. The hammering of his heart was so deafening, she had to have heard it. For the first time in his life, he didn't attempt to control anything. He wanted to be enveloped by her and to be passive and be warmed by her. He let her climb him and teach him, with wordless ways, what he must do.

"Mary," he whispered when she undulated in a slow, graceful rhythm astride him, her head dropped back and her eyes closed. "I want to see you."

But she shook her head. He wanted to know what she as thinking, but she had no intention of sharing that with him, either. He was reminded of how completely selfish sex is—calculated and colored by each person's need. When she reached beneath the shirt and touched herself, he found it unbearably exciting.

He felt her climax before it happened, and she folded over him and shuddered with a sigh. She wasn't prepared when he turned with her and brought her to that golden point again and again. When, at last, he entered his own self-absorbed quest, it was as if someone had carved a wonderful valley from the top of his head to the soles of his feet. He lost himself within her.

In Mary's dream, Jed was a cool, clear lake in the deepest heat of summer. She saw herself in the dream, moving slowly to his banks and standing in a pool of shade beneath a lofty tree. For long hours she watched him, then finally removed her gown and let it fall in a cloud of pagan-pure linen at her feet.

She was oddly unembarrassed to approach him so. In his unmarred reflection, she saw herself: her hands behind her back in a tableau pose, her nakedness not flaunted but offered. Her nipples were the color of rose petals that had been gently bruised, the rest of her skin pale and white upon the tawny water's surface.

She lifted her head so that her neck was a swan's neck, and she ran her hand over the swell of her hip as if she were made of finest silk. In a movement as fluid, as impossible of being captured as mercury, she stepped into him and moved quickly and smoothly into his depths.

Once he closed over her head, so cool, so clear, she kicked her feet and dived deeper. Her past sloughed away and swirled into the current to disappear. She drifted downward until she lay buried inside him like a jewel from some treasure lost in a storm. How safe he was, she thought, how still and quiet. It was here, deep in the warm interior of her dream, that she belonged. Here, in the soul of a man who was strong and deep.

Moving her arms, she swam swiftly to the surface, for she knew he would be there, waiting, and would hold her and kiss her eyes. She saw her limbs, supple and slim as she slipped through the water, and she wanted to laugh and send bubbles rushing to the surface, for she wasn't ugly and her belly wasn't ugly. She was beautiful and fertile, a woman no price could buy, for she had within her the best of all possible mysteries—the future.

Chapter Eleven

Vanessa had arrived. The news erupted like wildfire and spread as swiftly.

The fitness maven and her publicity-hungry entourage had moved en masse into the wing opposite Mavis Duvall. At the foot of the stairs that was the only entrance, grim-faced security men moved back and forth, walkie-talkies in their hands as guards checked purses and briefcases before allowing anyone to pass. Hoping to catch sight of the woman more famous than Jackie Onassis or the Princess of Wales, the lobby seethed.

No sooner had the elevator arrived and the cage opened than Mary realized that something was different.

What? The stir of Haman's guests had already calmed. This exceeded that. Even Gus, the lovable old elevator operator who shuffled around the château year after year, was sporting his best crimson uniform jacket and spit-shined boots. His hair had been freshly trimmed, and his mustache was waxed and curled with crisp vanity.

Now her precautions of having Jed go down the back stairs and enter through the lobby were laughable. No one would have noticed had she run across the lobby stark naked.

"Good morning, Gus," she said with an amused smile. "You look very nice. What's going on downstairs?"

Gus was ancient and wizened and wise. It wouldn't have surprised Mary to learn that the little troll read minds, too.

"Good morning, Dr. Smith," he said with the propriety of an age gone by. "Miss Vanessa has arrived."

"Ah." Mary was tempted to turn around and march back to her rooms and crawl beneath the comforter on the bed. Instead, she grinned. "Then I guess you've been much too busy to find out what the slopes are looking like today."

His pale old eyes twinkled. "Good powder on the high, they say, Doctor. More on the way."

"Wonderful."

A bell sounded, and as the door opened and Ellie Anderson and Juliet Haney traipsed into the cubicle, Ellie promptly offended Gus's high sense of decorum by tweaking his mustache.

"Good morning, Gus, old chap." She giggled.

The two girls eyes Mary's customary skirt, boots, sweater and lab coat with a bored appraisal. Mary bit her tongue to keep from telling Juliet the truth: *There'll be no more steroids for you, Miss Priss!*

Except that she didn't know yet quite how to accomplish what must be done. In some ways Jed's caution was advisable. Perhaps she should see a lawyer....

"Good morning, Dr. Smith," Ellie chanted like a first grader.

Juliet promptly echoed, "Good morning, Dr. Smith."

A thin smile found Mary's lips. "Hello, girls."

There was little about Ellie Anderson for anyone to like—her preposterous clothes, her thin, homely face pinched beneath a mop of punk-orange hair that would never see its natural brown again. Today her eyelids were sooty black and her pouty lips a clear, rag-doll red.

Juliet had to be the least likely counterpart to Ellie's wildness in the entire resort. When Juliet walked into a room, grown men tended to froth at the mouth. She was watching Ellie attempt to see through the cage to the floor below them.

"Come on out, Doc." Ellie was stooping and calling down, cupping her mouth. "We see you hiding down there."

Jed? Mary thought with a tingling start.

Gus gave the girls a hard look of disapproval while Mary hastily checked her own appearance. When Gus opened the cage, she kept her eyes discreetly low.

Jed had just come in from outdoors, the toes of his boots water-stained, a cable-knit sweater hugging his jeans and beneath it a pale blue shirt. The bomber jacket was slung over his shoulder and was hooked upon a finger.

He had nicked himself shaving, and a tiny piece of tissue was glued to the wound. Considering his right cheek, which bore a motley bruise and a red streak that marched across his nose, this latest wound was negligible.

Before he caught sight of Mary behind Juliet, he smiled broadly at Ellie.

"Gee, Doc," Ellie said with coy wonder. "What happened to you?"

Jed frowned. "A skiing accident. I don't want to talk about it."

Then he found Mary, and she lifted her brows in an amused shrug. Moving his tongue with thoughtful sympathy over his bruised lip, he backed out of the cage with the same gypsy grace as he'd stepped into it. "Ahh, I think I'll catch the next one, ladies."

"What's the matter, Doc?" Ellie crooked a finger enticingly. "Are you shy?"

"We can easily make room, Dr. Kilpatrick," Juliet said in her cool, perfect way.

Though Ellie and Juliet pretended to be oblivious to how lusciously displayed their nubile bodies were in the skimpy workout suits that dipped into the creases of their buttocks and molded their small breasts so tightly that their nipples were hard, buttony impressions, Mary recognized feminine posturing when she saw it.

"And if we can't make room," Ellie added with a thrust of her bosom, "I'll sit on your shoulders." She ran her tongue around her lips. "Or anywhere else you'd like me to sit."

Having the grace to redden, Jed flicked his eyes to Mary and grinned sheepishly at Gus.

"By all means, Doctor," Mary intoned with a mutinous smile as she, too, motioned him in, "do get on. If we can't make room, we can all get in Ellie's mouth."

When Jed stepped into the cubicle, Ellie looped her arm through his and rubbed against the side of his leg like a preening cat.

"Hey, Coach," she called to Scutter, who had ambled up, "Come on in. Water's fine. The more the merrier, I always say."

Scutter took one look inside the cage and shook his curly red hair. "Uh-uh. Thanks just the same. See you around, Jeddo."

With Juliet crowding him on one side and Ellie draped on his other, Jed's warning came through tightly gritted teeth. "If you want to live out this day, Scutter, I suggest you to get on this elevator at once."

With giggles and laughter, they were all forced to pack themselves like sardines. Mary vowed that if Juliet or Ellie so much as looked at her once, or bumped against her stomach or said a single word, she would poison their next meal.

"I guess you heard that Vanessa's here, Doc," Ellie reported as she arranged the collar of Jed's shirt beneath the ribbing of his sweater.

Jed's color, Mary thought, turned to an interesting shade of rust, and he brushed the girl's hand away. "Yeah, I heard."

"The big event's tonight. 'Course we—" the girl thumbed her chest "—we aren't invited. You can go, though. Who's your date gonna be? Miss Universe?"

"Actually, Ellie—" Jed made a point of avoiding Mary's eyes, "—if I go at all, which I probably won't, I'll go stag. I trust that doesn't upset your plans any."

"You don't have a date? My Gawd." Ellie took a sudden interest in her body suit and made the outline of her breasts even more prominent. She batted her eyelashes. "Why don't you come to our dance then, Doc? It's in the gym. Coach is gonna be there, aren't you, Coach? Actually, Doc, you can be my escort. I'm a cheap date. And guess what? I'm gonna wear the coolest dress you ever saw—no straps, no buttons." Giggling, she lifted her arms high over her head and flicked at the ends of her orange hair. "I'll bet you can't guess what'll be underneath."

Exchanging a pained look with Scutter, who was gazing with profound interest at the ceiling, Jed let out a whistling sigh. He moved to the back of the cubicle so that he was directly behind the two girls, and when Mary saw him ogle the tight little buttocks before him, she reached up and snatched the tissue glued with blood to his nick.

"Ouch!" he growled reproachfully, and fished for a handkerchief in his hip pocket. "I'm sure I don't have the faintest idea, Ellie."

The elevator was nearing the lobby entrance, and Ellie leaned backward so that her backside bumped the front of Jed's thighs.

"Garters," she said, and tipped her head far back so that it was in his face. "Flaming, lacy—"

Scutter was seized with a loud fit of coughing, and Gus brought the cage to a rough stop. With a wry curl of her mouth, Mary gave Jed a don't-look-to-me-for-help smile.

"Traitor," he mumbled, and his smile would have warped steel. To Ellie, he said "Someday, Ellie, someone's going to wash out that mouth of yours."

The girl pranced from side to side as the cage door slid open. "Wanna try it, Doc?"

"No, I don't."

"Too bad. I'd let you, if you'd promise to do it with your tongue."

"Sweet thunder," muttered Jed.

Scutter nearly exploded as he fell out of the elevator. He was followed promptly by Jed, who stopped in the path of traffic and pointed a finger at Mary as if he were aiming a gun.

"I want to talk to you, Dr. Smith," he snapped irritably, and touched his nick.

Mary smiled with delicious loftiness. "Well, I don't know, Doctor," she drawled sweetly, "my schedule is just filled to the brim. I don't have a single little ol' minute to call my own."

"I'll bet," Ellie slurred as she sidled out, followed by Juliet who moved into the lobby traffic like a princess about to be photographed.

To Juliet's back, Mary called, despite the visual warning Jed shot her, "I need to speak with you, Juliet. Come by my office, please."

"I'll try, Doc."

"Don't just try, do it."

The girl didn't reply. Hardly had they gone ten feet when they picked up an escort of four young men who were perfectly contented to trail along in their wake and make vulgar propositions.

Left literally holding her bag and feeling older and frumpier and more pregnant than ever, Mary glanced at Gus who was endeavoring to be the monkey who heard nothing, saw nothing and wouldn't have spoken had he been threatened with a firing squad.

"Yeah, Gus," she said grimly, and trudged out by herself. "I know exactly what you mean."

"Have a nice day, Dr. Smith," he called politely after her.

"Sure," she mumbled directly to herself. "It's already off to a whale of a beginning."

Jed had disappeared. Once she turned the corner toward her own office, Mary mimicked Ellie by turning down the sides of her mouth and chanting in a whiny singsong, "I'll let you wash my mouth out if you'll do it with your tongue."

"Your place or mine," Jed rumbled from out of nowhere.

Spinning around, her heart in her throat, Mary struck his shoulder with a fist, the action only half in jest.

"You—don't ever do that to me again! Grief, you scared me out of ten years' growth!"

"You would add cradle-robbing to my sins?"

From behind her glasses, loving him even more today than she had yesterday and wanting him twice, Mary gave him a brutal inspection.

"Just what might those other sins be, Dr. Kilpatrick?" she inquired.

"You're so all-fired smart this morning, why don't you tell me?"

She batted her eyes in Ellie's vampish way. "Oh, there're any number of ways to break commandments, Doc. Let's see, now—you've lusted and coveted and deceived and sworn and blasphemed and—"

With a lecherous grin, he leaned toward her. "You forgot murder, I believe."

"You're not planning that this morning, too, are you?"

"I don't know. Would you mind stepping down this corridor?" he retorted in a Bela Lugosi accent.

She smiled prettily. "I'm afraid I can't, Doctor. Haven't you heard that Miss Universe is here? I've a thousand things to do for tonight's bash. I'll see you in the restaurant for lunch. By the way, you're bleeding."

At noon the château's three restaurants were packed. As Mary waited to be seated, she had no fear of bumping into Miss Universe. By now room service would be threatening to kill the woman and Haman Stone would have a list of heads that would roll the minute she left the premises.

She followed the waiter to a discreet table and saw that Jed had not yet arrived. She opened her mouth to explain that she was meeting someone and could hardly believe her eyes to find Jed across the room, seated beside the most lavishly beautiful woman she had ever laid eyes on.

A stone dropped into the pit of her stomach. Flanking Vanessa was a phalanx of photographers, reporters, consultants and general flunkies. Seated at the next table were Haman Stone, his American guests and Annelise. Jed, in a posture that she had seen dozens of times, was slumped broodingly low upon his spine with his arm laid upon the table, his fingers thrumming an impatient drumroll upon the cloth.

The bandage reminded her of the love they had shared in the dark heat of the night. In that moment she was reminded of how close to hate that love actually was.

How like John Smith you are, she telegraphed him across the room.

The look that came down over his face was one of bitter pride. A photographer approached and requested a picture of Miss Universe. Leaning nearer Jed, her wonderful, famous smile excelling anything that was mounted upon the walls of her office, Vanessa draped her arm about Jed's shoulders and posed.

At that moment, Vanessa looked across the room and saw her, waiters and diners cutting back and forth across their line of vision. But still they looked—a stare as naked as two women could share with each other.

Mary's skin crawled. It was impossible, of course, that the maven could know she had raised a question about the legality of the world's most beautiful woman. Yet she felt as if everyone in the room looked at her and saw a fool. And worse, a tragic fool.

"Damn you, Jed Kilpatrick," she whispered as tears pressed hotly behind her eyes, threatening to burst past their dam and disgrace her.

To the waiter, as she pressed a bill into his hand, she said, "Keep the change."

The waiter blinked as she left. Why had she tipped him? he wondered. He hadn't even taken her order!

"That's her? That's Mary Smith? That's the little imposter?"

Jed steeled himself to the impact of Vanessa's magnificent bullet-blue eyes. Getting into a verbal wrestling bout with this woman before God and Haman Stone was the last thing he wanted, but when she had accosted him the moment he'd walked in, flashbulbs popping all around, pens scribbling, he'd suffered a waking nightmare of Mary marching up like David to Goliath and announcing that she intended to bring her up on criminal charges.

Why she had come to the restaurant was a mystery, for her private chef was in attendance in the château's kitchen. At a signal from her executive secretary, who was a dashingly handsome Godunovian blond, huge platters of fruit could roll out on room-service trolleys in an instant—imported strawberries and peaches and apricots, pears and grapes and pineapples.

But having meals in her suite wouldn't have satisfied Vanessa's insatiable appetite for being seen and admired. Wearing a black Halston knit, she had entered with great purpose while the maître d' and the captain bowed and scraped. Every person of importance rose to greet her, most of whom she ignored, with the exception of Haman Stone; to him she bestowed one of her dangerous TNT smiles.''

"I want to talk to you," Vanessa had said, and Jed had paled.

"Don't be so quick to judge, Vanessa," he said with a calmness he knew enraged her.

"Judge!" Her rippling laughter drew dozens of fawning stares. "Darling, don't be blind. It doesn't become you. The woman's an opportunist."

"At least she's not a black belt."

Her eyes angled for an appraisal of his bandaged hand. "I heard about that little incident. Frankly, I was appalled."

"Not nearly as appalled as I was when she tried to rearrange my face. Which raises an interesting question, Vanessa."

The maven inspected her diamond and sapphire ring. A waiter bowed obsequiously before pouring her special water into a glass.

Lifting the glass to her lips, she stared over the rim at Mary and purred, "By heaven she must be good to make you so loyal. She could do with a little toning about the middle, if you ask me."

"I think we could have this discussion some other time," Jed said. What had he ever seen in her?

She had helped him dry out. He owed her.

Mary was looking at him as if he were a leper, and he wanted to lunge to his feet. He watched her smile frozenly at the waiter. He wanted to go to her, to walk over hot coals to get to her and shake her until she stopped accusing him with those earth-brown eyes.

Without realizing it, he had begun coming to his feet.

"We will *not* have this discussion some other time, Jedediah." Vanessa was impaling him upon the sharp ends of her command. "Sit down, Jed."

Mary was thrusting money at the waiter. Without looking back, she was hurrying out.

Jed wanted to shout at her from the depths of his rage, *What does it take for you to believe?*

"Dear me, our little impostor is shy?" Vanessa smiled at him as if she held a big whip. "Why is she running away, Jed? Have you lost your touch? Poor baby. Never mind, I forgive you. I want you to be my escort tonight, Jed. Even with that face, which, by the way, I find unbearably sexy."

She placed her hand delicately on his knee beneath the table. Jed made no move to remove it. Her eyes were mica glints when she smiled.

"Really?" Lowering his voice to discuss the murderous rage boiling inside him, Jed returned her smile and said, "I don't think so, darling."

"You son of a bitch," she hissed in a radiance of swirling hair as she jerked her hand from his knee.

He grinned. "Yeah, I know. And if that surprises you, let me lay this on you. I know about your operation, Vanessa. And that innocent pretense of being surprised at what happened in the village last night? Save it. I also know what our mutual friend Mary Smith did for you all those years."

Vanessa's eyes went blank like dead planets.

"While you chew on that a while, love," he continued, "let me add one thing more. You see the woman across the room? If anything should happen to her...for instance, if she should so much as get bumped in an elevator or one hair of her head should get tousled, I would take it very much amiss, Vanessa. In fact, I would be so upset that I might do something really reckless. So be careful. And if you want some free advice, take your product off the market. That is, unless you'd like to become bedfellows with the Food and Drug Administration for the next few years."

With a flick of her wrist, Vanessa tossed the contents of her water glass into his face and, quicker than a switchblade, five photographers were crowding the table, flashbulbs exploding.

Smiling, not bothering to wipe a single drop from his face, Jed came to his feet. Leaning forward, he placed an insulting kiss upon Vanessa's cheek and whispered, "*Ciao*, baby. Sweet dreams."

With a jaunty snap of his heels, he left her sitting there.

By seven o'clock, a crowd was collecting inside the ballroom even though the orchestra had not yet begun to play. Press people and celebrities moved back and forth from the bar with programmed smiles. Gorgeously clad women kissed each others' cheeks while aides of the powerful men walked around in a somnambulistic state. A closed-circuit television camera was capturing the sparkle of jewels and cleavage.

For Mary, who could have attended the dance, since she was on staff, it was a nightmare. She had dutifully made herself as pretty as possible, wearing the red Bill Blass skirt and coiffing her hair until it was a frothy mass atop her head. All the tricks of makeup she knew had been called upon, although they couldn't begin to equal those of Mavis Duvall.

But what difference did it make? The waist of her skirt had stopped pretending to meet. The baby had lodged against her ribs and was slowly cutting off her breath. She had given Jed such a wide berth that she hadn't seen him after her infamous exit, and here she was in the kitchen again, wilting.

Why not work and be done with it? she thought. She felt much more at home with the villagers, anyway.

A full shift was on duty—the chefs from the village in their starched whites, the assistant cooks and the kitchen helpers who poured sweat as they hefted trays and pans and filled trolleys headed for the dishwashers. Around them, yelling over the chefs, were the hurrying waiters and waitresses, their serving trays balanced over their heads.

When the orchestra finally did begin and the guests were seated at candlelit tables, the dance floor beginning to move in an ever-blooming kaleidoscope of color, Mary was double-checking the refrigerators that contained the special à la carte menus and diets.

The waiters kept up a steady barrage of questions over the bedlam. Hardly did Mary get their trays aimed in the right direction than another problem erupted.

She hurried to where the helpers were making low-cal hors-d'oeuvre and allergy-free canapes.

"Aren't you finished?" she urged them, glancing at her watch. "They must go into the oven in exactly two minutes or we can forget it."

"We're hurrying, *fräulein*," one of the village women said without looking up.

Gently, Mary touched her shoulder in apology. "They're beautiful, Sarah. You're an artist."

The woman threw a swift smile over her shoulder and, putting the finishing touches on the crabmeat, swept up the tray and placed it into Mary's hands. *"Danke."*

"Danke, yourself." Mary laughed.

For two hours she worked, surviving one crisis after another. But even nightmares end, and soon there was nothing left but the cleaning up. The emphasis shifted, temporarily at least, to the bars surrounding the dance floor.

From the vantage of the swinging doors that opened from the kitchen, the huge room was festively decorated with lanterns and ribbons and balloons. The orchestra was set up on a raised dais. Butlers and maids hovered over tables, making sure the Baccarat glasses were kept filled.

Many of the glamorous young debs who decorated the room had been brought in by Haman Stone and would find their way into some power broker's bed for the night. Who would end up in Vanessa's bed?

With a vague feeling of being lost, Mary craved a few moments of quiet time. Tucking wilted strands of her hair into the upswept topknot, she walked wearily into her office with plans to freshen up. Maybe, she told herself, she might just have a good cry.

"There you are!" exclaimed a lilting feminine voice, and Mary spun around as someone touched her arm. She blinked in baffled surprise at Mavis Duvall. Slightly behind her was Annelise.

"Miss Duvall!" she exclaimed, and automatically hugged the lab coat she'd pulled on to protect her dress.

Resplendent in a floor-length sequined sheath of hot pink that made Mary's mouth water, the actress laughingly waved away the formality. She was, Mary discovered, more than a little drunk.

Over Mavis's head, Annelise signaled Mary that she would appreciate some assistance in keeping the famous woman from making too large a spectacle of herself.

"None of that Miss business," Mavis was lavishly declaring as she looped one arm through that of Annelise and the other around Mary. "We're here on official business, Mary Smith. Make no mistake about it."

"Really." Mary found herself propelled toward the kitchens she had just escaped. "I hope it's not serious."

The famous green eyes assumed a comical gravity that was Mavis's stock and trade.

"We've come to raid the refrigerator," she warned with mock gravity. "Do you have any idea what they're feeding us out there? We're talking gross here, ladies."

Mary shrugged. "You don't exactly inspire me with confidence, Miss Duvall."

Mavis lowered her voice to a conspiratorial whisper. "Do you have any idea what I want tonight? I want caviar and sweet rolls and crepes and lobster canapés. I want cherries flambé. Let Jean-Marc throw me off the set and bring in Streep. What do I care?"

Not sure whether to take the woman seriously or not, Mary consulted Annelise. The concierge looked more human than Mary had ever seen her in a mid-calf white silk gown and her lovely pearls. Her hair was spun gold.

"I'm sure Fräulein Smith has exactly what we want," she told Mavis.

"You're part of this calorie orgy, too, Annelise?"

"Of course she is." Mavis broke free of the looped arms and pushed through the swinging door to saunter sensually toward the rank of stainless steel refrigerators. Turning, she weaved a painted fingernail back and forth and aimed it inebriatedly at Mary. "And so you are you, sweetie."

Mary thought of all the months she had sacrificed to slimness. She couldn't break now. "Miss Duvall—"

"Mavis."

"Mavis," Mary complied. "I'm—I'm on a diet, for pity's sake."

"Diet, schmiet." With a twist of her famous torso, Mavis lifted her perfect brows and smiled her thousand-volt smile. "I don't allow conscientious objectors. Now, help me fill a tray. Then let's get loaded."

With a roll of her eyes, Mary looked at Annelise, who actually had an honest-to-goodness quarter-smile on her lips. "God help us all," she said.

"God helps those who help themselves," Annelise dryly retorted.

Mary went off in a fit of giggles. The woman had actually made a joke. "You're no help at all, Annelise."

Still giggling, Mary fetched one of the waiters' huge gleaming trays. As she held it, the actress blissfully piled it high with everything from the turkey reserved for the following day to exorbitantly expensive sugared fruits and mixed melons floating in thick cream, to the special eclairs flown in especially for Vanessa.

In horror, Mary signaled Annelise. "Those are for Vanessa."

"What? That bitch consumes sugar? Call the police! Better yet, get me a reporter!"

Over Mavis's head Mary and Annelise sent and received the same message—Mavis Duvall was insanely jealous of Miss Universe.

"If you're going to break the scales, Mavis," Mary dourly suggested, leaning around the actress, "you might as well take this." She deftly lifted out the raspberry mousse she had supervised herself only hours before. "I'll make another tomorrow."

"A woman after my own heart." Straightening, Mavis beamed. "Now, fetch a bottle of your best champagne, Annelise. Preferably whatever it is that you serve that viper."

"By all means." Mary liked Mavis more by the minute.

"The problem is, darlings…" Mavis stood with her hip thrown half out of joint and the neckline of her gown listing dangerously to one side so that half her breast was exposed. Giving it a highly unladylike yank into place, she laughed from deep in her throat. "Where the hell are we going to have this blowout?"

"If those really are Vanessa's eclairs on your tray," Jed drawled from directly behind them, "I suggest you head for higher ground. Might I suggest my office, ladies? It's a safe distance from the ballroom, and Scutter here can always stand guard at the door. If that doesn't work, I'll spill my own blood in your defense."

Nothing, but nothing, could have prepared Mary for the sight of Jed in a tuxedo. He stood in a pleasant slouch in the doorway, flanked by Scutter who had slipped away from the dance in the gym and was drooling like a tomcat that had discovered a nest of juicy sparrows.

Jed's weight was thrown to one hip, and the stripe of black satin that slashed his trouser leg glistened as he moved. His chest was an expanse of dozens of white tucks, covered by a black vest stretched skintight. With his bandaged hand, he adjusted his cufflink and arched his brows.

Mary's first horror was that Annelise would baldly refuse to be in the same room with Jed and spout Haman Stone's "house policy." "It's up to Miss Duvall, Doctor," she said quickly. "It's her party."

"Absolutely," Mavis declared, and looped her arm through Jed's. "Let's go party, you animal, you," she purred. "And don't you dare refuse."

Jed gave the actress a bow that Mary thought was a bit too enthusiastic and said as he grazed her own eyes from over Mavis's head, "I wouldn't miss this celebration for all the film in Hollywood."

"Annelise," Scutter said happily, "I'll help you carry the champagne."

By midnight, they had all eaten much too much and had drunk more wine than Mary had ever consumed in one sitting. Jed proved himself expert at impromptu parties. After snapping out a few freshly laundered sheets and spreading them on the floor and scrounging up some pillows from the infirmary and plugging in a radio, they had gorged like Romans.

Mavis told wild stories of having made up her face to look like a zombie or a dying craven, then entering a restaurant and causing a hilarious scene. For the first time Annelise appeared animated. She actually laughed at Mavis's antics and seemed to truly admire the actress's talent for creating illusions. She even amused them with her own story, a hotel scandal about a French call girl and an English lord.

As Scutter sprawled on his side and watched Mavis Duvall toy with his wristwatch, he didn't know which fascinated him more—the chances of Mavis asking him to her room later that night or watching the undercurrents between Mary and Jed.

Neither of them guessed how transparent they were. Jed liked to use his fingers when eating, relishing the feel of bread tearing in his hands and the texture of cheese, the sleekness of olives. Several times he dunked pieces into succulent concoctions and reached across to pop them into Mary's mouth.

If Mary wasn't his best friend's love, Scutter would surely have loved her himself. Maybe he did, anyway.

Trying to be discreet in front of Annelise, she would quickly avert her eyes, but would presently slide them back and stare breathlessly at the back of Jed's neck when he wasn't looking. Or adore the angle of his shoulder. No one seemed to notice that Jed carefully maneuvered himself in a sprawl so that Mary was innocently flanked by his long, tuxedoed legs. Or that his hand occasionally grazed her knee or brushed her thigh or, in shifting, that his knee bumped her hip.

At midnight, Mavis announced she had a headache and wanted to go to bed.

"I'll go with you," offered Annelise.

Flicking crumbs from her skirt, Mary pushed up from the floor, showing for the first time, Scutter thought, that she was growing heavier with child.

No one noticed. "Don't worry about the mess," she said. "I'll stay and clean it up."

"I'll help you," Jed volunteered as Scutter had known he would.

Jed didn't make a murmur when Mavis draped her arms about his neck and kissed him lingeringly upon the lips. When her hand stole to clap upon his buttock, however, he gently and laughingly detached himself.

"Don't turn into a pumpkin, handsome," she purred, and weaving slightly, reached for Annelise's hand. "God, am I going to hate myself in the morning."

Slightly disappointed when the two women said goodbye at the door, Scutter stretched and gazed helplessly at the disorder on the floor.

Grinning, Jed said. "That's all right, Scutter. You can go. Return to your kiddies."

With a wicked grin, Scutter made as if to stay. "No, no. I can't leave you with all this."

"It's all right, champ," Jed said more pointedly, frowning and smiling at the same time.

Laughing, Scutter was enjoying himself. "I get the message. I don't suppose it would be out of order to inquire if you'll be using the cabin tonight?"

Unfolding himself like an accordion while Mary adroitly made quick work of the leftovers, Jed growled, "Good night, Scutter."

"I get the message."

Jed walked to his office door and opened it, sweeping his arm in a meaningful invitation. "Good night, Scutter."

Scutter was still laughing when he stepped into the cold night air and headed for the gym.

"You know, I think Annelise could kill Haman Stone if the circumstances were right," Mary said.

"She hates him, but I hardly think she's capable of murder."

"Don't you remember those old black-and-white movies where beautiful women poisoned the villains?"

Jed yawned. "Stone's in enough trouble these days. If Annelise is patient, she won't have to do anything. He'll be his own undoing."

"Men like Stone don't get undone."

"Don't shake my faith in justice. It's fragile enough as it is."

"That's why Annelise will do him in herself. I feel it every time I see her. She's like a wolf trap, all set and primed. Wait and see. She'll bring him down."

They lay in the darkness of Mary's room, snuggled in her bed, and she was fitted neatly to Jed's back so that he was curled inside her form as safely as the baby that moved inside her. The measure of his love for her never ceased to amaze him. When he wasn't with her, he could close his eyes and see her face. When he was with her, he resented sharing her.

"I love you," he said quietly.

Outside the wind was moaning, and she hugged him tightly. "It frightens me to be so happy, Jed. The gods are angry when things go too well."

"You don't believe that."

"No, but it still frightens me."

Wisps of her hair lay across his face, and he drew in their sweet scent. Turning, he kissed her long and deeply, their tongues touching as if the newness were still there. He touched her cheek and the length of her swan's neck, the planes of her shoulder and he put his lips against the pulse in her throat.

As if she were learning him by braille, she moved her fingertips over him. His skin felt scorched as it slid against her, and she sighed. When he felt for her through her gown, for she still refused to take it off, she murmured his name. He knew so well where to touch now, and when she was ready. He found her through the silk gown, found the dampened curls. He moved back and forth, matching his strokes to her uneven breaths.

When she found him with her hand, he whispered, "Easy, easy."

The hoarse passion in her voice was more heady than any drug. "You're silky," she said, awed.

Groaning, Jed thought that the mere sound of her voice would push him past the brink. He battled with her gown and would have pushed up into her, but she shook her head. She made him last longer than he thought he could. She dissolved him with swirling pleasure until he, quivering with tension, penetrated her in one exquisitely slow stroke.

Mindless, unbound, loosened from earth and soaring, she opened her mouth upon his ear, her breath so harsh, so broken that he was blind with love. He felt when the release came that she had gripped him by his ankles and had hurled him headfirst through a plate glass window.

"I love you," she said afterward.

"I want to see you," he said. "I want to make love to you with the lights on."

"Not yet, not yet." And then she wept because she could not give him enough.

Chapter Twelve

The whole château seemed to suffer from a giant collective hangover.

By the time Mary and Jed were awakening in her turret, the night shift had already dragged itself home and the day shift was preparing to take over. Below them in the kitchen, early-duty helpers were making ready for the cooks who were changing from their street clothes into fresh, clean whites. Outside, the garbage was being collected for the bins that would be carried off in trucks to the dump outside St. Murren.

The night cleaners had already toiled through the restrooms and the kitchens, the downstairs and main lobby, vacuuming and dusting and buffing until the whole place gleamed and smelled of wax. In another half hour, wake-up calls would be going out. The hot water system was gearing up for hundreds of steaming showers that would be taken, for Vanessa's entourage alone placed as many demands upon the staff as a presidential visit. Behind his arrogant facade, Haman Stone was frantic that his guests from America would find everything to their liking.

Rolling over to look at the clock beside his bed, he rose and made his bed with the habit of forty years. He nervously laid out his suit with a freshly laundered shirt, over which he placed a tie. Considering the tie, he exchanged it for another. Below the cuffs that hung over the edge of the bed he placed a pair of sedate shoes and a new pair of black nylon support socks.

"Perfect," he said, and plucked a minute speck of lint from a cuff.

By tonight the château's financiers would have given him eleven million dollars and would be on a flight back to the States. A few weeks after that he would have manipulated legalities until the controlling interest of five hotels would be his. Bought with their money! Beautiful.

Until then, he was spread thinner than shellac. His nerves were screaming.

Picking up the phone, he dialed. "My room," he said to Annelise. "Be prompt."

"Patience? You speak to me of patience when I've skulked down back stairways for you and slipped in side doors. When I've restrained myself from attacking you in the elevator. When I've taught you to dance and had my nose broken and held your head when you were sick. And you speak to me of patience?"

Jed and Mary were having an early breakfast in one of the restaurants that was all but deserted. He had finished off a man-size meal, but she was toying with her melon, leaning back in her chair and watching him with warm, loving eyes while he stole bites off her dish.

"Yes, patience." She pretended to stab him with her fork when he burgled her last bite. "You remember, the virtue."

Jed didn't allow himself to dwell on the memories of the night, for his desire was too close to the surface. All he had to do was imagine them together.

"What virtue is there in not being able to have a regular cup of coffee in my own kitchen with my own well-loved wife and to walk out the front door like any other man in the pursuit of happiness?" he asked.

Pursing her mouth and cajoling him with strokes of his calf with the toe of her pump, she seemed to memorize him down to the last taste of melon upon his lips.

"That's why they call it patience, dear. You know I love you."

Jed grinned.

"And that I want you. This very minute."

He narrowed his eyes.

"That I can remember, and the remembering makes me hurt and dream."

He lifted his eyes to the ceiling and wondered if praying would help.

She smiled sweetly at the waiter who was leaving the check, and coyly inched her toe higher. Jed gave her a look warning her to behave herself.

"Oh-oh," she said with an irresistible droop that caused her hair to shift across her cheek and frame her so delicately, it broke his heart. "You're cross," she teased, and tapped her foot upon his.

"I'm weary of being single. Would you like me to drag you under the table and take you up on that offer?"

Mary adored the fact that he was relentless in his pursuit of her. She loved the way he held her chair when they left and made a sound of sexual agony against her hair.

She no longer worried what Haman Stone's policy was, or anyone else's. She didn't care what her own policy was! She wanted to be crazy for once in her life and fulfil her commitments to St. Murren and marry Jed as soon as arrangements could be made. She wanted to spend the rest of her life with him.

"Is there anything that doesn't weary you?" she mocked happily.

Taking her by the shoulders so that his perusal went from the top of her hair to the soft red sweater that fell about her knees to the straight black skirt hanging beneath it and the black stockings, the slim legs and trim pumps, he said huskily, "Yes. Oh, yes."

Her smile disintegrated as she considered him just as boldly, just as thoroughly, as sensually. Softly she whispered, "You're a dangerous man, Jed Kilpatrick."

He adjusted her nameplate above the pocket of her lab coat. "Only sometimes."

His grace, as he pushed aside the vent of his sport coat and replaced his wallet, had to be the most erotic thing she had ever seen, she thought as she arranged the ends of his tie where they had slipped outside his lapels. He had worn a dress shirt and slacks today, and he looked elegant by accident, but it was no accident, rather a carefully developed skill of making fashion work for him. She loved that he appealed to other women but that men were forced to respect him, too.

"I've decided to write the book," she said. "Did I tell you?"

He raised his brows in approval. "If you expect me to proofread, darling, you're going to have to make an honest man out of me."

"Your services run awfully high."

"I'm a specialist." He placed his hand at the small of her back as they left. "I don't come cheaply."

She laughed. "You're a thief."

"Who's a thief?" Scutter strolled blithely through the restaurant doors as they were leaving, then walked backward in front of them, returning to the corridor as they did.

"You," Jed said. "You're late."

Scutter huffed off his tardiness and wiggled his sandy brows. "You're looking awfully pretty this morning, Mary Mary."

"Ooooh." Looping her arm through his as well, Mary walked contentedly between the two men she liked most. "I'm glad someone noticed."

"*I* noticed," grumbled Jed.

Mary stage-whispered to Scutter, "Don't mind Jed. He's cross this morning."

"Keep it up," Jed warned, "and you'll be sorry."

Scutter chuckled. "Not half as sorry as a few financial types around here are going to be if Stone pulls this deal off. They're at it already this morning, snooping around. Jesus, Stone does his fleecing in style. Have you watched him operate? Every time you turn around, they're going into a huddle with their little pocket calculators."

Jed shook his head. "He's scared. He's coming down on his people."

"He always comes down on his people," Mary observed wryly.

"But this latest report comes from the ones who like him, which is to say they detest him less than the rest of us. No, the thread has definitely begun to unravel."

"Speak of the devil, gentlemen..." As they stepped into the lobby, Mary directed their attention to Haman

Stone emerging from the corridor that led from his office.

Stone's guests, the men who would carry their report back to Premier, Incorporated, were not yuppies. They were human computers in buttoned-up suits and sleeked-down hair, immaculate yes-men who lived on Maalox and wore thick glasses. This morning their skepticism was precisely in place as they made their assessments, their cynical, restless eyes seeing everything.

They saw, for instance, Vanessa entering from the main doors and striding through the lobby, gorgeously flushed from her early-morning run so that the pink of her ski suit matched her lovely cheeks. They saw the two beefy hunks trotting in her wake like flower girls behind a bride in some parody. They saw Mavis Duvall moving more slowly as she stepped out of the elevator, her hangover hiding behind enormous dark glasses and a face beautifully made-up to disguise the paleness.

They also saw the concierge descending the wide marble stairs.

"Annelise!" Mary breathed as her lips parted in shock.

Moving painfully, one step at a time, wearing her usual skirt and sweater and pearls, her twist of gleaming hair torn loose on one side and the sleeve of her sweater ripped from its seam and drooping to her elbow, Annelise drew the attention of everyone in the lobby like a magnet.

Jed and Scutter stopped in their tracks.

"I'll be damned," Jed said softly.

Scutter made a confused sound. "What in hell—"

Annelise carried her pearls in a cupped hand where they had broken. Her stockings were laddered with runs, and dark stains streaked her mauve wool skirt. Her face was shockingly battered. One of her eyes was blackened, and her lip was split. Her left cheek was bruised a motley purplish-green. Claw marks scored the side of her neck.

The hush spread to the farthest perimeters of the lobby. She steadied herself on the banister, and the pearls fell from her fingertips, dropping to ping and clatter down the long flight, step by step by mesmerizing step.

As if recovering from paralysis, one of the security guards took a step toward her.

"My God, Annelise," Vanessa exclaimed as she momentarily forgot that the attention was not upon her. She walked to the landing of the stairs and looked up. "Who did this to you?"

Mary sought Jed's reaction and was amazed to find it one of amused respect. He muttered, "Can you believe this?"

Turning, she reproached, "That's a terrible thing to say."

"Hell, the woman deserves an Oscar."

"What—" In disbelief, Mary looked form him to Annelise and back to him. "Surely you're not suggesting..."

"Well, look at her. No swelling. With bruises like those, her face should be twice its size. It's makeup. Very clever makeup, at that."

Annelise had stopped before Haman Stone. Several moments passed before the man slowly began to comprehend what she was doing, what she was accusing him of.

His jaw sagged, and his smooth, boyish face drained of color. Darting a look around him, he found no sympathy upon the faces of the financiers. They saw, not him, not the beaten, abused woman, but the value of

Premier stock zooming to the bottom of the big board like cold lead.

"My resignation, Mr. Stone," she said, and extended a folded paper.

"God Almighty, woman," he whispered. "What're you doing to me? Have you gone mad?"

"Tell us what happened," Vanessa demanded.

Without replying, Annelise moved slowly and painfully across the lobby to the corridor. Pausing in the opening, she turned back and gazed at Haman Stone who was still nailed to the floor, ruined.

"Ask him," she said.

As the hotel's security followed her, plus two of the reporters connected with Vanessa's entourage, Mavis Duvall glided toward Jed. Just when she had drawn even, she pulled her dark glasses down an inch and looked triumphantly into Mary's face.

She winked as she passed. Mary thought she murmured, as she swept by them, "It's all in the wrist."

They were left standing in one of those troubling moments when one wonders if what they've seen is real. Was it a hoax? Was a camera going to pop out from nowhere and announce that it was a setup?

Looking around to see if the same confusion was being felt by everyone else, Mary confronted the powerful force of Vanessa's presence. Vanessa! Feeling suddenly naked, she touched her throat.

The woman was staring at her with an unspeakable visceral hatred that Mary understood in the way that human beings know. Vanessa knew that her misdeeds had been found out.

Of course, she had to know sometime, and she, Mary, had been the one who'd vowed to do the telling, but now she could remember the lesson that Eve and John had taught her. She remembered how terrified she had been of her in-laws' far-reaching power and wanted to laugh. Never again would she fear them, not when she had just made an enemy of one of the most powerful, ruthless women alive!

With her eyes hardened so that their color was all but obscured and her flushed cheeks glowing fierily against her alabaster skin, Vanessa strode toward them. When she was close enough that her roughened breathing was audible, her hand flashed in the air, her scarlet nails looking as if they had already dipped into Mary's blood.

"Don't make me do it, Vanessa," Jed warned in a voice more lethal than Mary had ever heard him use.

The challenge was heavy and viscous between them. It was as if he had her in an unbearable arm-wrestling grip, and the veins in Vanessa's neck were taut, her teeth were gritted.

Abruptly she went gray and whirled on her heel. Mary sagged with relief. Beyond Vanessa, Juliet was meandering toward her mentor. Having come from the gym, she wore her maillot and leg warmers and a bright blue sweatband about her head. A towel was draped about her neck.

Mary thought she had never seen such a beautiful girl. Pausing to speak briefly and receiving a peck on the cheek from Vanessa, she glided to the steps and began climbing them.

"It seems the day for burning bridges, doesn't it?" Mary said softly to Jed, then looked at him with an expression that neither apologized nor sought his advice. "I have to tell her, Jed."

Jed supposed that she did. And since there seemed no better time for it, since he and Scutter were both present to keep an eye on Vanessa, he grimaced his resignation.

"I'll do it if you want me to," he offered.

With a shake of her head, she followed the girl, her slim legs so lovely they took his breath. Realizing that Scutter was watching, he tucked a smile into his shoulder.

"Yeah," Scutter said with a sound surprisingly like sympathy, "I know."

It was natural, Jed told himself as he let his body unwind from the tension of the past minutes, that neither he nor Scutter should have expected anything else to happen. There was that old saying that trouble came in threes, but he'd never been much of one for old sayings. Annelise had accomplished her purpose and gone, and Vanessa had been put in her place. Who could have guessed that the danger of his own annihilation lurked, not in those two hate-filled women, but in a girl of fifteen?

Juliet had climbed halfway to the top of the stairs, and he couldn't hear what was said. He viewed the scene as if looking at a television with the audio turned down: Juliet bracing her fists impudently upon her svelte hips, Mary earnestly explaining about the products the girl had been using, Juliet shaking her head in protest, Mary shrugging helplessly and trying to placate, Juliet shaking her finger, Mary turning away, Juliet grabbing at her arm and snatching her back, Mary spinning around, Juliet striking out, Mary stumbling...Mary falling, her stockinged legs flashing, Mary crying out...Mary rolling down step after step...Juliet screaming in horror...Mary, Mary...

Chapter Thirteen

It's a girl."

Every shred of Jed's medical professionalism had evaporated the moment Mary slipped under the anesthetic. Throughout the entire procedure, he had been certain she would die. He had stood above her and prayed with his eyes fixed and open, making blasphemous bargains with God if she would only live. He no longer cared about the baby, he only wanted her, and all the things about her that had tried and irked him, he loved most. His own life, his failures, his heartbreak seemed as nothing.

He hadn't known he was muttering out loud until one of the nurses looked up at him and asked, "Are you all right, Dr. Kilpatrick?"

Then he realized he'd been chanting, "Please, dear God. Please, dear God."

Once Mary was out of danger, he was washed with a whole new tide of horrors—something would be wrong with the baby, with their daughter! Then the newborn drew her first tiny breath, and he knew that life was the dearest possession there was, and he was ashamed for having run from it.

When he walked out of the emergency room, he was not the same man who had walked in. Now he sat beside her bed with tears glistening unashamedly in his eyes. He loved her more than life itself.

"Have you seen her?" she asked.

"Yes, darling."

"Is she all right? Is everything okay?"

"She's fine. She's very, very small, but she's perfect."

Mary gazed wearily around the room that was a bower of flowers and felt the strange flatness of her belly. But residual sleep kept beckoning to her, and she smiled.

"I'll have a scar."

Kissing her, Jed smoothed her tumbling hair. "Werner did an excellent job. A hairline, that's all. And you're fine. Nothing is wrong inside."

She remembered how gold his eyes had been that first cold morning in her turret when he had thought she was someone else. That had been a lifetime ago. "I'd give you a cigar, but I'm fresh out."

"Scutter's been passing them out all evening."

She touched his cheek. "Would you do me a favor?"

He traced the line of her eyebrow. "Of course not."

"Would you call my mother? Tell her about the baby?"

"What's the number?"

She gave it to him.

"Go back to sleep, darling," he whispered when she closed her eyes. "I'll be here when you wake up."

* * *

The next weeks were the nearest thing to heaven that Mary had ever known. She did not return to St. Murren. Haman Stone was no longer there, Jed said. Annelise was running the château until a new administrator could be found. Many of the villagers had taken back their old jobs.

When Jed took her from the hospital, he moved her to a house in Zurich that belonged to friends of his family. The house was lovely, standing in a row very old by American standards—the edifice a silver-grey stone that turned to a poetic violet at dusk. The rooms were large and airy with long, mullioned windows that drank in the sunlight. There, under the strict supervision of a hired nurse, Mary healed.

In a remarkable way, Jed began to build up his shattered medical practice. Once word was received that he was performing surgeries, calls began coming from all over Europe for his special skills. Most of them he accepted. Almost every evening, however, he was with her, though it often involved a harrowing juggle of schedules. The days took on a comfortable routine: in the mornings she wrote and missed the baby, in the afternoons, she rested and missed the baby; after dinner, she and Jed raced to the hospital to see the baby.

They named her Jessie. And their wedding plans, postponed until after Jessie came home from the hospital, inevitably began to revolve around her.

The wedding was a thing Mary took enormous pleasure in planning. She could hardly remember her wedding with John. Jed had a number of colleagues in Europe whom, he proudly informed her, wanted to meet her, and she invited his parents, who agreed to fly over.

Scutter would be the best man, naturally, and Dotty her maid of honor.

Curled up in her own bed for Jed had sworn to himself and to her that he wouldn't even sleep in the same room until she had passed the inspection of her doctor—she surrounded herself with bridal books and magazines she had never had the heart to read before.

And the shopping! What opinions Jed had about her trousseau! Once Jessie was happily and healthily ensconced in her crib, every moment they could bear to leave her, they frequented the finest shops Zurich had to offer.

The only ripple upon their lovely pond was when an investigator called at the château and asked Mary about the incident at the château. As honestly as she could, she told him her side of the story.

"Do you think I did the right thing?" she asked Jed from her rocking chair, as he leaned over her shoulder and watched Jessie going to sleep with the nipple of her bottle still in her rosy mouth.

Jed didn't reply at first. Reaching around her, he blotted the tiny rivulet of white and slipped a finger into the delicate little hand. Even in sleep, Jessie clutched, her fingers only a fraction of his and so very, very white and soft.

"Since when is the truth not the right thing?" he said, and drew the fragrance of her hair into his lungs.

"We haven't heard the last of it."

"Probably not."

Mary wondered if she heard apprehension in his voice.

As the weeks passed and her strength returned, along with her vigor, she continued to sit upon the bed in her lovely room after Jed and Jessie went to bed, and she studied the grain of the wooden floor and the walls washed with silver and pale green. She would rise and tiptoe into the nursery and stand over her beautiful daughter, loving her so much that tears brimmed in her eyes.

What was the matter with her? She had everything she had ever dreamed of. A lovely healthy daughter, a husband-to-be who adored her and was generous with his time and his money. He loved Jessie as if she were truly his. He delighted in her, and shared her pride. Sometimes she caught Jed holding Jessie when he didn't know anyone was watching, and he would enfold her protectively to his chest and his eyes would mist.

He missed his own children, she knew. He missed America. He missed his family. Once she dreamed that he stood over her as she slept and watched her for a long time before he turned and went to his room.

There were times, however, when he held her face a little too long before he left the house. Or he would hold her hand to his lips without saying a word. There were times when he would begin to kiss her and lift his head and hold her very tightly and whisper, "Don't let this ever end. Don't let this ever stop."

"It won't end," she whispered, troubled.

Once, when he cupped her face and searched her eyes for a reflection of them together, he said, "This is the rightness you wanted, Mary. Nothing can keep me from you. Nothing. No one."

But still, it wasn't their house, it wasn't their country, and their life wasn't really moving anywhere. It was just healing.

"Some things *should* end, my darling," she said as she stood at the entrance of her empty room one evening and saw her reflection in the freestanding oval mirror beside the bed—the tall, slender woman in the black, silk charmeuse Sanchez gown he had selected himself.

Drawing nearer, she inspected her breasts beneath the lace insert. They were more full, more ripe than before with their nipples that had been cheated of their infant suckling but not of their need for it. Yes, her waist was small again, smaller than before, but her hips were fuller, more feminine.

She angled her profile in the mirror and saw the jut of her pelvic bones and the delta of her legs. "This gown was made for one reason only, and you know it, Jed Kilpatrick. You knew that when you bought it."

Bending over Jessie's crib to make sure she slept, she walked deliberately out of the bedroom and across the hall and to a single door at the end. Opening the door, she left it ajar so that the light from the corridor filled the space with an infinite variety of shadows and sultry suggestions.

A painfully light sleeper, Jed lifted his head at the first scrape of sound. For a moment he wasn't sure he was awake when he focused upon the silent, dark-haired creature silhouetted dramatically against the light.

He didn't move. He didn't dare, for he was instantly, achingly hard.

The scent of her perfume was in the room, and as if drunk on it, he watched her eyes find his. "Are you watching me?" she whispered.

"Yes." His voice was serrated with passion.

Reaching behind the heavy mass of her hair, she released the fastening at the back of her neck. Gripping the gown, she slid it with infinite slowness up her long, willowy legs and firm thighs and over her head.

Her breasts were very white, as she was all over except for the symmetrical triangle of dark curls above her legs.

She touched her nipples and, pressing her lips tightly together, smoothed her hands down the sides of her waist and the sweet winking eye of her naval. Turning, she leaned against the wall, as if hugging it for warmth.

Slowly, painfully, Jed placed his feet on the floor. He wanted to go to her, to take her immediately and end the anguish that had smoldered inside him for weeks.

Not yet, not yet.

Rotating with infinite slowness, her every move calculated to torture him, she trailed her fingertips to the midnight curls at her legs. With a language all her own, she invited him into an intimacy more secret than any they had yet shared.

Jed was enthralled, he was spellbound as he watched, and she knew she was doing the very thing that would push him past control. She drew him to her—moth to the flame or flame to the moth, it didn't matter.

He thought he would not last until he crossed the room.

"You are a devil," he groaned, and leaned upon her as she stood there, kissing her until she reached between them and, curving a leg about his thigh, impaled herself and shuddered with instant release.

It was over quickly, and he carried her in his arms to bed. There, as she lay spent and glistening, he kissed her. He pulled her against him and entered her again. He loved her long and relentlessly. She said no, and he said yes. And when he looked at her afterward, lying so sensually in the tangled landscape of sheets, it was with the eyes of a dying man. She was the one then who refused to let him rest. She learned all the things about him that she did not yet know, the muscles and junctures and bands of taut flesh. She was scandalous and adorably bawdy, but in turn shy and so incredibly female that he would feverishly bend her to his will. And when she spread herself upon him so boldly, he rose up into her powerfully, like steel, and she reached beneath them and made him tremble.

"Don't you dare speak to me," she told him the next morning when she walked very carefully in to breakfast.

Laughing, he kissed her soundly and gulped a final swallow of coffee. "Am I allowed to say four words? I'll be late today?"

She angled him a speculative look that made Jed wonder if the day wouldn't be better spent at home. To hell with surgery! "Only those four," she clipped. "Now go."

"What a grudge holder you turned out to be," he said, and, chuckling, pecked her on the cheek and strode, medical bag in hand, to the front door.

Mary sighed contentedly as she slid low upon her spine in her chair, her legs stretched out beneath the terry robe that was still damp from her shower, her socked feet wiggling their toes. What had she ever done to deserve a man like Jed Kilpatrick?

When the doorbell rang, she laughed. Typical doctor. He'd forgotten something. The man needed a keeper. What would he ever do without her?

Rising, she walked through the house and said as she opened the door, "I knew you couldn't keep it down to four words."

"You're damn right," Vanessa said as she shoved it open and, motioning for Mutt and Jeff who were ever at her side, shut it behind them.

The human heart, Mary thought, was a miraculous piece of machinery. When fear attacked the brain in a rush so awful, so horrible that it wanted to shut down and die, the heart kept on pumping life into it. It refused to let the human organism extinguish itself.

Mary felt the blood withdrawing from her arms and legs, and numbness crept in. She felt herself withdrawing from the outer reaches of the space she occupied—away from Jed and Jessie and the house and the narrow limits of earth. She could feel the invisible hairs on her arms and her fingernails and knew that the words this woman would now say to her would brush her with death itself.

Aware of the men standing beside the door, she tried to concentrate upon Vanessa and speak. She swallowed and forced herself to move and breathe, but no words would come.

Vanessa was gazing up at the chandelier and at the fine walls and the furnishings that the owners had collected over a lifetime—priceless antiques.

"Very nice," she said.

Mary thought in horror of Jessie asleep down the hall. "What are you doing here?"

Stretching out a hand, Vanessa removed first one glove, then another, and as she started unbuttoning her coat—it was emerald green, very slim—she smiled icily. "Aren't you going to offer me anything?"

"No."

"Very well, I'll help myself." Tossing her coat aside to reveal a Pucci dress and at least a quarter-million dollars' worth of diamonds about her throat, she walked to the side bar and poured herself a glass of Irish whisky, of which she drank nearly half.

"Ordinarily I don't indulge myself," she said. "Today, however..."

"Jed is not here," Mary said frozenly, and closed her terry robe more securely over her bosom. The thin socks weren't adequate; her feet were numb.

"I know. I saw him leave."

"Then—"

"Patience, Mary, my dear. I'll get to it in good time. How's the baby. How's Jessie?"

She knew the baby's name! Dear God! All the blood that had left Mary returned to her head with a vengeance, and it felt as if the top of it would shatter. Afraid that she would lose her sense of balance and fall over, she stumbled to a chair and gripped its back.

Her voice was a rasp. "Say what you came to say and get out, Vanessa. Or I'll call the police and have you thrown out."

With a laugh that was too shrill to be sane, Vanessa threw back her head then lowered it to pierce Mary with eyes that were a shade of gray.

"You've seen the paper?" she snapped. "That's what I came about."

Confused, Mary shook her head. "No, I haven't."

"Then I'll tell you myself, though I might not be quite as objective as the reporter, you understand. It's a bit difficult being objective about getting screwed before the whole world."

Somewhere Mary found the wit to walk to the front door and, ignoring the goons beside it, fetch the morning paper from the box. Opening it, with the cold wind whistling across her feet, she scanned the front page.

"Fortunately," Vanessa hissed, "it's only in the investigatory stage. I'm on page two."

Mary didn't remember shutting the door. There, in black and white, almost verbatim, was her account of the incident at St. Murren. Above it was a photograph of

Vanessa, one of the older ones that was taped in her office at the château.

"At least the picture is good," the maven said, and snatched the paper away and hurled it to the floor. "Don't waste time reading it. I favor the bottom line so I'll come right to it. I want you out of this house, Mary Smith. I want you to disappear before this investigation goes one step farther. I don't want a single reporter from this city to be able to find you."

I'm losing my hold on life, Mary thought. I'm going to faint.

But she didn't. She shook her head and walked to the bar and poured herself a stout swallow of liquor and threw it down her throat. For a moment, she couldn't breathe and she couldn't think and she couldn't talk.

Vanessa did enough of all three. "Lest you start giving me all kinds of excuses why you must refuse, all about how much you love Jed and how you plan to be married and have a family, let me tell you something. I know all about you, Mary Smith. Since that day when Juliet knocked you down the stairs—God, how much simpler it would have been if you'd broken your neck—I've spent a great deal of time and money making it my business to know. I know all about your family, your sisters. I know, for instance, where you got your information about the steroid."

Despite the whisky, Mary felt fearfully sober.

"Have you spoken with Guy Rhodes in the last few days?" Vanessa said.

Oh, no! No, no!

Vanessa waved away her tears. "Oh, he's all right. With a bit of plastic surgery, he'll be fine. I'm not a barbarian, Mary, in spite of what you think." Leaning toward her with an almost rabid honesty, she aimed her finger at Mary's face. "You think I want Jed? What do

I want with Jed Kilpatrick? I can have any man in the world. You think I get off seeing people suffer. Well, I don't, but I've worked hard to get where I am, Mary Smith, and I'll do what I have to do to stay there. The terms are simple, if you don't leave here—this very morning before Jed can come home today and fill your head full of all that morality crap—I'll tell this reporter... what's his name?''

One of the men picked up the paper and handed it to her. Reading, Vanessa said, "Kurt. Yes. I'll tell good old Kurt that Jed knew all along that I was using steroids. Jed's already been involved in one scandal. Don't you know the press will eat it up? Now, I know you're going to do this, Mary. You love him, for one thing. And second, you know that I'll do exactly what I say. Look, I'll even foot the plane fare. In my private jet. That way you won't have to go through all that business at the airport.''

"And Jed won't be able to trace me." Mary covered her face with her hands. Jessie had begun to cry.

"Exactly."

The smile on Vanessa's lips were not inhuman. As Mary stood trembling, knowing already what her decision would be, she couldn't even despise the woman. Vanessa was what she herself was not—a survivor, purely and simply, without regard for anything except her own basic self. Vanessa could do whatever needed to be done, no matter who it hurt.

But what Vanessa could not know was that the love she and Jed shared would win, somehow, someway. She would go, yes, but Jed would come after her. He would find her. He *had* to find her.

"Are you going to come without causing trouble?" Vanessa said, and sighed as if very tired. "Or do I have to take the baby?''

Chapter Fourteen

It hardly feels like Christmas at all this year, does it? It's so warm. I can remember Christmas when my ears ached just walking through this drafty old barn of Mama's."

From the cutting board in her mother's large homey kitchen, Mary smiled gently at her sister, Dotty, who seemed just as much like an angel as ever with her painfully pale beauty and golden hair and soft white skin.

"I think it's the smells that take you back," she said. "Mama always made mince pies at Christmas."

"And the turkey dressing. Remember how the whole house would smell like dressing?"

"The whole house *does* smell like dressing," Joanna informed as she returned from the living room where Rick and her three children were watching football on television. A dish towel was wrapped about the center of her frilly beige dress.

Standing on tiptoe, she prowled in the cupboard above the sink. "Where is Mama keeping the relish dish these days?"

Mary wasn't wearing an apron. Why worry about spills when she was dying a little more every day? Jed had not come. She didn't know where he was. She didn't know if Vanessa had succeeded in getting to him or not. She had certainly gotten to Guy Rhodes. Someone had destroyed his lab and his face in the process. Nightmares ended, didn't they? Wasn't loving someone supposed to make you happy?

She didn't know about happiness anymore. She only knew what waiting was. People were placed on this earth to break their hearts, she thought, to ruin themselves and wait.

Very early, she had risen and climbed into the wide-legged slacks and classic, tailored white blouse. She had sleeked back her hair and tied it with a narrow challis scarf so she could wait another day and go to bed with a little less hope.

"Down there, I think." She pointed with her paring knife to the grumbling refrigerator. "Was Jessie dry?"

"Goodness, if she's not, she will be. I think Mama would change her even if she wasn't. If she'd made over either of my three the way she does that baby, I'd have moved her into the house permanently."

"Mama's older now. She's afraid of dying."

"Mama's too practical to die. Where are the olives?"

"In the fridge, Joanna," Dotty patiently informed. "Where do you think?"

Joanna laughed. "Daddy always said if it had been a snake, it would have bit me."

"Our father," Mary said blandly, "had a tendency toward clichés."

"'It's not over 'til the fat lady sings,'" Dotty chanted with a giggle.

Crunching a piece of carrot and chewing, Mary motioned to them with what was left. "I always liked the one 'When they passed out brains, dear heart, you thought they said trains and you didn't want to go anywhere.'"

When Treenie Calvert entered her kitchen, her capable arms full of Jessie, who was plumping out very nicely considering her premature birth, she hesitated in the doorway, her hand bracing the baby's back as she treasured the sight of all three daughters in the same room, none of them crying, none of them sick.

She and Wylie had never agreed on how to raise them, and she'd accused her husband of being a dreamer. But she didn't think she'd done any better. She was the one who had advised Mary to marry John Smith, and look what a disaster that had turned out to be.

Mary was much too thin these days and had been ever since she'd returned from Europe with the baby. Without explanation, she had called and asked if she could stay a few days, and Treenie had opened her house and her heart. But the days had turned into weeks, and some nights, when Mary was tucked comfortably into her old room at the head of the stairs with Jessie's crib next to her bed, Treenie heard weeping.

The next morning when Treenie asked, "How're you doing, old girl?" Mary would smile sadly and reply, "Pretty good, old girl. How're you doin'?"

But at least Mary was home, safe and sound.

"I think Jessie's hungry," Treenie announced and watched the quick flick of Mary's eyes to her daughter and the instant putting down of the salad fixings.

"Well, that's easy to fix," Mary said, her face transforming into something quite lovely as she indulged herself in a forgivable ritual of talks and sounds that no one would ever understand except herself and Jessie.

Over Mary's head, Treenie exchanged a wordless renewal of family bonds with her two remaining daughters. They must help Mary through the terrible thing that was eating away at her.

In the front room, Joanna's children were scampering noisily about, wheedling their father to let them open gifts. "Ask your grandmother," Rick told them. "It's her house."

Having more patience with the children than their own mother, Dotty wiped her hands and went to distract them. Joanna peeped through the oven door for the hundredth time.

She said, "It's cooking too fast, Mama."

"Nonsense." Treenie shooed her away. "Fetch some of your father's sherry and bring it to the front room. We'll put on some of those old records."

"Oh, no," Joanna wailed. "I hate those things."

"I love them," Mary said as she tested the temperature of Jessie's bottle on her wrist. "Come on, Jess, it's time you learned about the good old days."

Once the whole family was in one room, however, the children made such lavish promises to be good if they could open just one gift, everyone broke down and said yes. Being the only man left in the family, Rick was drafted to play Santa, and soon the floor was an ocean of torn wrapping, scattered ribbons, children's toys, sherry glasses and crumbs from stolen bites of fruitcake.

Before Mary could turn Jessie upside down on her knee and burp her, Treenie kidnapped her, and Dotty was left to turn up Perry Como's ageless, silver voice on the stereo. The sound of the doorbell was almost drowned by the happy bedlam.

"What?" Mary squinted at Dotty who was waving at her, sending hectic hand signals.

Dotty cupped her hands about her mouth. "The door, the door. Get the door, will you?"

Sighing and wading unenthusiastically through a pool of wadded Christmas wrapping and pausing to peel a scrap that had attached itself to her shoe, Mary bulldozed her way to the door.

She declared wryly as she opened it, "Well, don't stand there banging, come on in and suffer with the rest—"

He wasn't wearing a suit but the old familiar bomber jacket and a powder blue sweater. His jeans were paper thin and had the beginnings of a hole in one knee. Beneath them were chukka boots, and he was drawing off his gloves and stuffing them into a pocket.

With her heart plummeting, Mary opened her mouth to speak, but simply stood drinking in the sight of his face—the deep new lines on his forehead and lines from his nostrils to the corners of his mouth that seemed thinner somehow. A dash of gray was beginning to show at his temples, and he looked very tired, but very happy.

Inside her head she was squealing with delirium and she wanted to hurl herself into his arms and cover him with joyous kisses. But outside, where her limbs refused to work and the weary waiting of weeks had tainted her hopes until they were as crumpled and torn as the Christmas wrapping that cluttered the living room floor, she remained standing in the door.

"Hi," she said in hushed wonder.

His flickering smile collected all her worst insecurities into a heap. "Hi."

"You came."

"Did you think I wouldn't?"

"I—"

"Did you think that anything this life could do to me would be able to keep me from you?" His thirst slaked itself with long, thorough looks at her.

The framework of her body seemed to crumble, and Mary shrank behind her lashes. "How did you find me? A private detective?"

"Try the phone book."

Vaguely aware that Dotty and Joanna had come to see why the door was still open, Mary wanted desperately to let go of her doubts, but the weeks had given her time to think, and she wasn't blinded by desire anymore. Jed was no perfect Prince Charming riding up on a white charger. Her mind possessed a whole list of things she didn't like about him, but on the other side were things she loved, and she knew with a woman's wisdom that she would be balancing those two lists the rest of her life. And he, if he truly loved her, would be doing the same thing.

Was that what love was? Not going into it blind? Knowing the debits and the credits and wanting it anyway?

She moistened her lips. She studied her fingernails. "There are a lot of Smiths in the Annapolis telephone directory."

He said, grinning, "You didn't tell me your father's name was Wylie. I have a Christmas present for you."

Behind her, the two women were looking at each other and miming "phone book?" Joanna's three children peeped around the facings of the door to see the tall, determined man upon the stoop.

"Who's he?" they asked each other.

Mary watched Jed draw a tiny black box from his jacket pocket. He had brought her a ring this time, and she warily accepted the box from his fingers, her own fingers trembling with surprising violence as she pried it open.

Upon the velvet cushion lay a brass key. She blinked at it in bafflement.

"You once asked me for that," he said and compelled her head to lift with the force of his will. "There's something beneath if you want it."

She knew what she would find, but she had no way of predicting how overwhelmed she would be. The ring was the most breathtaking thing she had ever seen—sixteen diamonds set in platinum and bordered with gold. They lay together in her palm—the key and the ring, and she remembered holding another ring in her palm. A small one. A lifetime ago.

"I need one of those back," he said gently.

Dotty and Joanna were herding the children back into the house. Mary found him waiting eloquently with the bright December sun at his back. So profound were her feelings, she shuddered.

"You're still making me choose," she whispered as his fingertips touched hers, waiting for her answer.

He moved a step nearer, and they both felt the thrill of the closeness all over again. "When I found out what had happened, why you left, I could have killed someone."

With infinite care Mary lifted the brass key from the box and stared blindly at it. "I'm going to write about Vanessa, Jed. You have to know that. She may come after me, but I still have to do it. I've already talked to my editor."

"Do you think I would have come here without making sure of your safety first? Vanessa's no threat to you anymore, Mary. Write whatever you like."

"What?"

His words dispelled the awkwardness, and Mary pinned him with a look of unvoiced questions.

Shrugging, he raked his fingers through his hair. "Evidently she couldn't recover from your interview with the paper in Zurich. It was a real hornet's nest. She disappeared. Her board of directors is faced with crippling lawsuits, they tell me, and in a few more weeks there won't be anything left of her empire to come back to. But she wouldn't come back anyway. Her ego wouldn't allow it. Latin America is my guess. She could hide down there for the rest of her life."

The largest obstacle of all had been removed from their path, and their nerves strained to the snapping point as they both fixed their attention upon the dull sheen of the key. He was placing the future at her feet, Mary thought. Did she have the courage to pick it up?

"My life isn't conducive to a good marriage, Mary," he said quietly. "I make terrible demands upon my family and the people I care about. But I love you more than anyone will ever love you the rest of your life. We have that rightness, you and I. I want *us* to work."

With her eyes wide open and knowing full well what she was doing, Mary took the ring and placed it upon her own finger. As if signing a paper and folding it up, she slowly closed the box and extended it.

Keeping her eyes upon the diamonds catching the fire of a Christmas sun, she considered life's questions that had no answers, their future that made no promises. Except that they would place themselves into the scheme of it and live it together.

Taking the box, Jed placed the key inside it and slipped both into the pocket of his jacket. He waited until she looked up. Not smiling, he took her face lovingly between his hands.

"It frightens me to be loved so much by you," he said. "But kiss me now, and it will be all right. And then I want to see my daughter."

His lips were very sweet, very tender.

* * * * *

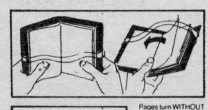
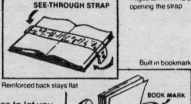

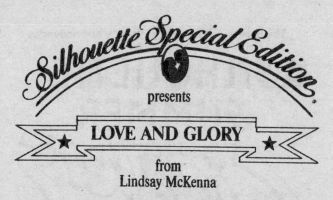

Silhouette Special Edition®

presents

★ LOVE AND GLORY ★

from
Lindsay McKenna

Introducing a gripping new series celebrating our men—and women—in uniform. Meet the Trayherns, a military family as proud and colorful as the American flag, a family fighting the shadow of dishonor, a family determined to triumph—with **LOVE AND GLORY!**

June: A QUESTION OF HONOR (SE #529) leads the fast-paced excitement. When Coast Guard officer Noah Trayhern offers Kit Anderson a safe house, he unwittingly endangers his own guarded emotions.

July: NO SURRENDER (SE #535) Navy pilot Alyssa Trayhern's assignment with arrogant jet jockey Clay Cantrell threatens her career—and her heart—with a crash landing!

August: RETURN OF A HERO (SE #541) Strike up the band to welcome home a man whose top-secret reappearance will make headline news . . . with a delicate, daring woman by his side.

If you missed any of the LOVE AND GLORY titles send your name, address and zip or postal code, along with a check or money order for $2.95 for each book ordered, plus 75¢ postage and handling, payable to Silhouette Reader Service to:

In Canada	In USA
P.O. Box 609	901 Furhmann Blvd
Fort Erie, Ontario	P.O. Box 1396
L2A 5X3	Buffalo, NY 14269-1396

Please specify book title with your order.

LG-1A